"Will You Ch...

Katie turned her head and saw Fletcher Ramsey in white shorts and polo shirt, walking across the exercise room full of women.

"Think his intentions are honorable?" asked another woman.

"God, I hope not," laughed a third.

"Nice calves."

To cap things off, someone let out a long, low whistle. Really, Katie decided irritably, we're as bad as a football team in a locker room. It sure wasn't hard to see where Fletcher Ramsey's confidence came from.

When he reached Katie at the other end of the room, he let out a nervous laugh. "Whew. That was the longest walk of my life. I will never torture a woman with the old once-over again!"

ANTOINETTE HARDY
lives on board a yacht in the harbor of Newport, Rhode Island, and has sailed in it with her husband up and down the Caribbean. "In every harbor," she reports, "I've found men and women who are fiercely independent, emotional, sensitive, capable, somehow larger than life—perfect for filling the pages of romance."

Dear Reader:

Romance readers have been enthusiastic about Silhouette Special Editions for years. And that's not by accident: Special Editions were the first of their kind and continue to feature realistic stories with heightened romantic tension.

The longer stories, sophisticated style, greater sensual detail and variety that made Special Editions popular are the same elements that will make you want to read book after book.

We hope that you enjoy this Special Edition today, and will enjoy many more.

The Editors at Silhouette Books

ANTOINETTE HARDY
Fit to be Loved

Silhouette Special Edition
Published by Silhouette Books New York
America's Publisher of Contemporary Romance

SILHOUETTE BOOKS, a Division of Simon & Schuster, Inc.
1230 Avenue of the Americas, New York, N.Y. 10020

Distributed by Pocket Books

ISBN: 0-671-53691-5

First Silhouette Books printing September, 1984

10 9 8 7 6 5 4 3 2 1

Map by Ray Lundgren

America's Publisher of Contemporary Romance

Printed in the U.S.A.

BC91

To all the ghosts in the old stone house

Fit to be Loved

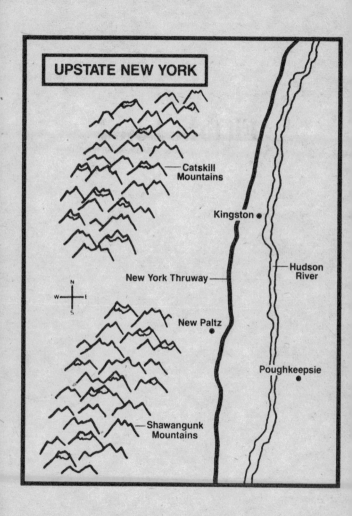

Chapter One

She took the phone off the hook, set the minute-timer to nine, adjusted her black leotards, and sat on the floor. A long inhale . . . exhale. Her last exercise class had dispersed, and it was time for an end-of-day cooldown; the next few minutes belonged to Katrina Bright, and no one else. Lying on her back, Katie brought her legs over her head until her toes touched the floor behind her in the classic yoga position known as the "plough."

She had put a selection of ballads by James Taylor on the cassette player, and the music, as much as the unlikely contortion she had assumed, did much to calm and soothe. It was her favorite time of day. Her pulse dropped slowly, her mind cleared, and, as always, odd little illuminations drifted in and out of her thoughts. She remembered, for example, that her green woolen mittens weren't lost at all but were back in the woodshed, where she'd left them. And that the birthstone for November was a topaz. And that she was out of eggs.

Before long the steady tick-tick of the timer replaced her random musings, and her thoughts became a hazy, pleasant blur. A male whoop of triumph came from the men's racquetball court across the hall, and then all was silent. Katie was perfectly comfortable, perfectly relaxed —until the sharp rap on the glass door to the exercise room.

"Wouldn't you know it," she muttered to herself. Well, whoever it was would have to wait; this was *her* time. She opened one eye, however, and was able to make out that it was a man in a business suit—probably some husband ready to surprise his wife with a gift membership to the Shape-Up Room. The wife might be pleased—but then again, she might not.

The next rap was sharper; the door swung open. Darn. Marcia had left it unlocked when she went down the hall to shower.

"Sorry to disturb you, miss," the man began in an obviously ironic voice. He expected to be waited on. Now.

"Inaminit." She didn't care if he were President of the United States. She would not be interrupted during a cool-down.

"Pardon me?"

"Be with you . . . in . . . a minute," she repeated a little breathlessly.

"Fine. Then I'll wait . . . right here."

Katie opened her eyes briefly; before she shut them again she registered that the visitor was tall, sandy-haired, clean-shaven, and standing almost directly in front of her, staring down the underside of her outstretched legs and hips. Suddenly she was neither comfortable nor relaxed. How could she be, with her knees next to her ears? And him next to her knees? Her neck began to ache unbearably; she would cut short her cool-down, just this once. Immediately she changed her mind. No—she would not. This was no emergency.

"Move, please," she demanded without opening her eyes.

"Oh, am I in the way?" he asked innocently. "Would you rather I wait in the hall, or maybe up on the roof?" She heard him move away, a smile in his voice.

She took offense at him for the smile, and for disturbing her tranquillity. Again she stole a quick peek; now he was pacing off the room!

"Three, six, nine . . ." he counted, completely unperturbed.

P-i-n-n-ng!

Thank God; the timer went off at last. Slowly and deliberately, but not so slowly and deliberately as usual, Katie rolled out of her plough position and stood up.

"*What* are you doing, pray tell?" she asked, hands on her hips. "And who might you be?"

"Obviously, I'm measuring the room. My name is Fletcher Ramsey. And your bun is falling down."

Automatically her hand lifted to the back of her neck. Her shining black hair was too long and too thick to confine to a bun, but every day she tried, and every day she failed.

"Is there something I can do for you?" she asked with frigid politeness.

His look traveled leisurely from her lifted eyebrows to the scoop neck of her leotard, down the rest of her five feet seven inches, and back up to her high-cheeked face. "Do you always lead with your left like that?" he countered, with a smile that stopped just this side of a proposition. Katie sucked in her breath impatiently and he added, "I'm looking for Katrina Bright, as a matter of fact."

"And now that you've found her?" She tried hard to swallow the challenge in her voice, but it was no use; everything seemed to be coming out hostile. *Serves him right for barging in.*

"And now that I've found her . . . I'd like to take apart her bun, hairpin by hairpin, and let her beautiful face enjoy a proper frame." His hands were in his pockets, and he didn't look all that dangerous. But his gray eyes projected far more warmth than the color gray should ever be allowed to have.

Her own eyes flashed more ice than fire. "Surely you're not all dressed up in a three-piece suit just to dismantle my hairdo. After all, New Paltz is a college town; jeans and a t-shirt would have been adequate." Why was she being so derisive? Obviously men had complimented her before; long black hair seemed to hold for them an irresistible appeal. Why was she behaving as though this particular one had just offered to dump a bucket of paint over her head?

A wry grimace brought a dimple into his left cheek. "What I *should* have worn is a bulletproof vest. I've just driven up from New York; any clues as to my business here, Kate?"

"Not a one."

He looked surprised. "You honestly don't know who I am?"

"Flesh . . . *Fletch*er Ramsey," she corrected hastily. For some bizarre reason she'd been speculating that he was a 42 Long in a jacket; and a 34 Waist, 34 Length in trousers—in college she'd worked part-time in a men's shop. "I'm sorry. From New York City, you were saying."

"I'm your new landlord, Kate."

"Ah." Instantly her hostility changed to wariness. In common with every other tenant in the world, Katie realized that one false step in front of a landlord could mean a raise in rent. She leaned against the edge of her desk and casually folded her arms across her chest. "So everything is settled, then?"

"This morning. Look . . . Katie . . ." Suddenly he laughed. "This is going to be harder than I thought. How close were you to Jimmy, anyway?" he asked abruptly.

"Why?" Her eyes narrowed suspiciously; a poker face was not one of Katrina Bright's endowments.

"Typical woman; answers a question with another question," he snorted.

She was stung by his condescension. "We were . . . close, but it hardly seems any of your business." Jimmy was her old landlord and her old friend, and though they had never been lovers, she was lost without him these last few weeks.

"You'd be a marvel in a witness stand," he said in exasperation. "Can you just answer the questions, yes or no? Did Jimmy ever go into any financial details? About this building, I mean?"

"Suppose I tell you what I do know, and then we can drop this little game of twenty questions," she answered coolly. "Some sort of corporation, of which Jimmy was a member, owned this building. Jimmy ran his racquetball section and paid rent to the corporation, even though he was part of it. I paid rent to Jimmy for the Shape-Up part of the building. For three years he was a wonderful neighbor and a marvelous landlord. I could hardly hope to do better," she couldn't resist adding. *There goes the rent.*

His heavy brows, darker than his hair, drew down in a look of irony. "I agree with you completely. As a landlord, Jimmy was strictly one of a kind," he said smoothly.

She knew it. He was here to raise the stupid rent. "I've always paid promptly on the first of the month," she offered feebly, anticipating what was coming.

He shook his head gently. "That's not enough, Katrina. You must have known that financially you were living in a fantasy world. For three years the rent was ludicrously low, a gift from Jimmy. He had the heart of a lion and the business sense of a child. In a way the two of you were both children, and this building was your playground."

She pushed herself away from the desk with a sharp motion. "That's not true! We both worked long hard hours to build up our businesses . . . painting walls on weekends, shoveling snow before it was light out. . . . For the first year, I washed all the towels myself!''

"No one is suggesting that you're not a workhorse, Kate. Or that Jimmy . . . Jimmy and I went back almost seventeen years. We were in the service together, and I owed him a big one. A very big one. When racquetball became his passion I . . . set him up with this place,'' he said simply.

She stared at him, not quite comprehending. She was aware, vaguely, that he needed a shave. His upper lip would be scratchy if he . . . if he kissed anyone.

"Don't you see?'' he asked softly. "I paid the bills. Gladly. There isn't enough money in the world to cover my debt to Jimmy. But he's dead now, and I'm a businessman, not a philanthropist.''

His voice was low and serious and sad, and for a moment Katie had the insane idea that he was going to take her in his arms and tell her not to mourn for Jimmy or for her little Shape-Up Room, because everything was going to be all right.

But he didn't. And Jimmy really was gone, killed in a motorcycle accident, and Fletcher Ramsey really was her new landlord. And she really had been acting like a child just now. Four years ago, when she first began pulling out of her tailspin, she thought she'd learned to face up to reality; yet here she was, twenty-nine, and still wanting to be cuddled.

She walked over to the bulletin board and, with a precise movement, replaced a pushpin on a newspaper clipping.

"So. What's the new rent to be?'' she asked without turning around. She still had almost two months on her old lease to streamline the business and squeeze a better profit. She could do it.

"Katie . . .'' he said quietly. He was directly behind her and she jumped, startled by his catlike approach over the carpeted floor. "There isn't going to be any new rent.''

"No new rent?" What was he saying, no new rent? A surge of adrenalin told her that her body had understood a split second before her mind. Still she fought the realization. "You mean . . . what do you mean?"

"I mean I don't know a damned thing about racquetball. My line of business is fast food, and this building is slated to be number five in a chain of Fletcher's Fish and Chips."

Unconsciously Katie brought her hands over her mouth. She wondered whether she was going to do something silly and hysterical like cry, but instead she surprised herself with a giggle.

"What's so funny?" he asked, clearly puzzled.

"Fletcher's Fish and Chips! Here? Where for three long years I've slaved to take ounces and pounds off women's bodies—and my own? You're going to slap that fat right back *on* all of us? Right here? It's too ironic for words. French fries! Batter-fried shrimp! Spare me." The giggle was long gone, and a sense of dull rage filled her. The injustice of it all! She could strangle him.

"Fish is healthy food," he replied calmly.

"Not the way you have it prepared. Deep-fried, dripping in fat. It's disgusting!" Although something deep inside of her said, "Get the facts, ma'am," she couldn't help venting her disappointment, fears and misgivings in a fit of righteous fury. She considered stamping her foot, but there was something in Fletcher Ramsey's eye that discouraged such melodrama.

"Have you ever eaten at a Fletcher's?" he asked reasonably. He certainly was a cool one.

"I have not and I would not. Besides . . . I've eaten at similar places; they're all the same," she fumed.

"Next week I'll show you that they're not."

"Fat chance!"

"Kate, for God's sake, stop taking it out on the fish. You'll be able to relocate the Shape-Up Room. You must understand that there's nothing personal in this."

"Of course not," she replied, trying heroically to match his calm. "Business is business." She could just strangle him.

She walked aimlessly around the room, tidying her desk; lining up the five- and eight-pound weights systematically; pushing all the waist-twist poles against the wall. "Of course, *you* will understand that the prospect of being out on my . . . leotards in January, surrounded by half a dozen sets of barbells and some full-length mirrors, is not reassuring."

He turned her words around on her. "There, you've just admitted that your inventory is small. It won't take you half a day to move. What you've spent the last three years trying to build up is a clientele—and they'll follow you, wherever you go. *I* would," he added with a little smile that was as endearing as it was sly. This one would have to be watched very, very carefully.

Seeing her hesitation, he stuck out his hand at Katie. "Truce?"

With an elaborate gesture she swung both her hands behind her back. "*Un*necessary," she answered regally. "No battle has been joined."

"Oh? What do you do when you're *really* sore at someone; pull out his fingernails and throw him in a dungeon?"

Something in his words struck a nerve. She wanted to say, "No; but I might throw his framed picture at a wall, shattering it into a million pieces." Which was how she'd handled her sense of hurt and betrayal five years earlier when her husband Peter left her. A dull red flush crept over her porcelain cheeks as she relived, for the first time in a year, the devastation she'd felt back then.

The flush on her face did not escape him. Nothing seemed to escape him. "Hey . . . if you've really pulled out someone's fingernails, I promise not to embarrass you about it again." His gray eyes glittered with humor.

Katie dropped her gaze from his. "Don't be a jerk. I was just thinking of my ex-husband." She sat down on the edge of a jogging trampoline, suddenly weak-kneed and drained. Sitting six inches off the floor, her chin resting on her fists, Katie knew that she was not exactly a picture of sophistication. But her whole world seemed to be falling down on her, all over again.

"What are those things, anyway?" he asked, pointing to the three-foot-wide jogger. "Trampolines for Smurfs?"

"Where on earth have you *been*, Mr. Ramsey," she said wearily. "These are rebound joggers; they're serious exercise tools." She eyed him warily as he slipped off his shoes and jumped on the second trampoline.

Bounce, bounce, bounce. His sandy hair, expertly cut and blow-dried, lifted and fell gently with each bounce. An irrepressible grin lit up his face. "Now *this* I like," he decided with the infallible authority of a ten-year-old.

"Get down off that before you have a heart attack," she muttered.

One eyebrow cocked up. He began jogging in place. "Don't be too sure; I don't have *both* feet in the grave, not yet."

"That's a pretty heavy-duty aerobic exercise you're doing. If you haven't warmed up properly . . ." she began automatically in her instructor's voice.

"Listen, woman, I could bounce this way until the cows come home. What's the big deal?"

"You couldn't last five minutes," she said in a tired voice.

"Wanna bet?"

"I'm not especially interested." Really, amusing as he was, she wished he'd go home so that she could lock up. It hadn't been a successful evening, all things considered.

"I can see why you have these joggers in a women's exercise salon," he said in an amused voice. "They're"—bounce—"cute"—bounce—"little"—bounce—"toys."

"Half the women in my class could destroy you in an endurance contest," she snapped.

"Half the *women,* sure . . . but what about you?" he asked baitingly.

"And what is that supposed to mean?"

"Well, just look at you . . . little Miss Muffet, sitting on her tuffet. Any full-blooded *woman* would've taken up my challenge immediately."

"That does it, Mr. Ramsey." She leaped up. "At this point I will do just about anything to get you *out* of here." Stepping on her trampoline she eased into a steady bounce.

He took off his jacket and tossed it on the floor, then loosened his tie. "No fancy stuff, mind," he threatened cheerfully. "Just a basic jogger's bounce for this contest."

"Fine." Face to face she glared at him. He really did have nice eyes, she noted impartially. They were probably his best feature. Expressive, and changeable . . . although his mouth wasn't bad either. The teeth looked healthy and white . . . but his nose . . . it seemed not quite . . . straight.

"Why do I have the feeling I'm a pony at auction?" he asked, grinning and bouncing.

"Your nose is crooked," she answered coolly. By chance or by design, they were bouncing in perfect synchronization.

"Broke it in a toboggan accident when I was eight. My mother said no one would ever notice."

Her breathing was beginning to come more deeply. He'd been working two minutes longer than she, so it was hardly a fair contest. Too bad for him. What was she doing, anyway, in a jogging contest with her landlord? "What *is* the point of this?" she demanded caustically.

"It's a great way to assess the human form, for one thing," he said with a warm, appraising look.

Her pulse was gradually moving closer to her optimum aerobic rate, but his look may have kicked it up another beat or two. Her rounded breasts bounced gently up and down beneath her leotard. She thought of changing directions on the trampoline; but would a side view be all that less interesting? Or a rear view, for that matter? What an idiot she was.

"You're right, however," he continued somewhat breathlessly. "There should be a stake to this wager. Keeps the . . . interest up."

He was tiring. She could feel it.

"A weekend with me if I win," he panted.

Her eyes opened wide. "Don't be absurd," she snapped.

"Ah, well, it was worth a try. A day, then—and that's my . . . final offer." Beads of sweat lined his brow; Katie studied his face for danger signs of overexertion, but he was holding up.

"I doubt that you could stand me for a whole day," she confessed quietly, almost to herself. Ramsey looked at her curiously and lost the beat; now he jogged up when she jogged down. "And if *I* win?" she asked.

"Anything you like," he answered generously.

"If I win, I'll never have to see you . . . again," she said, suddenly furious with herself for having thrown away her dignity, and furious with him for not giving up.

For the first time since he'd walked into her life, a look of displeasure crossed his face. "Whatever turns you on," he said dryly.

There seemed to be nothing more to say, and both combatants settled into a steady, rhythmic pace. Katie could jog all night if she had to, but she didn't think she'd have to. Surely he'd give up soon. She was wearing comfortable leotards; he was fighting the restrictions of a business suit. He must be boiling, even without his jacket—although now he was taking off his vest. And his tie. And rolling up his sleeves. He looked awfully determined . . . but tired, and hot, hot, hot.

After a bit Katie was no longer feeling invincible herself.

Ordinarily she indulged in a little fantasy when she jogged on the trampoline: she pretended she was a robot, made with nuts and bolts, and when someone pressed the "on" switch, her legs moved up and down and her arms swung back and forth, like a wind-up soldier. That was how she ignored the pain and had toned herself into the superbly thin woman she'd become.

But tonight nothing was going right. Fletcher Ramsey, with his warm expressive eyes, his damp heat, his heavy breathing, was altogether too human to ignore. He made robot fantasies impossible, and she began instead to focus alternately on his humanness, and hers. Her own forehead was wet with perspiration, and her hair, she could feel, was tumbling out of its confinement in long, damp locks.

The muscles of her thighs began to ache more and more, and she became aware that she was not raising them as high as she had been. She wanted to look straight ahead so that she could maintain a comfortable posture, but *he* was straight ahead, and so she dropped her look. But when she looked down a new feeling overcame her—long, sweet plunges of intense, rippling . . . awareness. She didn't know what to call it; yet with each raising and lowering of her legs, she became more breathless, almost giddy. But the sweet aching that washed over her was tempered by an overwhelming sense of confusion and embarrassment. If she kept up any longer she might even . . . she would surely moan out loud.

Abruptly she stopped. "You . . . win," she said, panting heavily and swaying slightly.

Instantly he was standing next to her, steadying her. His hands felt hot on her shoulders, and her shoulders felt hotter still under his hands. Everything was on fire. "Kate . . . are you o.k.?" He lifted a tendril that had flopped over her brow.

"I guess so," she murmured. "It wasn't the same . . ."

"Let me take your pulse." He turned her wrist upward

and after a few seconds said, "Looks like you'll live, Miss Muffet."

But the fire wasn't going down. She was breathlessly aware of his damp finger on her pulse, and still shaky from the strange, sweet agony she had somehow irreversibly associated with him. And he was still holding her pulse. Holding it, and then dropping a warm, light kiss on it, and then a kiss on the edge of her collarbone just inside the leotard, and then at the base of her neck . . . on her ear, her cheek, her chin and on her mouth. And on her mouth again; and Katie, damp and flushed and breathing heavily, thought that they must be making love, because these kisses weren't anything like the affectionate pecks she and Jimmy had exchanged over the last three years. These kisses were deep and urgent and wildly electric, terrifying in their intensity. Something long dormant leaped to life in her as his tongue invited, then dared, then took possession of hers.

It had been so long . . . not since Peter . . . not even Peter. . . . Her hands were in Ramsey's damp hair, and his hands pulled impatiently at the thigh-line of her leotard top; but underneath she wore leotard panty-hose—all road-blocks to the hell-bent fury of her longing. She could cry with frustration. . . .

"Should I clear my throat or something?" came a bemused voice behind them. "A-*hem*. Howzat?"

"Marcia!" Katie said, even before she whirled her head around. "I didn't know you were still . . . here," she said, mortified.

"Wa-a-ll, I decided to give myself the works—I did the sauna too."

"We were . . . we were . . ." Katie groped.

"Settling a bet," Ramsey finished kindly for her. "You'll never guess who won," he added with a sympathetic smile at Katie.

Katie stumbled through the introductions in a semiconscious state. "Marcia Welkins, this is Flesh"—again!—

"*Fletch*er Ramsey. Marcia runs the Shape-Up Room with me."

"Don't you believe it, Mr. Ramsey. She's the owner and the brains here. I just collect a salary for staying in shape."

"And a very nice shape it is," Ramsey responded gallantly. "But you can call me Flesh; everyone else seems to," he said with a sidelong glance at Katie.

"I wonder why," Marcia said, looking him up and down with an altogether lecherous expression. Marcia was a modern young woman; words like "shy" meant nothing to her.

As usual, Marcia was the bracing splash of cold water that Katie needed. She provided perspective. Looking at Ramsey through the younger woman's eyes, Katie was able to see that he was . . . an appealing hulk. She'd fallen under his spell momentarily and the rest, as they say, was biology. And that was all.

"Mr. Ramsey is our new landlord," Katie said with sweet irony. "Not for long, however. After the first of January our customers will be lining up to put it on, not take it off."

Marcia looked at her blankly.

"Never mind; I'll fill you in later." To Ramsey she turned and said, in dismissal, "It's been an . . . interesting half hour, Mr. Ramsey, I won't deny it."

"Well"—he smiled—"we've had our ups and our downs, haven't we? I'll see you . . . again," he said softly—and chucked Katie under the chin. Infuriating devil!

He was hardly out the door when Marcia whipped around breathlessly. "*What* is going on around here? I was only out of the room for a few minutes! Clothes all over the floor . . . a new landlord . . . January first . . . What is going *on* around here? Wait! Don't say a word! Let me make tea first. Tea first!"

Marcia dashed around the room, a short, manic bundle of brown-eyed energy. It exhausted Katie almost as much as it amused her to watch her younger friend in action. Water, the teakettle, the hot plate, two mugs, one spoon and a sugar bowl—Marcia shuffled them around almost faster than the eye could see. Even her leotards—pink stockings and a pale blue top—were upbeat. People who liked Marcia called her perky; people who didn't, called her feisty.

"Marcia . . ." Katie began.

"Shhh! Not a word till the tea."

Before long two giant blue mugs glazed with big smiling whales sat steaming in front of them. Katie reached over and gave a solid yank to her friend's new-washed hair. "You! Playing up to that . . . that curmudgeon!"

"Yeah, right; I should've given him the cold shoulder— the way you did," Marcia added slyly. "O.k. Start at the beginning." One heaping spoon of sugar went sliding into Marcia's mug. Then another. Katie never had been able to break Marcia of her habit of taking sugar in her tea.

"I'll start in the middle, actually. There I was, halfway through my cool-down, when he walked right in. Well, you know how we've all resolved that unless it's a fire or something, we don't allow interruptions. Anyway, he began measuring the room! Because he's starting a new business here on the first of the year." Katie sat back indignantly and sipped her tea.

"That's it? That's supposed to explain the scene I walked in on? Katie, would you mind . . . *fleshing* it out a little? Literally, if you'll forgive the pun."

"You know," Katie said irrelevantly, "I can't figure out why I *can't* say 'Fletch.' It's almost a speech impediment. Fletch. Fletch. Fletch. Did you know that he makes fish and chips? That's what's going to be built here. A Fletcher's Fish and Chips," she said contemptuously.

"*That's* what Fletcher he is? Those things are all over the state."

"There are only four—not such a very big deal," Katie argued.

"But they've all been built in the last three or four years. At this rate he'll be the new McDonald's by the time he's forty-five."

"How old do you suppose he is? He acted like such a . . . kid," Katie mused.

"The fast-food business is not child's play, Katrina. I'd say get ready for some hardball if you plan to deal with him."

"Oh, I have no such plans. He only dropped in to throw us out; I'm surprised he didn't just have his lawyer nail an eviction notice to the front door. I suppose it's the personal touch that's got him where he is," she added ironically.

"*I* thought he was getting pretty far with his 'personal touch,'" Marcia said pointedly.

"Oh . . . that. I really don't know how all that started," Katie said in confusion. "He taunted me into accepting a jogging challenge and after a while—well, it must have been too hot in the room because I began to get very . . . dizzy . . . light-headed . . . and I had to quit."

"And you wrapped your arms around him so that you wouldn't fall over backward?" Marcia pursued relentlessly. When she saw her friend's embarrassed look she said, "Never mind. I only wish I'd got it all on videotape—it'd make a hell of an exciting change from our exercise-analysis movie. I'd title it *Hunger,* of course."

"Not a word to anyone, if you value that mop of hair," Katie warned in a low and dangerous voice.

"I suppose you think you scare me?" Marcia challenged imperiously. "You want to know what scares me? The thought of you throwing the *next* five years of your life down the same hole as your *last* five."

"Only two of those years were actually a dead loss," Katie objected mildly. "And even then, I learned all there is to know about the consoling powers of chocolate," she said with a rueful smile.

"You can't take a pound of chocolates to bed with you on a cold night," Marcia warned.

"*I* did," she laughed. "Do we want more tea?"

"It appears we do," Marcia said resignedly. The two of them had decided long ago that water boiled twice as fast for Marcia, and so the brewing became her job; Katie did the cleaning up.

"Look, I'm perfectly serious, Katie. Granted, Peter was not much more than a charming rat. And granted, his running off with a model was maybe a little hard on your ego. Crushing, in fact. So your losing control for a while and eating your way into twenty extra pounds was perfectly understandable. *That*, I have no problem with. What I am having trouble with is the way you continue to punish yourself for your collapse after Peter left. You don't eat, you don't drink, you don't smoke. You act as though you're still twenty pounds overweight, when, if anything, you're underweight. And except for a little . . . friendliness with Jimmy, you've shunned the male sex. When're you going to start letting your hair down?"

Katie held out a long lock of undone black hair in each hand. "I did, tonight, or didn't you notice?"

"I mean, figuratively speaking," Marcia corrected.

"I *did* tonight, or didn't you notice?" Katie gave her a wry grimace.

"Well . . . so how did you feel about it . . . him?"

Katie let out a long, weary sigh. Instead of answering Marcia's question directly, she said softly, "I think it would be too much like the old days, when I'd open up a new box of chocolates. One cream-filled chocolate would lead to another, then to another. Whether I was reading, or doing the dishes, or folding the laundry . . . part of me would always be aware that I had a box of chocolates going. I'd want to go back to it, then back to it again. I'd pretend I didn't care, but I wouldn't be able to leave the box alone, couldn't forget that the candy existed. I'd become dependent on it, addicted, in fact. I was never safe, never free until I finally learned not to bring the damn box of chocolates into the house. The same holds true of a male bonbon like Fletcher Ramsey," Katie concluded firmly. "He looks habit-forming."

"Now that's truly silly, Katie. Just consider him a little treat when he's around, like the sugar in my tea," Marcia argued, sipping from her mug.

"And when he's gone—like Peter, like the box of chocolates? What then? No, the best thing is to do without, so that if you don't have . . . whatever it is . . . you won't miss it."

Marcia threw up her hands. "That is the most cockeyed logic I've ever heard. When do you dream up this stuff?"

"At night, in my bed—when I'm chewing on a celery stick. Come on, let's close up. We can talk about the future of the Shape-Up Room tomorrow. I'm ready for bed—even a cold one."

Chapter Two

$\mathcal{K}$atie burrowed more deeply under her down comforter and slid her toes under the furry lump that huddled under the covers with her. Thank heavens for Moose. He kept the mice down, purred often and radiated heat like a warm brick. At Katie's stirring movement, he crawled laboriously from the foot of the bed to her pillow, paused at her nose to verify that it was indeed Katrina Bright that he'd just spent the night with and laid himself across her shoulders. It was Moose's way of saying, "Food. Now."

"It's too cold, you spoiled beast," Katie moaned, and dug in more deeply. She didn't have to be at the Shape-Up Room until the afternoon, and on this of all mornings, she longed for sleep. If she slept, she wouldn't have to begin working on a relocation scheme. And if she slept, she could go back to the dream she'd been having. But what *was* the dream? Fletcher Ramsey had been in it, and Katie felt, after the dream, as though she knew him very well. But what had she dreamed? No, it was no use . . . she couldn't remember. She might as well get up and feed the cat.

Oh, but it was *so* cold. She shivered as she pulled on a pair of knee socks under her long flannel gown and wrapped an oversized bright yellow terrycloth robe around her slender frame. She was well into her first autumn in an Old Stone House in New Paltz, New York—and she was beginning to wonder whether she'd make it through an actual winter. Stone houses dotted all the hills and side roads of the Catskill Mountain region. Most of them dated back to the early 1700's, and although many of them had been fashionably and comfortably refurbished, the one Katie was renting was, as Mr. Barker the real-estate agent had assured her, "nearly original." True, it had plumbing and electricity. But the heating system consisted of two lonely kerosene space heaters at opposite ends of the ground floor. Any heat the upstairs bedrooms enjoyed had to filter up through the cracks of the wide pine floors.

Hands jammed into her bathrobe pockets, Katie pattered down the steps behind her cat. Impulsively she laid her hand on one of the stone walls of the kitchen. Stone cold. So much for Mr. Barker's theory of thermodynamics. "The walls are two and a half feet thick," he'd said. "Great for heat retention," he'd said. "Costs next to nothing to heat," he'd said.

She turned up the dial on the back of the space heater. By January she'd surely be in the poorhouse. She winced. January. Where would the Shape-Up Room be in January? She looked around the huge kitchen, thirty-five feet long and more than half as wide. How about right here? Of course, it was not exactly an empty room. Besides the usual large appliances and metal cabinets, there was an over-stuffed maroon sofa, an antique rocking chair, and a long bench at one end; and an enormous mahogany dining table and six chairs at the other. She would have to move out all the furniture every morning, roll up the braided rug . . . no, it was a silly thought.

The cat threw his full sixteen pounds at her leg in a rub that was more threat than entreaty. "Hurry up," he warned. Katie bent over and scratched his ears, then kneaded her fingers in his thick white fur. "A few more weeks, Moose, and I won't be able to find you in the snow." If ever a cat deserved the name "Snowball," it was Moose.

Katie fed the cat and curled up in the sofa, near the heater, to savor her boiled eggs and single slice of toast. It was still early morning, but the November sun shone bright and clear through the small multipaned windows. On the deep stone windowsills, geraniums flashed bright red and pink in their clay pots. Pulling up a green and blue woolen afghan around her, Katie decided that the kitchen sofa was more comfortable than the living-room sofa—which was just as well, because she spent most of her time in this room.

The stone house was too big and too drafty, of course, but it was the most wonderful house she'd ever lived in. If she squinted, she could imagine a New England colonial family getting ready for the day's farming. Probably they had a cow and chickens and a big shaggy dog. For a quarter of a millenium, people had lived and loved here, and Katie had grown fond of every one of their ghosts.

During her first weeks in the stone house last spring, she'd made up her mind that one day it would be hers. The owner lived in Albany; his wife, thank heavens, was strictly a city girl. Eventually the house would go on the market— but would Katie be in a position any longer to afford it? Fletch was right—she was living in a fantasy.

Fletch? Since when had she put herself on a nickname basis with him? Since her dream that morning, that's when; all of a sudden the elusive dream came rushing back in vivid detail. In it she had been trying to find her way home in a snowstorm. She was wading through deep drifts of snow and the flakes bit into her cheeks and brow. She had lost her hat, and her long hair whipped around her face. Suddenly Fletch appeared alongside her, talking normally and acting as though there were no blizzard at all. She asked him if he knew which direction her home was in, and he'd answered simply, "I haven't any idea where your home is."

Then—and this part made less sense—he began gently to smooth her wet, wind-tossed hair away from her face. When he wrapped his arms around her, her clothes began to disappear beneath his touch. He didn't actually take off her clothes; they just . . . went away, and she was standing naked in his arms. But he was still wearing his three-piece suit. Then it wasn't snowing any longer, and a kind of peaceful numbness settled over her for a bit. And then he began to stroke the sides and back of her naked body with his warm hands, and she felt sensation return, although slowly at first. But then, as his hands explored her body further, the pleasant sensation quickly developed into an electrifying current and she shuddered his name, "Fletch" —and that was when she awoke, shivering.

For one long moment Katie shut her eyes tight and relived the sensual joy she had known in the dream. It had been so long since she had dreamt of pleasure. When her marriage lay in ruins she had dreamt, for months and months, of falling, and plane crashes, and—dreariest of all—being an actress on a stage without a script.

She stood up to make another cup of coffee. Well, her dream about Fletch was a better dream than those others, but it still took place in a blizzard, she observed with characteristic irony. And then her tight, disciplined intelligence took over. *You dope. What do you expect to dream about when you turn the heat nearly off—the South Pacific? And of course you'd be likely to dream about him. He dropped into your life like a hand grenade; he held you, kissed you, took outrageous liberties. Snap out of it.* A sexy dream after meeting Fletcher Ramsey was as natural as indigestion after a double-anchovy pizza.

She took a sip of black coffee and grimaced. *Now if I had that colonial cow out in the back, I could have thick cream in this coffee,* she thought with sudden longing. For the last three years she had taken her coffee black. It was one of her greatest disciplines; she really didn't like black coffee.

At noon Marcia called. "Katie! Yesterday—was I hallucinating?"

"No, Marsh, you were not," Katie sighed. "We really have been thrown out on our keisters."

"Oh, the on-our-keisters part I accept. *I'm* having trouble believing the in-his-arms part." Her laugh was sly and friendly.

Katie groaned. "*All* true, I'm sorry to say." Clearly Marcia was going to fan that memory red-hot for a long time.

"Well—what're you going to do about it?"

"Which part?" Katie returned dryly. "His arms, or our keisters?"

"Our keisters, of course." Obviously Marcia had a plan; her voice was throbbing with excitement.

Katie intercepted her. "As a matter of fact, you little nag, I've already called Mr. Barker. He promised to look through his rental listings, which means he has nothing obvious at his fingertips."

"Not to worry, boss. I've just tripped over a possibility. Mrs. McPhail was in this morning, and I was crying on her shoulder about relocating. She says she has a charming country barn on her property that she'd be willing to let cheap. I'll pick you up in ten minutes and we can check it out."

"And meanwhile, who's going to rally the troops back at the Shape-Up?" Sometimes Marcia forgot those little details.

"Jessie said she'd sit in for an hour. Be ready."

Fifteen minutes later the two women were barreling out of New Paltz, heading west toward the rolling Shawangunk foothills. Geologically the Shawangunk hills shared none of the characteristics of their taller neighbors to the north, the Catskill Mountains. But Katie preferred to think of the flattened hills as little children of the Catskills. She was extremely fond of New Paltz and the countryside around it, and in the bright, crisp November sun it was easy to see why.

They drove through several miles of New England apple orchards, and Katie thought with longing of the crisp MacIntosh, juicy Delicious, and cheek-sucking Cortland apples that had been harvested so recently. The nicest stomachache she'd ever had she'd got by plucking and eating too many apples on a ramble into town once. She sat back with a smile. As far as Katie was concerned, the mid-Hudson River valley, where New Paltz and dozens of other small towns and cities were snugly nestled, was God's country.

Marcia had been chattering happily about the fantastic business opportunity an unreconstructed barn represented. No New York landlord gouging them on the rent; just a sympathetic lady who wanted the Shape-Up to succeed. No premiums to pay for an ideal location. . . .

"Which brings up a good point, Marsh, old girl—where *is* this barn? We're twenty minutes out of town and climbing steadily."

"It's on this side of Lake Minnewaska, that I know. Keep an eye out for a shingled farmhouse with green shutters; the barn's in the back."

They missed it the first time and had to double back; the

farmhouse was barely visible behind a thick, high grove of bushes and trees.

"I hope Mrs. McPhail won't object to having a large billboard set up discreetly in front of her bushes. It's either that or a traffic cop if we want anyone to find this place." Katie's hopes were plummeting fast.

Marcia had been told that no one would be home, so the two tramped through overgrown grass and around a small junkpile to the back. It was a barn, all right. Katie could see bales of hay up in the loft where the broken shuttered door had blown open. Marcia's face fell, but only a little. "It looks like it could use a little work, of course. But Mrs. McPhail said it does have electricity, at least."

"Do you suppose this is what she meant?" Katie pointed a booted toe at a heavy orange electric cord which ran from the basement of the farmhouse and disappeared under the barn door. "Really, Marsh, we may as well go back," she said flatly.

"Oh, we've come this far, let's just take a peek." Marcia grabbed one end of the barn door and slid it open a couple of feet. They peered into the unlit interior.

"I hear something . . . *flapping* in there," Marcia breathed, her eyes opening wide. She moved away from the door.

"Bats or an owl, probably," Katie said calmly as she stepped inside. As her eyes adjusted to the light she made out an ancient, rusted farm tractor, a pile of kegs with broken barrel hoops; several bicycles missing front or rear wheels; a load of lumber haphazardly stacked; and a dismantled wooden lawn-swing. Toward the back things were packed even more densely and chaotically. Most of the rusty metal looked like unnameable farm tools from the horse-and-buggy era.

Katie popped back out and pulled her green woolen hat down over her ears. "If you want my opinion, Mrs.

McPhail should forget about being a landlady and go into antiques and collectibles. It was sweet of her to think of us, but . . . no, Marsh, it won't do.''

They got back into the car and headed back to town. Marcia wasn't quite ready to give up. "If we worked *really* hard and cleaned it all out . . .''

". . . and insulated it and installed a heating system and electricity and a bathroom facility—then we still probably couldn't get people to drive way out here. No thanks. I've been told I have no head for business,'' Katie said, smarting again from Ramsey's cold-hearted analysis. "I may not be a Fletcher Ramsey, but I'm no starry-eyed Pollyanna either. There must be *some*thing more suitable in this bustling metropolis of six thousand.''

"*Six* thousand? Haven't you forgotten someone? Seven thousand more of us, to be exact? I realize we college kids are often considered *persona non grata* by you townspeople; but really . . .'' Marcia huffed playfully.

Marcia was a math major at the State University at New Paltz, and the ancient town-gown rivalry that existed in any college town was an endless source of jokes for them both. Actually, Katie was neither town *nor* gown. Originally from upstate New York, she had completed her freshman year at New Paltz by the time she'd met and married Peter. She dropped out, broken and dispirited, in the second semester of her sophmore year. Then a year ago she'd begun taking courses again, at night. At the rate she was going, Katie calculated, she'd have her liberal arts degree in twelve and a half more years.

Katie picked up and returned Marcia's town-gown challenge. "Don't you go all high-falutin' on *me*, Ms. Welkins. You forget—I knew you before your contact lenses and the body perm.''

"Two of your very brightest ideas . . . Ms. Bright,'' Marcia conceded smugly. She looked at herself in the rear-view mirror and stabbed at her curly brown ringlets.

"You know, Katie," she said in a softer voice, "you really have made a difference in my life. Because of you I'm no longer an obnoxious, brainy type. Because of you, I'm a *pretty,* obnoxious, brainy type." She looked sideways at Katie. "Because of you Chuck . . . Chuck wants to marry me. And in *spite* of you," she added quickly, "I want to do it."

Katie turned to her friend in open amazement. "Marcia! You're kidding!"

"I knew you'd fall right in with the idea," Marcia said dryly.

"You *know* I don't mean that. Chuck is a wonderful guy, perfect for you. It's just that you've been so . . . so *liberated,* all the time I've known you. You've marched for every feminist cause in the book. *I* didn't spend four hundred dollars last spring to go down and picket the White House for more women in the Cabinet. A wedding . . . a veil . . . it's not very . . . militant, that's all," she groped.

"Yeah, I know. But lately we've been getting more . . . I don't know . . . serious. Tax-wise, it doesn't even make sense to marry. We just . . . want to do it."

"And you're afraid I'll . . . what? Kidnap the minister?"

"Well, it's not as though you've been singing the praises of matrimony for the last two years," Marcia said defensively. "I've never said much, one way or the other, about marrying; I was afraid you wouldn't think I was being supportive when you . . . after Peter."

"Oh, but there's no comparison between us and you two, you silly dimwit! For heaven's sake, you've been *living* with Chuck for two years. You're from the same background; you like the same food, share the same hobbies. Statistically, at least, you're a perfect match. But Peter . . . Peter swept me away, you know that. I wasn't thinking."

She pulled at a thread in her mittens, then looked out at

the rolling orchards. "Who was *I*? Just a runny-nosed kid from Oswego, not nearly so grand as"—she rolled her eyes—"*Chicago*. Peter seemed so suave, so . . . citified. He knew which wines went with what; who got presented to whom first. Once he even had to show me where to set the lobster picks when we were giving a fancy dinner," she groaned. "I didn't even know lobster picks *existed*. I would've used . . . forks," she said in a low voice.

"Katie, if you pull an anxiety attack on me, I promise I'll roll you right out of the car and make you walk home. Listen to me. Peter was obsessed with appearances, and he ended up with exactly what he deserved—a shallow, vain creature who dumped *him* before the year was out. All's well that ends well, if you ask me. Peter is out of your life and . . . dammit, I *knew* this would happen once I mentioned marriage."

"In that case, let me give you my . . . really, Marsh . . . my deepest, fondest, best wishes. And if I'm not the maid of honor, I'll pull out all your hair."

"Don't worry. I'd be too embarrassed to ask any of my fellow picketeers," Marcia answered wryly.

Marcia threaded the car expertly through the meandering lunchtime crowd of students. The college was a block or so from the main drag, a street of cafes and bars, with an occasional clothing or tourist shop thrown in. Life did not exactly proceed in the fast lane in New Paltz, Katie thought gratefully. And yet, there was an undeniable sophistication apparent in many of the students. Katie could tell by their dress—by the expensive leather shoulder bags of the women, and the carefully handcrafted boots of the men—which students were from New York City. For these city sophisticates, the college was ideally located—far enough from parents for a sense of freedom; close enough to drive home for the weekend, when the inevitable homesickness hit.

Marcia was bubbling over on another subject. "I can

hardly *wait* for Thanksgiving,'' she said happily. ''Somehow or other Chuck has managed to get us involved in the Macy's Thanksgiving Day Parade. I gather we're going to be up all of Wednesday night blowing up a giant Mickey Mouse balloon—or maybe it was Fred Flintstone. Who cares? It'll be a lark, either way. Have you made up your mind about going home yet?''

''My parents have made it up for me; they're going to be basking in the Florida Keys on vacation, which is just as well. I read somewhere that the average American consumes eight thousand calories on Thanksgiving Day. I don't need that kind of temptation—or the hassle my folks give me when I don't clean up my plate.''

''But I hate to see you spend Thursday and Friday alone. Come down to Long Island with us.''

''Thanks, Marsh, but three is still a crowd. Anyway, Helen's invited me to a vegetarian Thanksgiving. Helen should be an ideal hostess—she's totally blasé about turkey; she's currently on a little health-food kick; and she's rich enough to make an un-turkey dinner interesting. It might be fun.''

''I thought you weren't too keen on Helen Ritter and her crowd,'' Marcia answered, surprised. ''Where to now? Home or Shape-Up?''

''Home, I guess. Helen's not bad, once you get to know her. It's just that with that silver spoon in her mouth, I have a little trouble understanding her sometimes.'' The two women grinned at one another. Helen Ritter, whose father had made it very big in TV-game circuitboards, was inclined to put on airs. Marcia had had to remind Katie that Helen, just like everyone else, got into her leotards one leg at a time.

Katie spent the next two hours huddled near the kerosene heater with the cat on her lap and the telephone at her feet, calling every real-estate agent between Kingston and Newburgh, trying without immediate success to find a new location for the Shape-Up Room. She began to feel like a missionary forced out into the cold with her little flock by a villainous, mustache-twirling entrepreneur. Only there wasn't any mustache in this case . . . just the barest stubble above a laughing mouth and under an almost imperceptibly off-center nose.

Chapter Three

"Ready? To the left and right. Back. Forward. To the left, right, back, forward. And again . . . back, forward."

Feet together, stomach flat, Katie led the last class of the day through their exercises. There were seven women in the group—Thursday night was the strongest television night of the week—but the group was fiercely loyal. Katie had become friendly with three or four of them, and she knew that the battles they were fighting were even longer and more uphill than her own.

"All right, deep knee bends now. Up, down, two, down. By the way, a tip—for those of you who like your coffee light. Did you know that you can trade the cream from four cups of coffee for at least four apples? Eight, down, nine, down . . ."

"I'll trade all four apples back to you . . . for a chocolate sundae," one of the younger women shot back between exhalations.

Katie laughed. "Don't talk to me about chocolate . . . up, down . . . sundaes. Unless . . . down, up, down . . . you want to see a grown woman cry."

Sharing the pain. That was what these classes were really all about. And Katie needed the class as much as its members needed her. "O.k., all together now. Backs flat on the floor, hands behind your heads, knees bent. Time for sit-ups." A groan rose from nearly everyone.

And so it went, as Katie put her heart and soul into every exercise she demanded of her class. When she said, "Get that leg up *higher*," she raised her own leg higher. When she said, "Let's go five more," she did five more, too. And when she concluded with a smiling "Not bad, for a bunch of tootsies," her brow was as dripping wet as everyone else's.

As the class broke up a woman Katie's own age, and a newcomer to the Shape-Up program, came up rather shyly to her and asked about an exercise to relieve lower back pain. Katie demonstrated one or two of them. As she rose up from the floor she saw reflected in the mirrored wall her own tall figure, dressed in navy-blue leotards with tiny white vertical pinstripes and circled with a thin white belt. And she saw Fletcher Ramsey, in white shorts and polo shirt, walking across the room toward her.

It had been exactly one week since she'd last seen him. And although he was instantly recognizable, for a split second she was reminded of Jimmy, who often timed his racquetball game to end with her last class so that he could take her home. But Jimmy had never got from the rest of the women in the exercise room the reception that *this* guy was getting. Six or seven female heads turned toward him simultaneously; two or three of those heads came equipped with voices.

"Will you check *him* out," murmured one.

"Think his intentions are honorable?"

"God, I hope not," laughed a third.

"Nice calves."

And, to cap things off generally, someone let out a long, low whistle. Really, Katie decided irritably, we're as bad as a football team in a locker room. It sure wasn't hard to see where Fletcher Ramsey's confidence came from.

When he reached Katie at the other end of the room, he let out a nervous laugh. "Whew. That was the longest walk of my life. I will never torture a woman with the old once-over again. If you send me out of here before these women all leave, I swear I'll collapse of embarrassment," he threatened with a crooked smile.

"Everyone should be treated like a sex object once in a while," Katie whispered in a deliberately pleasant voice. "It keeps one from getting intellectual." Then, raising her voice, she announced, "Ladies, I'd like you to meet our landlord—for the next few weeks—Mr. Fletcher Ramsey. Mr. Ramsey . . . has a few words he'd like to say to you." And she yielded the floor to him with a graceful gesture. Why she decided to put him in such an awkward position, she had no idea.

The bantering glow in his gray eyes erupted into flame as he said quietly to Katie, through a forced smile, "Naughty girl. That *isn't* nice." Aloud he said, "Yes . . . well . . . I'd just like to say . . . uh . . . that I hope we'll all be very happy here." Then he paused, looked at Katie, looked at the other women, and said, "Oh . . . and one other announcement. Miss Bright and I . . . are engaged to be married." And he put his arm around Katie and kissed her long and full on the lips.

From behind his hot, sweet kiss Katie heard a wild cheer go up among the women. With a vigorous shove she freed herself. "We are *not* getting married," she burst out vehemently.

Ramsey turned to their audience. "See? How she treats me? For months I've begged her to let me make an honest woman of her. For months she's refused." He turned to an

outraged Katie and in a mock-earnest voice said, "Katie
. . . over dinner . . . just give me a chance."

"Hey, give the guy a chance, Katie," one of the women
chimed in. "So go to dinner—so what's a dinner?"

"I *don't* dine *out*," Katie answered crisply.

"Then at least have a drink with me, Katie," Ramsey
followed up at once.

"I do *not* drink," she snarled.

"*I* do!" someone volunteered.

Ramsey took Katie's fist, raised it, and kissed the
clenched knuckles. "Your place, then? Or mine? Katie . . .
we've just got to talk." He really was getting into full
swing.

She whipped her hand out of his and said in a voice
seething with fury, "You out*rage*ous man. I wouldn't go
out . . ."

Leaning over to kiss her again, he whispered quickly, "I
said I'm not leaving until that gang does. I can keep this up
all night if necessary."

And he would. Damn him, he would. He had to have the
last word, the last bounce, the last everything. Quickly she
swept her scattered wits into a little pile in the middle of her
brain. "Well, then . . . since what I do this evening seems
to be a community concern . . . I *will* see you," she
announced coldly.

But he was faster than that. "Dinner?" he corrected.

"I *said* . . . all right. Dinner."

Another loud cheer.

"I'm so glad you approve, ladies. Now . . . good-*night*,
perhaps?" Betrayed by her own sex.

In high spirits the women ambled out of the room. Katie
turned back to Ramsey, still nursing her fit of pique.
"What're you doing in a racquetball outfit?" she said
peevishly. "You look ridiculous." Actually, he didn't look
ridiculous at all. Stripped of his three-piece suit, he looked

leaner, trimmer, fitter than she'd imagined. Make that a 32 Waist.

"You, on the other hand, look adorable, Kate. I like the belt," he said as he ran a finger along her encircled waistline. "Still, with that hair I'd have to vote for basic black," he said in an allusion to the first time he'd seen her.

"What do you do—load up your popgun and fire off all your compliments at once?" she sulked.

"I would've fired some of them off last week, but you shot *me* out of the room like a human cannonball. But never mind; we've plenty of time to exchange endearments. First, I've got to shower; one way or another I work up a sweat every time I walk into this building."

"What *have* you been doing, anyway?" she couldn't resist asking.

"Playing racquetball, of course." He took an imaginary swing at a ball. "Great fun. Don't know why I've never found time for it before. But really, I'd be brutish not to shower. I'll be back in ten minutes."

"Don't bother. *I* won't be here."

"Certainly you will. Tonight we dine on Fletcher's seafood *du jour*."

"*That* swill? You're wasting your time, Ramsey. Go away."

"Are you showering?" he asked, unfazed.

"I bathe at home."

"Suit yourself," he said politely and walked toward the door. On his way out he scooped up five or six long waist-twist poles.

"Where are you going with those?" she called after him.

"Just securing the fort, princess." He opened one of the double-glass doors, walked through it, and slipped the half-dozen poles through both door handles on the outside. With a friendly wave to Katie, trapped inside, he headed down the hall toward the men's showers.

"I don't believe it." Katie made a dash for the doors and pushed with all her might. Nothing. She leaned her back against the glass, breathing heavily. She'd call Marcia. She'd call the police. She'd break the damn door down; what did she care if the landlord objected? *But wait. Think. Relax.* He wasn't worth the aggravation. Surely she'd had her fill of melodrama for the night. She would walk calmly to the outside of the building with him—and then bolt.

She wrapped a denim skirt around her leotards, pulled a creamy lambswool sweater over her head and slipped into a pair of soft suede boots. By the time she'd tucked her hair back into its bun and run some clear gloss over her lips to protect them from the cold, he was back. The poles came out, he came in and the two were once more face to face, ready for another round.

Katie stood with her back to the mirrored wall, both hands resting on the exercise bar behind her. She was thinking that it would help her side a lot if he'd look, oh, *plainer* than he had managed so far. But again he was distractingly attractive, this time in faded jeans, a navy turtleneck and a gray tweed jacket.

"Well . . . you said jeans and a t-shirt was the uniform around here. It's too damn cold for a t-shirt," he said with a half smile. "Surely this will do?"

"Makes no difference to me," she sniffed. "I won't be anywhere near the outfit tonight."

"Kate . . ." he warned, moving within two inches of her face. She leaned away until her head was pressed against the mirrored wall and her back arched in retreat. The palms of his hands slid over her white knuckles, and he began to unpeel her grip from the exercise barre finger by finger. His hair was still slightly damp, his chin just shaven, and he smelled clean. His eyes flashed good-humored impatience.

"Kate, you'd wear out a stone. Now, look. We can do this easy, or we can do this hard. You can come along like a nice, fair-minded person, or we can repeat our little vaudeville show to a new house tomorrow night. And the night after. I want you to sample the Fletcher's menu, and you will. If you still want to blow up all my restaurants after that, fine. Shall we go?''

Taking her elbow, he marched her out into the sharply cold night. ''It's been a pretty fierce November so far, don't you think?'' he asked pleasantly.

''Yes.'' No one said she had to be chatty.

He glanced around. ''Your car isn't around, I take it?''

''No.''

''Good; I'll be able to take you straight home afterward.'' He paused at the only car that remained in the parking lot. ''Here we are.''

''You're kidding, of course.'' She looked at him openeyed. *''This* is your car?''

''You only date fellows in Maseratis, perhaps?'' He blinked at her innocently.

''Of course not,'' she said, taken aback. ''But . . . but *this . . .''*

The Chevrolet was seven or eight years old, and the right rear fender was badly crumpled. So was the left front fender. The passenger door was white, but the rest of the car was red. The radio antenna was bent over double and pointed forlornly to the ground. A long piece of chrome trim had become detached and was bobbing gently in the wind. A Maserati, it was not.

''Don't worry; it'll get us to Kingston, all right. Old Charlotte runs like a top.''

''Do you bring this along special for when you have to negotiate with your tenants?'' she asked as he swung his weight lightly into the driver's seat.

He laughed. ''You'd be more understanding, if you ever had to leave a car parked in the city. I used to have a Corvette; it lasted three days before it was stolen. The Mercedes lasted a week. Finally I got tired of it all, bought this Chevy—it was nearly in perfect condition, a real peach—and spent a weekend doing cosmetic surgery on it. I thought the white door was a particularly nice touch,'' he added serenely.

"The broken windshield wiper sure wasn't.''

"Oh, that idea wasn't mine—just a passing kid who got inspired, I suppose.'' The engine started effortlessly. "There's no music, of course. I didn't dare risk installing a radio or a tape deck.''

Katie stared at him, completely bemused. "You're amazing, you know that?'' He was absolutely nothing like her ex-husband. Peter would've worn a shopping bag over his head rather than be recognized in a rattletrap like this. Even physically, Fletch was different. He was fair; Peter was dark. He was lean; Peter was burly. And Fletch laughed easily and often. He was supremely confident, yet not swaggering. Peter . . . well, Peter swaggered. At the time, she'd found Peter's style impressive.

"I repeat . . . why am I amazing?'' Fletch had been speaking to her.

"What? Oh . . . well, you don't seem to care about . . . appearances . . . about what people think of you.'' They had rolled onto the New York Thruway, and, as Fletch had promised, old Charlotte the Chevrolet hummed right along. "And Lord knows,'' she added as the memory of his wedding "announcement'' sprinted across the back of her mind, "you're not afraid to make a scene.''

He was quick to understand. "I'm sorry I put you on the spot in front of your class, Kate.''

"It was my fault, really. I put *you* on the spot first,'' she conceded grudgingly.

"Yes, but *I* put *you* on the spot last week when I . . . this is silly, Kate. All I'm trying to say is that basically, I'm a survivor. I've always lived by my own wits. I act quickly and instinctively, and sometimes I don't predict the fallout very well. I think I pushed you a little too far with that engagement nonsense.''

''That's all it was—nonsense. Don't worry about it,'' she said, wishing he'd change the subject.

''I'm not so sure,'' he smiled, moving into the high-speed lane. ''Those ladies seemed desperate to see you fixed up with a husband.''

''I've had one, thanks; they're not all they're cracked up to be.''

He turned to her with quickened interest. ''So you prefer the freewheeling life of a single?''

''I didn't say that, either.'' She groaned inwardly. *You're sounding especially intelligent this evening,* she told herself. He'd probably grill her all the way to Kingston, if she didn't control more of the conversation herself. After all, there was little harm Fletcher Ramsey could still do: he'd already evicted her, embarrassed her and abducted her. She had nothing to lose by being civil to him.

She sat back in her seat, a little more relaxed somehow. ''When did you first decide to open a new Fletcher's' Fish . . . and Chips . . . in New Paltz?''

''Years ago. It's all part of a master strategy. Basically the restaurants will follow the Hudson River from north to south, Albany to New York City. As I get ready to slice into the Big Apple itself, I'm counting on 'Fletcher's' being a household word.''

Katie was impressed. There was something about his do-anything attitude that convinced her that ''Fletcher's'' *would* be a household word. ''How on earth did you decide on fish and chips? Are there fisherman knocking around somewhere in the Ramsey dynasty?''

''None that I know of. But I used to take my daughter, during my weekends with her, to a local seafood joint. It wasn't great, but we used to play a little game of 'If this were *our* place.' She wanted fatter French fries. I wanted flakier fish. We had it all planned out, how when she grew up she was going to manage the restaurant and be nice to the customers and all. I believe *I* was assigned to the deep-frying and the dishes.''

He had a child, then. And once, a wife. She smiled politely. ''And does your daughter still plan to run your empire when she grows up?'' Katie couldn't bring herself to ask about the wife for some odd reason.

''Cindy *is* grown up—or nearly so. She's nineteen. It's hard to believe that when I was her age I was married. And miserable.'' His voice had dropped to a soft musing tone, but there was nothing in it of self-pity.

''Nineteen?'' The number hung in the air between them. Katie herself wasn't certain whether she was asking about the daughter, or asking about the father.

''Cindy was born nine months after prom night. Corny, isn't it? Almost, but not quite, amusing. It was pretty tragic at the time, I can tell you. College, career—everything out the window. And all because of a few bottles of beer—and the family station wagon, of course. Sometimes I think my whole life would have been different if Dad hadn't lent me the car that night,'' he said quietly.

Katie sat mesmerized, occasionally forcing herself to look at him as he rambled on—she wanted to be as natural as possible. *He* certainly was. He spoke so easily of what must have been a shattering event. Not flippantly, but . . . comfortably. Fletch made her feel as though she were an easy person to talk to, and it was strangely flattering.

''But then, of course,'' he continued in a lighter vein, ''Cindy would never have been born. And Cindy is, as the song goes, the light of my life. Fabulous kid. Smart as a whip. She's in pre-med at Boston University, and doing great. And, thank God, she has no plans to get married for a while.''

Katie felt the conversation had moved to safer ground—

maybe. "Would it be the end of the world if Cindy did marry?" she asked curiously. He seemed so hostile to marriage. Any marriage.

"Marriage sidetracks dreams," he said flatly. "By the time I got out of the service, found a job and educated myself part-time, a third of my life had slipped away. A third of it."

"It's not as if you're doing badly," she contradicted. "It's not as if you don't know . . . where your next restaurant will be." Suddenly she felt wildly impatient about the slow progress her own life was making. She'd let a week slip by and all she'd done to find a new place for her Shape-Up Room was to look at a run-down barn and call a few real-estate agents. She wanted to race back to New Paltz and . . . what? Drive around town looking for "For Rent" signs? *There* was the real problem. She had no imagination, no wildly brilliant scheme. And yet she'd do anything to just . . . get moving.

He broke into her thoughts. "Kate . . . are you going to carry a grudge against me forever?"

"I don't know," she answered honestly. "Right now I couldn't care less that you're the one responsible for the little detour my career is taking. I just want to get back on track again." She paused, surprised at her benevolence. "You've really got me all fired up; have you considered going into the business of bottling and selling enthusiasm?"

"First let's see if I can talk you into my Fisherman's Platter."

"If you can do that, Ramsey, you can probably sell oil to the Arabs."

"Here's our exit; we'll soon see."

They drove directly to the business section of Kingston. Plucky Kingston. Overrun at least once by just about everyone—French, English, Indian—and slowly rebuilt, Kingston was an appealing amalgam of historic, decrepit, restored and modern buildings. If you closed one eye, you saw Rip Van Winkle. If you opened it, you saw computer programmers in three-piece suits hurrying home after a late night at the office.

Ramsey's restaurant seemed well located on a main thoroughfare. The building itself was sided with weathered vertical planking; the doors and windows were painted sea blue. Green awnings over the windows and the drive-in section gave the restaurant a more distinctive look than the typical red-brick fast-food palace.

Katie liked it. It suggested the ocean to her, without being overly nautical. But she wasn't ready to admit it. "The colors clash with your car, of course," she said as he opened her door.

She stood up, several inches below his height in her low-heeled boots. He scanned her face intently, searching for signs of humor, then relaxed. "How would you like me to bite your nose?" He grinned, dropping his forearms on her shoulders and letting his hands dangle idly behind her. He was so close. Their smoky breaths mingled in the cold night air, and Katie was suddenly, irrationally aware of his aftershave cologne. It was a husky, appealing scent and hinted of forests and lakes. If she closed her eyes she could imagine that they were standing at the door of, say, his hunting lodge, instead of in the parking lot of a . . . Fletcher's Fish and Chips. She closed her eyes briefly, just to imagine and then opened them wide again. What was she *doing?*

Fletch, meanwhile, was dropping a kiss on the tip of her nose. "That is the prettiest nose this side of the Hudson, Kate."

She gave him a sly look. "Well . . . at least it's on straight."

And then he did bite her, gently, on that nose.

Inside the restaurant there were only a few diners; it was

late. To her astonishment Katie wished that it had been more crowded, more obviously a success.

But Fletch seemed happy enough. "Hey, not a bad showing . . . eight, nine . . . *eleven* customers."

"That's good?"

"For 9:15 on a nonshopping night? My god, it's terrific. There must be a convention nearby."

They slid into a booth. Katie knocked on the varnished tabletop. "Real wood."

"I got a little carried away on this one," he admitted sheepishly.

"Oh, you don't have to be ashamed, surely. Do you?"

"You do if you're in the fast-food business. But last year I got this crazy idea that the food would taste better if the surroundings were more attractive."

She wrinkled her nose. "Doesn't say too much for the food."

He rested his chin on his fist and gave her a scrutinizing, memorizing look. "Kate . . . why do you wear your hair in that stupid bun?"

"Because that way it stays out of my eyes during exercises," she answered patiently.

"It's not that your face alone isn't fantastic; but it's just such a waste," he said philosophically. "Well, never mind. What're you having?" he asked, pointing to the "menu"— an oar paddle on which the selections were neatly painted. "They're a little hokey," he laughed, "but I got a great deal on the oars, and then I didn't know what to do with 'em. I still have nineteen pairs."

"I think they show great . . . enterprise. But Fletch, I really have no intention of eating here. I'm not hungry," she hedged. Everything smelled delicious. She was starving.

"I'd suggest the fried flounder," he said calmly, ignoring her.

"I don't *want* fried flounder," she answered politely.

"Scallops. Bet you haven't had fried scallops in years," he continued helpfully.

"I don't *want* fried scallops." Her voice had dropped ominously low.

"Kate. Why do you think I dragged you up here?" he asked in a reasonable tone.

"I'm blessed if I know," she answered impatiently. "Look, Fletch, the carpet's thick, the windows are clean, the help looks friendly. The food smells . . . fine. Can't you leave it at that?" She hoped to finish on a severe note, but somehow her words came out sad, almost plaintive.

"Good grief, Kate," he said, baffled. "What's the problem here? A hundred extra calories? So skip breakfast, just for once. Are you afraid it's indigestible? Do you want an ambulance and a stomach pump standing by? Just say the word." His gray eyes, so expressive, were saying something new—that he didn't take kindly to the word no. This time there were no cute bets, no cheering audience, no friendly blackmail—just a contest of wills, his and hers, pure and simple.

"No."

"Why, dammit? Why won't you eat this stuff?"

"Because . . . because I might . . . like it."

"Oh." He stared at her blankly. "That's a good reason."

"It *is* a good reason, Mr. Ramsey. It's the best reason in the world. I might—let's just say for instance—I might order your blasted flounder. Tomorrow too. And the next day. I might want some French fries too, why not? Then . . . all that salty food . . . I might want a chocolate shake to wash it down. Then my stomach would be stretched, and I'd have the rest of the day to fill it—and the night. I love to eat when I read. And I read all the time. . . . And also when I think . . . or have nothing to do . . . or no one to talk to . . . where would it all end?"

"Just from eating fried flounder?" he said gently. "I didn't know, Kate. I'm sorry." He cupped her pale face in both his hands and beamed a warm smile of life back to her. "All right, then, how would you feel about . . . broiled?"

He was hopeless. She dropped her gaze away from his watching face. Broiled. Her mouth quivered. Then . . . one corner turned up, and the other. The emerging smile lit up her fine-boned face. Her full lips, normally set in a serene and steady line, surrendered and fell into a wide grin, revealing straight white teeth. Her high cheekbones took on an even more accented line, and her eyes were filled with good-humored sparkle.

"How much do I have to eat?"

"One fillet and . . . a salad? Will that fill you to bursting?"

"If I can't manage it, I can always take home a kitty bag." Another smile. Where were they all coming from?

"Can I trust you to wait here while I order?"

"Where on earth would I go?" she answered, wondering.

"Oh, I don't know . . . home . . . the nearest health spa . . . out for a jog. Don't move."

He went past the line and spoke briefly to one or two of the young girls working behind the counter. He could have easily been their father, Katie realized, but the enchanted smiles they were giving him were anything but filial. Yes, indeed; this guy was a heartbreaker.

Fletch disappeared into the kitchen, and Katie had time to kick herself once or twice for her incredibly stupid performance. The kids behind the counter probably could teach her quite a bit about maturity. Hysterics? Over fried fish? They'd be rolling on the floor with laughter. Why had she become so upset? Katie didn't like being coerced, naturally; that was one factor. But there was more.

Ever since she'd got over Peter, she'd associated food with rejection, with self-pity. And since she'd met Fletcher

Ramsey—was it really only last week?—she'd been reminded more and more of an earlier time when she was happy, willing, with an appetite for life, and food, and love. All that had been shut away under lock and key for years. Her life now was simpler, safer, generally more peaceful. There were no real downs—but then there weren't any ups, either.

Fletch appeared from out of the kitchen, a look of intense concentration on his face as he carried an enormous stainless steel baking tray loaded with dishes.

"And flowers! Say, this *is* a classy joint," she teased.

"Correction . . . *a* flower," Fletch said as he transferred the plates and cups to the table. "I didn't dare swipe any more from Nancy's birthday bouquet or there'd be hell to pay."

"Who's Nancy?"

"One of the kids who works behind the counter. It's company policy to send women employees flowers on their birthdays."

"What a nice idea," Katie said, pleased.

"Don't give me too much credit; I'm also aware that it helps keep the turnover down."

"Oh, right. The personal touch," she said dryly.

"Beats a cat-o'-nine-tails any day," he agreed cheerfully.

On her plate a fillet of flounder lay attractively arranged and prepared.

"Salt, pepper, paprika and lemon juice," he explained. "And . . . I admit . . . one teaspoon of butter. Thirty-three and a third calories. I looked it up. We can sponge 'em off if you like. But wait! Look! At least thirteen or fourteen of them have slid off the fish—they're over on that side of the plate, huddled together and terrified. Poor little calories. Here, let me soak 'em up into this hot, delicious roll I'm about to wolf down. Mmm-*mmmn*," he cooed, as though Katie were a cranky toddler in a high chair.

"*Not* very funny, Mr. Ramsey," she said.

"So why are you smiling?" he asked as he tore off a piece of the steaming roll with his strong white teeth.

"I'm just an illogical nerd, I guess."

"You're an undernourished nerd, that's for damn sure. I could see it if you had a weight problem—all this fasting and counting. But you could be on the cover of *Vogue*—you could be a professional model."

"Don't be silly," she interrupted quickly. "My torso is too long and my upper arms are too . . . fat." A *model*. Ha. The irony of it all.

"Too fat?!" he objected incredulously. "What's *thin?* Being able to slip your arm through a napkin ring? No, Kate. What you need is some meat on your bones and some color in your cheeks. They're far too pale."

Not for long, however. His fierce, unrelenting scrutiny caused a gradual, inevitable pinking of the very cheeks in question. Really, he was just so thorough about everything. "You have to understand, Fletch, that I'm a Reformed Eater. One buttered roll, and I'll bounce right off the wagon. Please just understand that," she said softly. Without waiting for his response she continued breathlessly, "The fish was really pretty good; but it's getting late, and I'm leading the first class tomorrow."

"We're on our way, sweet pickle. I have to be on the road pretty early myself." He stood up and handed Katie her cape, a pale green knit of Irish wool. As he watched her slip it over her head he said, "Now there's a sensible design; lots of room for your giant arms." He affected a very tolerable poker face, but the gray eyes were dancing. One glance into their depths, and Katie felt as if he'd waltzed her around the room.

"Stop charming my socks off and tell me since when do you broil fish—it's not on the menu." Her voice cracked like a teenager's on "charming." How charming.

"But it *will* be on the menu, and soon. There must be

zillions of skinnies like you out there, dodging calories left and right. Picture this: 'The Calorie-Counter's Platter.' Broiled fillet. Carrots. Broccoli. More carrots.'' He eyed her hopefully.

She considered. "Can you bring it in under four hundred calories?"

"I don't know. Can I?"

"I don't see why not, Mr. Ramsey," she conceded. "You seem able to do anything. It certainly would be a hit."

"Great. Fantastic. I'll do it. You're wonderful." He put his arms around her, lifted her off the floor and kind of . . . waltzed . . . her around the room.

Chapter Four

$\mathcal{T}$he trip back to New Paltz was like a glass of champagne
—tickly, and a little light-headed. It was clear to Katie that
Fletcher Ramsey was one of life's darlings. Life would
never deal *him* a hard knock on the head. At worst it would
pinch his cheek and send him scampering off with a
warning.

Amusing her with stories of his hitch in the service—a
time when surely he must have been coming to terms with
his bad marriage—he made it all sound like "Hogan's
Heroes." After the army his first job was selling cafeteria
equipment; apparently he nearly starved, but he sounded
pretty cheerful about it. Then he became a sales representa-
tive for a pizza franchise in California—that was where he
learned about the fast-food business. That was when he
went to night school. And that was when he got in a car
accident and broke a hip, an arm and two ribs. He made
lying in traction sound like sunning on the deck of a cruise
ship.

When his daughter was ten she ran away, and here, at last, his voice became serious as he recalled the hysterical phone call from his divorced wife. But even that turned out to be just another pinch on the cheek: after telephoning every hospital and police station in the state of California, he got a call from the security office in Disneyland. Cindy had spent the day, and all of her pocket money there. She needed carfare.

As far as Katie could tell, that day nine years ago was the last unhappy one Fletch had known. "You're really on a roll, aren't you?" she mused, taking in his clean-lined profile in the dim glow of the dashboard. There was humor and alertness in the set of his chin. It wasn't at all a stubborn-looking chin. Which just shows how wrong a chin can be, she thought.

"You're right about my being on a roll," he was saying. "It scares me sometimes. I get an idea and click, zing, off I go; it's all coming so easily. This sounds silly," he confessed, "but I'm finding I drive more carefully nowadays. My great dread in life is that I'll end up in traction again; it'd drive me nuts to be immobilized now."

He made it all sound so exciting. Click, zing, and off you go. Mind over matter. Nothing ventured, nothing gained. Shoot for the moon. Every upbeat cliché in the book could have Fletcher Ramsey as Exhibit A. Why *couldn't* she be more like him? Why sneak through each day as though it were sprinkled with land mines? She should just . . . go for it. But . . . go for what?

Fletch had slipped into a quieter mood, apparently at ease with her thoughtful silence. He reached across the darkness between them, took her hand in his, gave it a little squeeze and held it. It was an oddly old-fashioned gesture, throwing her back to her years in high school. But when she tried nonchalantly to withdraw her hand, he gripped it more tightly and continued to hold it; *that* wasn't at all like high school.

Why was she fighting him, anyway? Undeniably she was intensely attracted to him. Even now her pulse fluttered like a captured bird in his strong grip. The renewed contact sent shock waves of awareness rippling up and down her arm. She remembered his rather spectacular kiss in front of her class, and that reminded her of the deep, long dream-kisses she had imagined in her sleep last week. And *those* reminded her of the kisses that started it all, the hot, wild, electric kisses after the trampoline nonsense. How had she *ever* managed such wild abandon? It was practically schizophrenic.

They had come to the country road on which the stone house was situated. "The road winds a bit. We're right after the next curve; my driveway is in that clump of brush."

The night was moonless and black, but starry. They turned into the pitch-dark lane which was marked "Private Drive." "I nailed that sign up out of desperation, because tourists kept mistaking this for a country lane. At least once a week I'd find myself headlight-to-headlight with a car that was bigger and meaner than my little VW."

"What *you* need is a car with front-wheel drive. This driveway is in terrible shape," he growled. "Ever consider having it blacktopped?"

"It's not mine, for one thing. And for another, there are some huge boulders—yowch!—sticking up in it. That was one of them."

"Is that a fact," he muttered. "What the devil do you do when it snows? This driveway isn't plowable."

"I think that might be a reason—one of the reasons—why the rent was so low. The last tenants told me that two different snow-removal services broke their plows on the drive and refuse to come here anymore. Personally, I'm praying for a drought this winter. Careful, there's one more boulder after the next curve."

The end of the driveway opened out suddenly to reveal the front of the stone house, aglow in the soft light of two lanterns on either side of a double dutch door. An enormous, towering pine tree on one side of the entrance soared up into the stars; on the other, an ancient oak spread its branches protectively over the steep slate roof of the house.

Katie reached behind the bird feeder in the oak tree and brought out a house key. She had hoped to slip out of the car with a simple good-night, but Fletch was too quick, too chivalrous. So now they were both at the door and he was raving, quite naturally, about the house and expecting a tour.

"This is quite an interesting—really, an incredible—place, Kate. In the middle of a forest, almost. So isolated, so quiet." A clattering clash came from behind the house. "And so spooky! What the devil was that?"

"The raccoons, undoubtedly," Katie said calmly. "We're having a running battle over who'll control the garbage. They outnumber me, of course, and I'm beginning to think that pound for pound, they're stronger than I am, too."

"I refuse to believe that you live here alone, Kate. You've got a bodyguard in that house. Or a Doberman . . . Good lord," he said softly, pointing into the thick branches of the oak tree, "what is *that?*" A furry creature swung up onto a limb and scurried down the far side of the tree.

"Huh! The possum's back. I wonder where he's been." She slid the key into the door.

"Kate," he said, turning her around to face him and studying her with a half-earnest, half-humorous expression. "You're not . . . a witch, are you?" He made his voice sound like a cross between Cary Grant's and Vincent Price's. "Tell me the truth. Is there anything . . . ghastly . . . inside that house?"

She laughed, a little startled by his comic melodrama. "Only my cat."

"Black?"

"White."

"Ah. *That's* perfectly all right. Open the door," he demanded fearlessly.

The heavy double door swung soundlessly into a twenty-five-foot square foyer, sparsely furnished. Katie dumped her shoulder bag onto an old-fashioned drum table laden with pots of yellow and wine red chrysanthemums.

"That's the trouble with you city slickers," she drawled, pulling off her gloves and tossing them on the table alongside her bag. "You run up against one little creature of the night, and your knees start shaking. Good thing you didn't notice the bats," she said grinning.

He moved closer to help her pull the cape over her head. "Kate, you dear, sweet thing, has it occurred to you that I too am a creature of the night?" he said softly.

"Oh?" she said in a blurred voice from underneath the cape. "Is that why my knees are shaking?" Whether she meant it as mere banter or as a clinical observation, Katie really was not sure. But when the rest of her cape came off, she found herself gazing into his searching eyes—and she realized that, as a rule, Fletcher Ramsey *expected* women's knees to shake.

"Let me . . . ah . . . turn up the heat before I give you my nickel tour," she said as she eased away from him. She hoped he understood that to her "nickel" meant "brief; of short duration."

In the kitchen she switched on a brass ceiling lamp that hung low over an oak bench doubling as a coffee table. Fletch ambled over to the functional little gas stove, lifted up the heavy iron teakettle, and asked, "Tea? Coffee?" with all the smiling courtesy of a gracious host.

She decided to spell it out for him. "It *is* late."

He waved the teakettle back and forth in front of her. "But just imagine—no calories. How can you refuse?" he coaxed, as if Katie were trying very hard to back out of her own front door.

He was so damn impertinent; so damn . . . likable. "Well, all right—but just a small cup—coffee."

A week ago she'd been sipping coffee and racking her brain for more details of a dream in which her guest had played a starring role. Her heart gave an erratic lurch as she looked up at him. *Well, there he is, woman. The man of your dream.* He stood at the stove with a catlike, easy grace, waiting for the water to boil, then became restless and began prowling the kitchen.

Passing over the rather unpretentious furniture, he paused to finger two or three pretty pieces of Colonial bottleware, and a rainbow-colored tin rooster Katie had picked up in Mexico. But Fletch seemed far more interested in drinking in the massive construction of the stone house. His eyes scanned up and down the huge overhead beams, hand-hewn into shapes a foot and a half wide and nearly as deep. He ran a loafered foot lightly across the uneven, twenty-inch-wide planks of the pine floor.

Leaning with both palms on the deep stone windowsills, he peered through warped and ancient windowpanes into the blackness outside.

"It's all so . . . tre*men*dous. This house will stand forever. It just reeks of history." His voice was quietly awestruck. "But more than that," he said as he returned to the sink and took two cups from the drying-rack, "it's so obviously haunted by . . . friendly spirits."

Bull's-eye. He'd hit on the essence of the stone house for her, and she was ridiculously pleased with his perceptiveness. Not everyone reacted in the same way to the house. Her mother, for instance, had taken one look at the immense beams, some of which still bore peeling whitewash from another century, and said, "You *like* it here?" Marcia . . . Marcia thought living outside of walking distance to the town's only singles bar was madness. And

Katie's father had sent her a check, still uncashed, to cover the cost of installing any burglar alarm that could be heard at least a mile away—which was where the nearest neighbor lived.

"Where's the coffee?"

"Oh . . . up on that shelf above the sink," she said, pointing to a curious arrangement of her own design. A wide board hung suspended by white chains attached to the overhead beams. A set of art-deco canisters, some mason jars filled with dried beans, and a dozen apothecary jars filled with spices were crammed two and three deep on the shelf. The effect was of cheerful, homey clutter. "I know the shelf looks a bit medieval," she said self-consciously, "but how do you attach kitchen cabinets to lumpy stone walls?"

"*You* could not. A construction contractor could. Look, I plan to have a crew of men in New Paltz in January remodeling the Shape . . . the building you're in," he corrected. "If you can get hold of some kitchen cabinets, I'll have the crew spend a weekend here installing them. No sugar, no cream, right?" He handed her a pretty red-patterned porcelain cup edged in gold, then went back to pacing the kitchen curiously, no doubt measuring the walls with an eye to installing kitchen cabinets. In his friendly, straightforward way, Fletcher Ramsey had taken over the place. First the Shape-Up Room; now here.

"Thank you, but I think not, Fletch," she declined with studied coolness. "Number one. I couldn't afford your men. Two. I couldn't afford the cabinets. Three. I don't think I'd *want* the cabinets. And four, my landlord may have his own views on the matter." She tucked one leg beneath her on the sofa and tried to look proprietary. "Would you like some skim milk in your coffee? I'm afraid I don't have any sugar."

"Black is fine," he sighed. "I'm sorry I rolled over you just now, Kate. This house is catching. I can't help wanting to . . . make it right, somehow. Like those boulders in the driveway—I'd have them out of there before the first snow fell, if it took a stick of dynamite to do it.''

''Oh, I see—buy what you need, blow up what you don't. A convenient philosophy—but it doesn't work that way for us ordinary folk. Some of us have to work around life's little boulders. We can't always eat and buy and take whatever we want.'' It was impossible to keep a note of resentment from creeping into her voice.

He paused in his ramble around the room and stood above her, a surprised look of comprehension on his face. Placing his heavy stoneware coffee mug on the oak bench, he sat down next to Katie, one arm resting behind her on the sofa, the other lying across the knees of his faded jeans. It was a relaxed, easy position, but there was in it that hidden reserve of coiled energy that Katie somehow associated with him. She was aware of his nearness, aware of his warm breath, aware of his aftershave—and aware that she was cornered. To slip away this time, she would have to climb awkwardly over his legs, or over the oak bench.

An ironic, amused smile played across his face as he leaned, almost imperceptibly, toward her. Katie sat stiffly still, hardly daring to blink.

''You funny little sorceress,'' he mused as he slipped his right hand beneath her bound-up hair and gently rubbed the exposed area between hairline and sweater. ''If I thought I could eat whatever I wanted, I'd have your stockings off and be nibbling at your toes right now. And if I thought I could *buy* whatever . . . darling, my wallet's filled with money and credit cards, but you're not the kind that takes currency, VISA—or kitchen cabinets. As for *taking* what I want . . .'' He laughed. ''Short of knocking you out cold, I'm damned if I know how I'd manage it.'' Almost absentmindedly, he continued to rub the back of her neck. ''So there, you see—we rich folk can't have it all, after all,'' he said soothingly.

His pensive, resigned little speech allowed the sentry that was standing guard in the back of Katie's mind to take a little break. All evening long, but especially since Fletch had walked through the dutch door, she had been tense and watchful. As far as Katie was concerned, a box of assorted chocolates had tiptoed through that door a little while ago, and she wouldn't be comfortable until it tiptoed right out again. But if he really had no intention of making any moves on her, then she could just relax a little. In a long moment of silence she gave herself up entirely to the warm, circular motion of his palm on the back of her neck.

"Mmmn," she breathed. "You know, our masseuse has just run off with the circus or something. How would you like a part-time job at the Shape-Up Room—to help you make ends meet, and all that." She let out a long, luxurious sigh.

"I'd figure I'd died and gone to heaven," he laughed. "I might even work for minimum wage. Here, let's do this right," he said as he swung Katie around slightly and set his other hand to helping reduce her spine to warm honey. Her back, ramrod-straight all evening long, relaxed into a rounded curve as soft, purring sounds came from deep within her.

"Lower . . . please," she murmured, floating blissfully back to her childhood days, when like a languid cat she'd throw herself across her aunt's lap and demand that her back be rubbed. She felt five years old again. "Don't stop," she begged contentedly, just as she once had to her aunt.

"Angel, your sweater is stretching from crew neck to boat-neck style. If you let me slip it off, I can work my way down a little farther, to the edge of your leotard top."

The sentry inside her head was still enjoying a well-earned nap, and Katie said, "Mmmn, just don't stop."

Still seated behind her, he gathered the ribbed waist of her sweater in his hands and pulled the soft lambswool over her shoulders. Helpless with contentment, Katie raised her arms above her head and waited, almost drowsily, for him. He laid the sweater across the back of the sofa and resumed the deep, soothing rub.

She was sitting cross-legged on the sofa, her spine bent forward, her hands resting limply in her lap. The intense tactile sensation had nearly obliterated her other senses. Her eyes were closed; her ears heard only the purring evenness of her own breathing; and she barely registered his forest-fresh nearness. It was heavenly. From the base of her hairline to the apex of her leotard top he worked, his palms fanning out farther and farther across her back.

"On second thought," he said in a husky, confused voice, "maybe I'd better pass on that job as masseur—I don't seem able to keep my mind on my . . . work," he rasped, his hands beginning to slide up and down the sides of her body. Up, down, up and down—it was her dream from last week, coming true.

She felt his mouth at the nape of her neck, kissing the sensitized area just below her hair. His hands had drifted from the sides of her body around and underneath her arms, encircling her waist, moving lightly over her breasts, searing through the thin covering of her leotard. "This damn leotard, always there, like a second skin," he said in a low, sensuous grumble.

The vee in the back of her leotard was cut lower than some of her other tops—and ended in a zipper besides. Still dazed, Katie heard, from some other planet, the distinctive "un-zip" sound of the nylon closure. And then his warm, restless hands were inside, trailing fire along the flat of her stomach and midriff, cupping her swelling breasts, holding her nipples between thumb and middle fingers, lightly teasing, playing, drawing them into an erect, aching state.

He had abandoned a neutral zone for an erogenous one, and the dreamy contentment Katie had been savoring was suddenly converted to explosive yearning, as her initial gasp of shock dissolved into a moment of panting wonder, and finally into low, deep moans. The earlier sensual deprivation now became a whirlpool of intense sensations; of warm wet lips, and aftershave, and strong, well-formed hands; of raspy wool on her soft bare back; of the husky, maddening sound of his voice as he murmured endearments between kisses.

It was all happening so fast; she felt as though she were alone on a runaway train. How could she get off—she had to jump off—without hurting herself? With a sob of panic she half turned to face him. Her unzipped top dropped off one shoulder and she was dimly aware that she was trying to re-zip it as she struggled to express her fear through mournful, misty eyes.

"My God, Kate, don't look at me like that." He took her hand from her shoulder and, spreading it palm upward, held it to his lips. He kissed one eyelid, then the other. "Close your eyes, sweet, please. I wouldn't hurt you . . . don't, don't be afraid," he whispered, smoothing her hair and tracing a silken line around the contours of her face and neck with a gossamer touch. *"Don't* be." His lips, warm and reassuring, alighted on hers in a kiss of melting sweetness. He ran his tongue over her dry, parted lips, explored her mouth tentatively, and then drew away, after dropping one, two, three light kisses on her lips.

"It's been a while, hasn't it." It was a statement of fact, made without sarcasm.

"Not . . . not so long," she said perversely, mortified by her childish behavior.

"How long, Katie?" he pursued gently.

"Oh . . . a while," she answered illogically, bringing the conversation around full circle. She was oddly distressed by his deduction. "All right; I'm a little out of practice," she said, lifting her head defiantly. "So maybe all I need is, you know . . . a push, to get going." Now why had she said *that?* The last thing she wanted was to be pushed—here, there or anywhere.

"A push?" He studied her face curiously. "You honestly want me to give you a . . . push?" His smile was puzzled and tentative as he held her by the shoulders and eased her, with a slow-motion shove, onto her back.

But Katie was looking over his shoulder on the way down. "Oh, my goodness—not *now!*" she cried, sitting bolt upright.

"Not now?" he repeated. "For God's sake, Kate . . ." he groaned.

"I don't mean you, Fletch, although . . . I mean that too. But I mean . . . Moose," she said, pointing to her cat. Moose had just trotted into the kitchen, holding a squirming mouse gently in his jaws.

"Moose? Don't you mean mouse?" Fletch asked as he watched, fascinated, while Moose dropped the furry blob on the braided carpet for a little game of hide-and-seek.

"Yes . . . no . . . that's Moose's mouse. I mean, the mouse is the mouse and Moose is the . . . cat," she stammered incoherently. "He did this to me once before. Keep an eye on him . . . them," she said, jumping up to get a towel from the bathroom. She returned and explained breathlessly, "The last time, I threw a towel over the mouse and set it free outside."

The mouse had made a beeline for the nearest wall and was scurrying along it as fast as his little paws could carry him. He ran into a corner—no exit there—and began scurrying down the next wall as Moose almost casually monitored his progress.

"Your cat looks like an old hand at mousing," Fletch said as he took the towel from her. "Are you sure we don't want to leave this to the professionals?"

"That little 'professional' eats 'em up and leaves their tails in the shower stall," she explained grimly. "Usually it's done in the night, so at least I can call myself an innocent bystander."

He nodded sagely. "The law of the jungle; eat or . . ."

With a deft motion he dropped the towel on the mouse, gathered the creature in its folds, and with Katie leading the way outside, shook out its contents near the pine tree. "Think he's learned his lesson?" he asked as they watched the mouse scamper off into the night.

"Probably not," she answered, shivering. Even with her top zipped up, far too much of her was exposed to the icy wind. She dashed back into the house, overwhelmed by the cold air and by recollections of her recent idiocy. "Fletch," she began wearily, "I feel like I'm in round fifteen of a heavyweight fight. Can't we just call it a night?"

"Not enough carbohydrates, that's your problem," he said sympathetically. "I, on the other hand, don't know when I've had more fun." He did look absurdly, maddeningly fresh; his hair wasn't even mussed. Definitely a night creature.

The two were just inside the unlit foyer, and Katie hoped that in the semidarkness she would, for once, be free from his piercing scrutiny. The cat appeared, threading through their legs with a huffier "gniaow" than usual. "We've just thrown out his dinner," she laughed softly in the shadows.

"Cheer up, Moose," he said wryly. "Tonight we'll *all* be going to bed hungry. Well, good-night, fair Katrina," he murmured. "And good-night to all your little critters— possums, 'coons, mice, cats, bats. All that's missing is the hoot owl."

"I don't think I've ever heard one," she said thoughtfully. "Would you settle for a pheasant? One tried to fly through the kitchen window the other day."

"Your menagerie is absolutely charming, Kate, but why don't you have any . . . people . . . here with you?" he asked impulsively.

"Oh, but I did," she answered, surprised. "Jimmy lived here with me. He never told you? He kept his apartment, naturally, but he ended up spending more and more of his time here. He loved being out of doors. That pile of firewood overflowing the woodshed was all cut down by him this summer. He had so much fun doing it. He figured he was . . . another Paul Bunyan.'' Her words dissolved in a bittersweet rush of memories.

"No. I didn't know. He never said a word." Fletch's voice was as still as well water.

"Oh . . . well, maybe he didn't think it was important.'' She sounded unconvincing to herself.

"Or maybe he thought it was *too* important," he said evenly. His hand was on the iron door-lift as he turned to her. "Well, Kate, you had me bewitched, after all. For a while there I figured you were shy, troubled . . . I don't know what." He laughed a short, bitter laugh. "And all the time you were just afraid that I was jumping over Jimmy's grave to get at you. Sorry," he said coolly. "It was an honest mistake." And he closed the door on her hollow-cheeked, baffled face.

"Jimmy?" she said blankly to the dark.

It took a moment for Fletch's cryptic remark to sink in. She opened the door to object; Fletch was seated behind the wheel of the car, his whole body a study in dejection. Katie stood there, fluttering her hand at him in a kind of distress signal. "Jimmy and I weren't . . . that way," she called out awkwardly.

He rolled his window down. "No. Of course not."

And before she could decide for certain that he was being ironical, Fletch was horsewhipping poor old Charlotte down the driveway at an axle-breaking speed.

Katie locked the door, flipped off the lanterns and wandered back into the kitchen. How could Fletch possibly have thought that she and Jimmy were lovers? Jimmy had been a brother to her, from the day she'd moved into the Shape-Up Room to the day of his motorcycle accident. He'd been a brother, and a friend—but nothing more. The chemistry just wasn't there. It had never occurred to her to accept Jimmy as her lover. It had never occurred to Jimmy to ask.

How odd that Jimmy had never told Fletch that he was living off and on at the stone house. Some buddies. Then something clicked suddenly in the back of her mind. Could *Fletch* be the one Jimmy meant when he had occasionally referred to an "old army buddy?" The memory of a hot August Sunday came winging back to her. She and Jimmy were clearing brush behind the house and they stumbled on a well, abandoned and overgrown. Katie had leaned over the low stone parapet and peered down the well to see if any water were visible, and Jimmy had yanked her back violently.

Amazed, she turned and told him how silly he was being. He explained that when he was stationed in Germany, he had once talked an army wife out of jumping into the Rhine River. Ever since that time, Jimmy couldn't bear to see people walking on bridges, or even on overpasses—and now, he said, he was going to add wells to his list of phobias. If the army wife were Mrs. Fletcher Ramsey, then Fletch really did, as he said, owe Jimmy "a big one."

Absentmindedly Katie opened a can of food for the cat, who was assuming tragic airs: standing on his hind legs, paws digging into her knees, Moose gazed up at her with one blue eye, one yellow eye, and howled piteously. Katie spooned out the brown glop and addressed the cat. "Fletch was wrong, wasn't he, killer?—*You'd* never stand for going to bed hungry." Only her. Only him. Her breasts tingled and her legs went limp as she recalled the hot trail of fire Fletch had traced so recently across her body.

"Damn it, anyway!" she cried, slamming the utensil drawer. Moose looked up sharply from his food bowl and flattened to the floor. "Oh, Moose . . . shhh . . . I didn't mean you, silly. Shhh," she cooed, petting and reassuring him. "Not you."

Chapter Five

Katie was six days nearer to January first; six days nearer to being out on her keister. In the last week she'd viewed four different business locations, ranging from hopelessly inadequate to breathlessly unaffordable. And today . . . today the muffler on her Volkswagen bug blew out—again. Wondering how such a tiny little engine could produce such a hideously loud roar, Katie turned self-consciously into her driveway. What wouldn't she give for a new car!

In the slanting rays of the late afternoon sun she was startled to see a convoy of cars parked in the clearing in front of the stone house. Her landlord's Oldsmobile was there, and a blue van with "Security Electrical Sales and Service" painted on its side panel. The van almost, but not quite, concealed a red Chevy parked demurely alongside it. Katie knew without looking that the red Chevrolet had a white door.

She ran her car onto the edge of the grass, got out and,

with all the wariness of a young fawn, approached her landlord, who was deep in conference with two uniformed workmen. Something was definitely up. The two workmen were pointing to the upper-story windows, and her landlord was squinting in that direction and rubbing the back of his neck uncertainly. "Well, I dunno; I don't think he'll go for that," he was saying.

"Hi, Mr. Durette; I haven't seen you for a while," she greeted him politely. Mr. Durette—who loved his stone house, even if Mrs. Durette did not—always made a point of stopping by whenever he was in the area to reminisce about the childhood he'd spent in the house.

"Yep, yep; been real busy lately," her landlord said. "Just about everyone in Albany seems t' want new drapes." He pushed his bifocals up over the few gray hairs that were left on his head. "Recession's over, I guess."

"I'm really glad to hear that, Mr. Durette. But . . . what's going on?" she blurted, waving an arm at the van and the two workmen, who were trotting through the dutch door—*her* dutch door. Well, Mr. Durette's dutch door. Not *their* dutch door, anyway.

Mr. Durette had finished rubbing the back of his neck, and now proceeded methodically to begin on his chin. "Yep, yep. It makes sense . . . you being alone and all. Hate to admit it, but times aren't safe as they used t' be. Mr. Ramsey tells me a lady was robbed and threatened not three miles from here. Find that kind of hard t' believe, though, I have to admit," he added.

"Fletcher Ramsey! How would he know something? . . . Wait a minute. Did you say, three miles from here? You don't mean Mrs. Johansen, surely?"

"Jansen, Johansen . . . yep, that might be the one," Katie's landlord agreed sagely.

Katie didn't know whether to laugh or scream. "It's true that Tommy Oliver sneaked into her kitchen and tried to steal five dollars from her purse. And it's true that when Mrs. Johansen caught him, Tommy did threaten to spray-paint her garage door if she told his mother,'' Katie added. "But really, Mr. Durette, since Tommy's only ten years old . . ." she trailed off impatiently.

Ramsey. Obviously, it was Ramsey. She pulled off one glove, then the other, and jammed them into the pockets of her tan suede jacket, aching, just aching, to do battle with Fletcher Ramsey. "What does Tommy Oliver have to do with all this?" she demanded suspiciously. After all, it would help if she knew precisely *why* she was about to do battle.

But Mr. Durette hadn't finished. "Yep. And another thing that Mr. Ramsey pointed out to me is Mrs. Durette's spinning wheel. Why, that's worth I don't even know how much. Not to mention all the stuff locked away in the storeroom. Especially Mrs. Durette's grandfather clock. Not an easy thing to steal, I grant you, but . . ."

Katie wasn't listening. She was marching grimly and purposefully toward the house, intent on one thing only: to flush out Ramsey, who was lurking within it somewhere, and send him packing to New York City. Bent possibly on murder, she shoved open the dutch door.

TUH-WEET! TUH-WEET! TUH-WEET!

Katie gasped and jumped back as though she'd been splashed with ice water. *TUH-WEET! TUH-WEET! TUH-WEET!* Eyes wide open, hands over her ears, she whirled around frantically, searching for the source of the deafening siren.

In a way, she found it: Ramsey came barreling down the stairs, a Christmas-morning grin on his face, shouting, "Hot damn, fellas! It works!" When he saw Kate he stopped short, still grinning; he didn't even possess the common decency to look sheepish.

"Fletch! What the *hell* is going on here?" she shouted over the piercing, incessant wail.

"Burglar alarm!" he shouted back happily.

"I know it's a burglar alarm, damn it! *Turn it off!*" she roared. The sound seemed to be vibrating through every hairpin on her head, every filling in her teeth. A genuine air raid would have been far more discreet.

Fletch reached up over Katie's head to a little black box newly mounted on one of the huge ceiling beams and flipped a switch. Instantly the siren stopped, and Katie collapsed with relief onto the telephone bench.

Fists jammed in the pockets of her jacket, long legs stretched straight out in front, she glowered up at Fletch from under the turned-up brim of her angora cloche. "You've got five seconds to explain why you're running around installing little black boxes in my house. After that I call the police and have you arrested for trespassing." Her confusion, shock and relief had been replaced by brightly burning anger.

"Trespassing? Nothing of the sort," he returned indignantly. "I'm here at the express request of your landlord as a kind of . . . overseer to this installation."

"Overseer, my foot. This burglar alarm is your idea," Kate said flatly. She jumped up, jittery with anger. Once again he'd made *her* feel like the interloper. She was still wearing her hat and jacket; *he* was standing against the railing, casually sweatered, hands in the pockets of his corduroys, the perfect Lord of the Manor. It was amazing how well he went with the house.

"All right, Kate. I admit, it was my idea. For one thing, I was astonished the other night when you casually revealed that the upstairs storeroom was filled with valuable colonial pieces. How many hungry collectors have you dropped that little tidbit to? Maybe someone in your exercise class? Someone you hardly know? Do you think burglaries can't be 'arranged?' The next thing you know, you trusting little twink, there'll be a couple of thieves on the roof cutting your phone lines, and then where will you be?" Fletch's voice had become lower and more urgent as he pointed out, with brutal reasonableness, the rather vulnerable lifestyle Katie was enjoying.

At the same time, the complete . . . presumptuousness of the man hit home as one of the workmen, excusing himself, passed between them with his toolbox on his way upstairs to the bedrooms. Fletch, Mr. Durette, the workmen —she was surrounded by a bunch of overprotective males. The thought of the uncashed check from her father for a burglar alarm flickered through her anger. Didn't anyone understand that she was twenty-nine years old, an adult, for heaven's sake?

"Mr. Ramsey," she said sweetly, "I appreciate the gesture, but basically I think it's a . . . dumb idea. In the first place," she said, raising her hand to the little black box above her head, "I can't even reach the shut-off switch." Her smile was of the superior sort.

"Ah. Hmm. So you can't," he agreed awkwardly. For the first time since she'd met him, Fletcher Ramsey actually looked at a loss. She liked him more for it, somehow.

"In the second place," she continued, pressing her advantage, "I *have* taken classes in self-defense; I'm not nearly so helpless as you think. And in the third place . . ."

But she wasn't allowed to finish. Mr. Durette, with one of the workmen in tow, had come up to them. "Feller wants t' know if you want a control box upstairs, too. I says we'd better check with the man who's payin' the bill," he said pointedly.

Fletch glanced at Katie in time to catch her look of surprise and said hurriedly, "Sure, no problem. Put it in."

"*You're* paying for all of this?" Katie challenged him, amazed. She'd assumed that her landlord was picking up at least part of the tab.

Fletch shrugged without answering, and Mr. Durette went back to rubbing the back of his neck. "Yep," he said, studying a worn spot in the linoleum before carefully shifting his foot over it, "Mrs. Durette is bound to sleep better at night, now that she knows her spinning wheel—and you, young lady—are safe and sound. Yep." He glanced at his watch. "Well, good golly, would you look at the time? If I'm not on that Thruway in ten minutes flat, it'll be burnt meat loaf for supper. Well, Mr. Ramsey," he concluded, pumping Fletch's hand whole-heartedly, "been a real pleasure meeting you." To Katie he turned, smiled, winked and said, "You could do a heck of a lot worse than this one. Yep." And he drove off in his immaculate, brand-new Oldsmobile four-door sedan.

Katie unbuttoned her suede jacket and allowed Fletch to help her out of it. "I suppose you told *him* we're engaged, as well?" she growled.

"Not in so many words, no," Fletch answered composedly. He hung her jacket on one of the brass hooks of an old oak coat rack that stood in the foyer. "Y'know, this coat rack could stand refinishing. I know a place that'll dip it and strip the old varnish. . . ."

"I *like* the rack to look old, dammit! It looks used; it looks . . . needed. Just leave it right where it is, please," she snapped.

"Well, suit yourself, of course. But . . . you can see that the grain of the wood is really beautiful underneath all that crazed, beat-up varnish," he went on in his friendly, informative way.

"God! What does it take to slow you down—a bullet in the leg?" Kate snapped as she pulled off her hat, almost too exasperated to be angry.

Her hair, which she'd left unbound, spilled out over her shoulders in a tumble of ebony gloss, and Fletch drew in his breath sharply. Katie was momentarily confused. "I . . . what's wrong?" she demanded, irritated anew.

"Nothing, absolutely nothing," he answered softly as he lifted his hand, almost unwillingly, and stroked the sheen of her hair. His touch was gentle as a child's, caressing the

soft, smooth coat of a cat. The sheer lightness of that touch
left Katie reeling with dizzying awareness.

This wouldn't do. She should argue. She should push
him away; he had no right to do any of this. Black boxes,
black hair—everything was the same to him, items for
amusement, nothing more. Katie inhaled deeply, then
forgot to exhale, and her words came out on a rush of air as
she took a step away from his stroking touch and his
dancing eyes. "I want you to . . . have that alarm removed
right now. I can't afford it." She made it sound, as nearly
as she could, like an ultimatum.

"But Kate," he argued with eminent reasonableness,
"the lion's share of the bill will be for labor—and that's
already spent. Taking all the equipment out again won't
make the bill go away."

Logic. He was always threatening her with logic. It
wasn't fair. "Well *now* what am I supposed to do?" she
fumed. "Rob a bank just to pay you back?" She had begun
aimlessly to wander through the ground floor, surveying the
damage. There were tools on every windowsill; ashtrays
filled with cigarette butts; an opened lunch bucket with balls
of crumpled waxed paper and a half-eaten apple. The
invading army had settled in comfortably, it seemed. "Can
you believe this?" she muttered to no one in particular.

Her pained sense of being overrun by events had penetrated his consciousness at last. "Kate . . . I overstepped,
didn't I?" he admitted quietly. He was perched on the arm
of the living room sofa, the one she didn't like, watching
her wander from window to window and stare in dismay at
the little high-tech sensors that were mounted on each.
"I'm sorry, Kate; I guess I thought you'd be . . .
excited?" he suggested helpfully.

"Oh, it was exciting, all right," she said grimly, turning
around to face him and folding her arms across her chest.
None of the invaders had bothered—amazingly—to light
the kerosene heater in the living room, and it was bone-

piercingly cold. As a rule Katie kept the living room closed off from the rest of the house; why have all that expensive heat floating up into a locked storeroom? She shivered slightly. Stone houses did not expect their inhabitants to wear silk blouses and dress skirts in November; Katie longed to change into warm slacks and a sweater. "Will your men be here much longer? If so, I'll have to turn on the heater," she said in a tone as cool as the air in the room.

"Save your kerosene, sweet; I'm sure the men are nearly done." Fletch went off to check on their progress.

In fact, the men had just finished. The head invader turned out to be both friendly and conscientious. After obtaining Fletch's assurances that he understood how to operate and explain the alarm system, the foreman emptied the cigarette butts, gathered up the tools, the lunch pails and his assistant, and left after handing Fletch, not Katie, his business card.

"Well. That's that," Katie sniffed, glaring at the little white card that got tucked absently into Fletch's hip pocket.

Fletch had been watching Katie with an almost querulous expression on his face, the natural warmth of his gray eyes mixed equally with problem-solving fervor. Kate felt like a skittish pony about to be introduced to its first halter, and she edged away from Fletch to the old-fashioned roll-top desk on one side of the massive brick fireplace.

Fletch wandered over to the opposite side of the fireplace and stood next to Mrs. Durette's spinning wheel, the one item that Katie had managed to wheedle out of her landlord's storage room. "This is a lovely piece," he said appreciatively. "Any idea what period it's from?"

"Shaker, I think," Katie answered briefly. Fletch's beautifully formed hands, the hands of an artist, really, curiously fingered some soft, unspun strands of flax that still remained on the wheel, and Katie felt the hairs on her head tingle with recollected appreciation of his gentle touch.

Oblivious to her scrutiny, he looked up at her suddenly, snapping his fingers. "Here's the solution, Kate: you pay for the actual equipment; I'll pay for the installation cost. That's fair, don't you think?" She could almost see the light bulb turn on above his head.

It was fair, she had to admit. After all, if Fletcher Ramsey had money to burn . . . and her father had sent her a check anyway . . . and her landlord's wife would sleep better . . .

"O.k.," Katie sighed, "you win. But I still say it's a dumb idea." She began searching through the pigeonholes of her desk. "Actually, my father sent me a check recently for a burglar alarm," she confessed, feeling ridiculously guilty about it. "Can I just endorse it over to you? It's for two hundred fifty dollars. Will that be enough?" she asked naively.

"More than enough," Fletch answered blandly. With a good-natured grimace he accepted the check she handed him and folded it into his wallet. "Damn it, Kate—I don't want this check," he complained gently. "That . . . pride of yours! It stands between you and the rest of the world like a chain link fence," he said exasperatedly.

And that's where it's going to stay, Katie thought, and quickly changed the subject. "Now that I've paid for some of this alarm, how about showing me how it works?" she said lightly, wandering back to the foyer, away from his damnably speculative look. She stepped up onto the telephone bench, and scrutinized the black control box. "Let's see," she mused, glancing over the bewildering displays of switches, "this looks simple enough." It looked like the cockpit of the Columbia Space Shuttle.

"It's very simple," he agreed, missing the deadpan sarcasm in her voice. "For the burglary part, you have two types of sensors: the perimeter type, to detect a window or door being opened, and motion-detectors, which do just what the name implies. Understand?"

"Certainly." She couldn't get over the warm sincerity in his eyes. He must have been a heck of a good pizza-franchise salesman.

Fletch was standing a foot below her, and the reversed difference in their heights, combined with the intensity of his look, gave him an oddly beseeching manner. He might have been proposing to her. She, on her pedestal; he, desperately trying to persuade her to . . . to what? To make use of a burglar alarm?

He was saying something about eight break-in zones and pointing to a series of console lights. "Are you listening?" he asked her suspiciously.

"To every word." His hair, seen from above, was a shimmer of golden light, and her desire to fill her hands with it was becoming overwhelming.

"Now this," he continued, "is the panic button. If for any reason you're frightened or need rescuing, just punch this one," he said, his voice softening.

She lifted a tapered forefinger to the big red button, fingering it gently. *I'd like to punch that panic button right now,* she thought dizzily. Obviously, he was making love to her. All this talk of burglar alarms . . . just words. Glancing down at his suddenly serious face, with its brows drawn together, Katie was aware, as never before in her life, of the need for . . . touching. And so she continued lightly to finger the switches on the control panel, afraid, still, to transfer her touch to the face that held her spellbound.

"Katie? Is any of this making sense to you?" he chided softly.

None of it was. She nodded yes. What could possibly make sense about being enthralled by a take-charge meddler? What was the matter with her?

"I almost forgot," he said, more distractedly than before. "There's a . . . whatchamacallit . . . a smoke alarm as well."

"Oh, dear; no more cigars in bed?" she quipped. *Help.*

"And, uh, this option . . . this thingamajig here is an automatic-dialing feature; the police or whoever get a recorded message if the alarm goes off." His voice was illogically husky, and in an almost unconscious response to it, Katie stepped down off the bench and stood before him.

He took a long ribbon of her black hair in his hands and idly twisted the strand around and around his forefinger. His face drew slowly nearer to hers. "Kate, you're just so frustrating. What'm I going to do with you?" he murmured.

"You're going to stop mothering me, for one thing," she whispered, watching with mesmerized fascination as his lips drew closer to hers. "And stop . . . fathering me . . . and stop . . . whatever it is . . . you're doing to me," she faltered, closing her eyes and lifting her mouth to his, meeting the inevitable kiss halfway.

The kiss was gentle, the kiss was sweet, as tongue met tongue, lightly questioning, tentatively exploring. There was pleasurable wariness in the first seconds of contact between them; Katie didn't know quite where to put her hands, and Fletch held her only by the twisted silken strand of hair that he'd wound around his forefinger.

But that was enough. Kate remembered now the delicious chemistry of their mouths together, as their lips parted and met again, this time in a deep, satisfying kiss. His hands had slid down to hers. "Here, do like this," he explained with ironic tenderness, lifting them up and behind his waist. "And I'll do like . . . this," he continued, enfolding her in his arms, his hands searing a trail across her shoulders through the thin silk of her blouse. Brushing aside the glossy folds of her hair, he nuzzled fire along the ultrasensitive curve of her neck, across her jaw until his lips again met, then claimed, hers in a long, clinging kiss.

With a growing sense that she had just undone the gold band on a box of Godiva chocolates, Katie allowed herself to yield, just this once, to sweet temptation. She would taste, just this once, the divine sweetness of his kiss, savor the sensations that were rushing through her limbs. How could it hurt? Just this once. . . .

"Katrina," Fletch murmured huskily between lazy, gentle nips on her lower lip, "you could become real habit-forming, miss."

"I'll bet you say that to all the women you plan to burglarize," she answered a little breathlessly.

"Nope, just those I plan to protect."

His mouth came down on hers more tenderly, yet more passionately than before, and Katie gave herself up completely to the unique paradox of pleasure. She shivered again, this time in a hazy awakening of desire, and lifted her hands behind his neck, pulling his mouth to hers, pressing her body closer to his, instinctively seeking the warmth of his arousal. Fletch responded instantly to her signal of need, embracing her more tightly, his hands wandering hungrily over the contours of her spine, her shoulders and then, curious and eager, around to her breasts. With one hand he undid the top pearl button of her burgundy blouse, then the next; his fingertips skimmed the pale flesh along the line of her bra. Katie waited dreamily, without thought, for what would come next. *Just this once. . . .*

They were standing in near-darkness now. The thin November sun had run off somewhere to huddle for the night, and Katie shivered a third time, tense with longing. He held her shoulders, then smoothed her hair, his gray eyes beaming warm desire. With a nod of his head upstairs, he said quietly, "Can we?"

"I . . . yes. We can." *Just this once*, she told herself, continuing to apologize to the tyrant inside her, the one in charge of denial, discipline, pain. *I only want to, just this once.*

Fletch took her chin between his thumb and forefinger and, tilting her face up to his, brought his lips in to hers in a kiss so reassuring, so tender, that when he murmured,

"Katie . . . let's enjoy one another," she wondered how it could possibly be otherwise. It seemed so very reasonable that she should allow herself the pleasure he was offering her.

She led the way up the worn, green-gray carpeted stairs, her hand in his, aware that her blouse was unbuttoned; aware, intensely, of the tips of her swollen breasts. She felt overwhelmingly desirable, and an overwhelming desire. There were no limits to the enjoyment that they might give one another . . . just this once. It had been so long. She had chosen before, but not too well, and now, after years of bitter self-recrimination, she was choosing once again. Only this time it was someone sensitive, unbelievably tender, with a quicksilver touch. For years she had been waiting, without realizing it, for Fletcher Ramsey to come along.

At the head of the stairs she said softly, "My bedroom's to the left."

"Yes, I know. Kate, I forgot to tell you . . ." he began.

But Katie had let go of his hand and was pointing bewilderedly to two chest-high stereo speakers sitting on the floor like massive watchdogs staring at her bed. "What are *those?*" she asked, blinking with astonishment. "Surely not part of the burglar alarm!" The speakers were huge, more suitable for the stage of a rock concert than the floor of her charmingly cramped bedroom. They covered most of the pattern of the small oriental rug that Katie had laid so lovingly at the foot of her bed. They were nearly as tall as the tiny oak bureau that was wedged tightly under the slanted roof of the house. They were in *her* bedroom, aimed at *her* bed. They were so big, so wide, so . . . *wrong*.

"Are those yours?" she asked with deadly control.

Fletch let out a resigned sigh. "Yes, they're mine. And before you leap behind that chain-link fence of yours, let me explain that I'm moving out of my New York condo and don't have room for them anymore. The downstairs rooms of this house are so enormous that I just assumed the upstairs rooms would be, too.''

"But it's not a question of proportion, for pity's sake! It's a question of . . . of your just assuming! You assume I need protection, kitchen cabinets, fattening up. You assume that you have the right to walk into my bedroom and set up stereo speakers. . . .''

Marching up to the speakers, she reached behind and yanked the wires off the back of each. "And why set them up by my bed?'' she blazed. "Did you *assume* I liked to make love to the *Rolling Stones?* Or were the speakers for your benefit?'' With a sweeping flourish she checked the ceiling. "What? No overhead mirror? No closed-circuit television? Why such noble restraint?'' Bending over, she tried to lift one of the speakers, which seemed to weigh at least a thousand pounds; she left it where it was.

Fletch watched her with interest, his weight on his left leg, his right forearm resting on the pine headboard of the bed. "Are you finished, lady?''

"Yes. *No,*'' she fumed, almost enjoying the sudden ferocity of her response. "Let me just check my bed.'' She walked over and sat on it, bouncing up and down ostentatiously on the cheerful patchwork quilt. "Gee whiz! I was sure you'd have slipped in a waterbed by now. But then, I guess I did return a little early,'' she said scathingly.

"Now, are you finished?'' His voice was low and calmly menacing.

Katie remained seated on the edge of the bed, her arms defiantly straight on either side of her, glaring straight ahead at a spot on the wall. She said nothing. Let *him* figure out if she were finished or not. Jerk.

Fletch eased out of his too-casual slouch and stood above Katie, staring down at her for a long, silent moment. Then he bent over her, gripping each of her wrists in one of his well-formed—and exceedingly powerful—hands, and brought his face nose-to-nose with hers. The piney freshness of his aftershave teased her nostrils, conjuring visions of what might have been if . . . if the speakers weren't sitting close by, like two uninvited neighbors, watching the proceedings with relish.

His warm breath scorched her cheeks. "I've witnessed some pretty cockamamie tantrums in my life, but this one beats all," he said. "You've got a lot going for you, Katrina darlin', a lot. But you've got some growing up to do. All right, you're beautiful. And okay, you're endearingly eccentric. But you'd better be careful, living alone out here—and I don't mean careful of your virtue, or your antiques. I mean be careful that you don't turn into a wild-eyed hermit. You're already so paranoid, distrustful. . . . That's not a chip on your shoulders, it's a block of wood," he growled.

Katie stared furiously at his gray eyes—gray ashes, on glowing embers. He'd hit her where it hurt, and she blinked back tears of outrage. Twisting her hands out from under his, Katie brought them up to his chest and gave him an energetic shove, surprising him and knocking him off balance.

"You!" she spat. "Who do you think you are—Hugh Hefner? You're so sure you can make a voluptuary out of me. Well, don't waste your time, chum. You may have every right not to renew my lease; but you have . . . zilch . . . when it comes to me and to my stone house. I like who I am, and this is *my* castle—and I don't like the idea of being enthralled in it electronically. So just find yourself someone else to be your little . . . bunny," she finished up contemptuously. There was something—if not blissful, at least satisfying—about blowing off a good head of steam. It was a novel sensation; Katie did not consider herself a blower-off of steam.

"Feel better now?" Fletch asked perceptively. He was standing before her, fingers laced through one another and resting on the top of his sandy hair, looking . . . she didn't know what. Like a prisoner of war, begging for mercy? Or just plain bored?

Suddenly deflated, Kate shifted her gaze to a bright yellow square in the quilt and pulled at a loose thread. "You just don't respect . . . people's privacy," she muttered.

"So you seem to enjoy telling me," he answered dryly. He continued resting his hands on his head in the same baffling position. If only she understood more about body language; right now she didn't know if he wanted to take a poke at her or make love to her.

The answer was: neither. "O.k., pickle-puss. So you're determined to stay in your lair, licking your wounds for a few more years," he said evenly, lifting up one of the speakers easily and heading out the door and down the stairs. "I don't know what that guy—what's your ex-husband's name?—" he called back over his shoulder.

"Peter."

"—what that guy Peter did to make you so antisocial."

"He ran off with a skinny New Yorker, if it's any of your business," Katie shouted angrily down the stairs after him. She'd already unraveled one side of the yellow patchwork square, and now she was working on the next. Really, she could murder him. Fletch, not Peter. Or maybe Peter too. They were both useless. Men! She heard the downstairs door open; waited for a moment with suspended breath; heard his light step coming back up the stairs; and resumed breathing.

Her gaze never left him as he walked past her to the other speaker, lifted it up and turned to her. "You really don't want me to stay?" he asked her softly.

Mindlessly she smoothed the yellow square, which she had somehow dislodged from the rest of the patchwork, over her knee. Her emotions and her reason had fought a bitter fight, and both had collapsed exhausted; she had nothing to say.

"Because if you do want me to stay, just say so; this speaker's heavy," he complained with charming candor.

She shook herself mentally. Here they were, negotiating again. He must be devilishly successful in a company boardroom. His style was irresistible: a little friendly pressure; just tell him what you wanted; the only thing was, he'd have to know—now. Yes or no. Suddenly it dawned on her—that's how you got what you wanted in life. You made an offer, and you tried to close on it.

She'd come within a hair's breadth of letting him close with her. "If you don't mind, I'd like to think about it for a bit," she said coolly, sounding like a customer turning down a used car.

He snorted in exasperation. "That's another problem hermits have; they lose their ability to make simple decisions."

"Quite the expert on the care and feeding of hermits, aren't you?"

"I sure as hell will be, before another month is out," he promised with a wry smile.

"Don't bet on it. Do you need a hand with that?" she asked with icy politeness, inclining her head toward the huge speaker still cradled in his arms.

"Of course—oof—not," he answered irritably, shifting its weight awkwardly. "All right, Kate. The speakers are going. I'm going. But before we do, just answer me this—are you eating more nowadays?" There was amused challenge in his look.

The question was totally unexpected; she stared at him blankly a moment while it sank in. "Yes, I am—a little," she conceded, absurdly annoyed with him for noticing. Pizza with Marcia on Wednesday; three or four hearty breakfasts—it must be adding up. She'd taken his earlier advice to heart and had relaxed her diet a little. She felt a lot more energetic; but if the extra calories were beginning to show *already* . . .

"I thought you might be," Fletch observed impartially. "Some of the gauntness is gone from your cheeks and— even better—there's a becoming rosiness in them."

"Probably I'm blushing," she answered calmly, feeling the rosiness increase. "I hate being under scientific observation, and right now I feel like a frog on a dissecting table."

"You don't look like a frog," he argued amiably. His eyes held hers in a close embrace. "You look more and more like a real woman. What a cruel joke on us all," he drawled, "that you're not ready to act like one." And he was gone. With the speaker.

Katie stared dully at the yellow fabric square in her hand. It wasn't a hanky, though she'd used it, over the last hour, to wipe her eyes and blow her nose. Where had it come from? Then she noticed the empty square in the quilt.

"Oh, for crying out loud!" She threw it on the floor, disgusted with herself. If her grandmother, who had laboriously hand-stitched all the squares together, could see her now!

In a few short weeks Katie had nearly forgotten every bitter lesson she'd learned after a year with Peter Bright. In no time at all she'd allowed Fletcher Ramsey to pervade every aspect of her personal and professional life. Having been dropped on her nose by one Svengali, she was now being picked up and dusted off by another. Wonderful.

And yet . . . and yet. Peter was *nothing* like Fletch. Peter's constant advice and criticism had been rooted in his firm belief that women needed all the help they could get. "Just like a woman" was a phrase often on his lips. Fletch, on the other hand, expected her to do well, wanted her to succeed. Hadn't he assumed that she would relocate as easily as she might rearrange the living room? Who could resent someone who thought you were superwoman? So all right, unlike Peter, Fletch wasn't a chauvinist. But he was . . . bossy. Well, not bossy exactly, but . . . a meddler. And also, of course, the sexiest, most arousing man she'd ever met. He was even, damn him, fun to fight with.

With a feeling half of despair, half of wry amusement, Katie dragged the edge of the quilt over her thinly dressed body and let out a small, forsaken sigh. If she didn't know better—if she hadn't thrown Fletcher Ramsey bodily out of her stone house—she'd swear she was falling, just a little, in love again.

Chapter Six

Two inches off the hips, two off the waist, one off the thighs and one off the bust," Katie ticked off methodically as she recorded Jessica Wyatt's new shape. "Jessie, that's absolutely fantastic!"

"One off the bust!" Jessie wailed, comically holding her hands flat over her rather small breasts. "I can't afford it!"

"You look terrific—solid as a rock. You've lost very little weight in the last six weeks; so that means all the difference is in muscle tone." Katie spun Jessica around by her shoulders and faced her to the mirror-covered wall. "Look at you. Are you really complaining?" she challenged laughingly.

Side by side the two women scrutinized their reflections. Jessica was a little shorter than Katie, and far less evenly proportioned: her size-eight top sat a little lightly, it was true, on her size-twelve bottom. But she had done the most

with what she had, and the twinkle in her hazel eyes told
Katie that she wasn't complaining, really.

"After my first baby the extra weight seemed to just slide
right off; I never even thought about it. But after the second,
I dunno . . . it kind of . . . stuck." Jessica turned to Katie
with a look of gratitude that bordered on wonder. "And you
did it, Katie! I'd never have made it without you."

"Don't be silly," Katie said flatly. "If anything, I should
be thanking *you*. Marcia and I have been looking for
another woman for weeks to help us out with the classes."
She slid Jessica's record sheet into a new file labeled
"Employees." "How about some tea?"

"Do you have any coffee?" Jessie hedged.

"Yup. Jessie, you're going to be a natural at this. What I
need to know now is whether you want to develop your own
specialty, like jazzercise, or aerobics."

Jessie tugged uncertainly at the back of her short,
blunt-cut hair. "Oh, golly, I don't know. Music of some
kind, definitely. . . ."

The two were plunged deep in shop talk when Marcia
entered—dressed, packed and ready to go. She plopped her
canvas duffel bag on the floor next to her and announced
briskly, "Last chance, Bright. The Thanksgiving Express
leaves in ten minutes. Sure you won't change your mind?"
Turning an authoritative eye on Jessie, she said, "Classes
will be light before the holiday. You can handle it alone,
Jessie, can't you?" Marcia wouldn't think twice about
ordering Santa Claus to deliver Easter baskets.

Jessie's gulp was audible. "My first day?" she asked
weakly. "Do you think so?" The question marks were
pleas for mercy, and Katie was nothing if not compassion-
ate.

"Marcia? Do you remember *your* first day leading an
exercise group? When four guys from the racquetball court
crashed your session, demanding equal rights?"

"Indeed I do." Marcia grinned. "One of 'em ended up

my fiancé.'' She poured herself a cup of tea, chuckling contentedly.

"Now you laugh; then, as I recall, you were in a petrified rage. No; if Jessie doesn't mind, I think I'll stick around this weekend,'' Katie added reassuringly.

Jessie did not mind. Relaxing visibly over her coffee, she chatted about the limited job opportunities in a college town, and about how lucky she was to find something flexible enough to work around her two young children. "The ironic thing is,'' she added, "my second cousin is program director of a TV station in Connecticut, and he's looking for someone to star in an exercise show every morning. . . .''

"Katie!'' Marcia interrupted, slamming her mug down so hard that tea slopped over the rim. "Perfect! You're going to try out for that job.''

Katie was flipping through her renewal list, vaguely convinced that the number of renewal memberships was down. She looked up absently at her friend. "Are you insane, Marcia? I do own and operate a business—such as it is,'' she added ruefully. Definitely the renewals were down.

Marcia was not easily deterred. "Just let me ask two things. One. New location?'' she demanded crisply.

"None, so far,'' Katie admitted.

"Two. Profits?''

"Not to speak of,'' Katie sighed. As a matter of fact, her Volkswagen was still mufflerless.

"*Voilà.* You go on the interview.''

"*You* go on the interview,'' Katie interjected.

"Why should I? I've got to finish school with Chuck so that we can job-hunt together in California. And anyway, I'm not as good-looking as you are. So. You go on the interview, get offered a fabulous sum . . .''

Jessica intervened. "Oh, I don't know about 'fabulous,' Marcia. My cousin's station is pretty small. Very small.

Tiny." She looked sorry that she'd ever brought the subject up.

"No matter," Marcia went on breezily. "It's just a foot in the door. Katie—the interview itself would be worthwhile. It'd test your poise, confidence, adrenalin level; you have nothing to lose and everything to gain. *Do it*," Marcia urged fiercely.

One thing about Marcia—like Fletcher Ramsey, she liked to close. She was as impulsive as Katie was deliberate and analytical. Many of Marcia's schemes were incredibly impractical. As for this one . . .

"You're right. I'll do it," Katie said simply. "Why not?"

Why not indeed? she asked herself a little later after she had called for and arranged an interview for the following evening. Glumly, she stared at the dismal tallies for the fourth quarter so far. Renewals, down twenty percent. New memberships, off fifteen percent. New Paltz was a small town; either word had got around about her relocation difficulties, or she'd exhausted the market. Where was the baby boom when you needed it? she thought wryly. Ha. Where else? Hanging around ice cream shops—and Fletcher's Fish and Chips—getting fat. If she could just reach a larger share of the market . . . Advertise. That's what Ramsey would say. Spend money to make money, that's what he'd say. What Katie needed, what she'd lacked all along, was a bankroll.

Her thoughts hovered over the neatly arranged membership forms that covered her desk. How little profit they represented. Just how much would the television job pay? she wondered. Thirty thousand? Three hundred thousand? What would it be like to have all that money . . . and weekends off . . . a new Volkswagen . . . a Porsche, maybe . . . the stone house, for her very own . . . fame . . . autographs . . . a movie contract? . . . Katie let her fantasies float gaily in the air like iridescent soap bubbles before mentally pricking them, one by one, with her finger. Wrong. Wrong. Wrong. She'd go on the interview tomorrow night, but it'd be just for laughs. No Porsche, no autographs.

Then on Thanksgiving she'd sleep late, relax, make a big fire, play with the cat . . . and think of Fletch. It was dumb, it was stupid, but whenever her mind was free to drift, it drifted in his direction, like a compass needle to north. She relived over and over again the soft, luxurious passion of his kiss, and regretted over and over again the fury with which she'd rebuffed him. Her fortress of uninvolvement was crumbling fast, which no doubt had explained her desperate anger.

But couldn't she have been more graceful about declining his concern for her welfare? Did she have to play the sarcastic shrew with such happy abandon? Anyone watching the bedroom farce the other evening would have thought Katie was an expert at Punch-and-Judy relationships. But just the opposite was true: Katie had been taught by Peter that "civilized" couples did not argue; that it was ill-bred to raise one's voice unless one were hailing someone on a nearby yacht. And so with Peter she withdrew, then withdrew a little more, whenever a subject arose on which they didn't agree.

Which was why Fletch, with his appealing candor and tell-me-what-you-want attitude, took such getting used to. Katrina Bright still wasn't sure what it was she wanted, let alone how to tell him she wanted it.

But in the meantime she had to do something to slow her rapid slide into bankruptcy. It was time for another six-week introductory offer: *Special! Limited Time Only! Save $$$!* The only problem with a six-week loss-leader was, while Katie's clients were saving $$$, she'd be losing $$$. But it couldn't be helped; she desperately needed to expand her membership base. And so Katie tossed off what she hoped was a brilliant ad for the campus newspaper and was on the phone, intently spelling "introductory" for the girl in Classified, when a visitor entered.

The young woman carried an enormous book knapsack over her shoulder, and like every other student, she wore jeans and a sweater. But the denims were carefully faded designer jeans; the sweater, cloud-soft cashmere. Even the knapsack, heavily laden with hardback books, was a piece of beautifully crafted mountaineer-wear.

Vaguely bothered by a sense that she knew the student, Katie peeped out from her preoccupation with the phone call now and then, trying to pin the girl down in her memory. She was not one of Katie's "Shaper-Uppers"—too tense, too harried-looking. Nor, despite her understated sophistication, did she resemble the large New York City population on campus—not, well, pushy enough.

"That's right," Katie said to the Voice of Classified on the other end of the line, " 'Offer ends December 31st.' And then my phone number. How much will that come to altogether? Yes, I'll wait." Katie beamed a bear-with-me smile at her visitor, tapping the eraser end of her pencil on the desk.

And then she recognized the girl. She knew those gray eyes, knew that impatient look; knew the nose, the line of the jaw; knew the graceful artist's hands, one of them tucked in an almost hereditary way into the pocket of the girl's jeans. It had to be Cindy Ramsey.

"Oh! You're . . . I . . . can I help you?" Katie blurted, promptly hanging up without learning the amount of her bill.

"I hope so. They told me Fletcher Ramsey might be here. Is that true?"

It was an accusation, not a statement, and Katie's instinctive impulse was to deny that she'd ever even met the man. "He's passed through here once or twice," she answered cautiously. "But I wouldn't really know how to get in touch with him; I think he's on the go a lot. I'm Katie

Bright, incidentally," she added with a smile, hoping to confirm the girl's identification.

The clear gray eyes held Katie's look captive, then let it go. "Yes. They told me." Another accusation. Really, the girl should give up pre-med and head straight for a court of law, Katie decided. She'd make a wonderful district attorney. "I'm Cindy Ramsey," the young woman conceded at last, "and I was hoping to catch my father." She bent over and lowered her book bag to the floor with a heavy thump.

Katie jumped a little at the sound. "That sounds like an awful lot of homework," she volunteered. She was drawn to the father's likeness, determined to be friendly despite Cindy's puzzling hostility.

"It's Thanksgiving 'recess,'" Cindy answered with ironic emphasis. "And I've got an incredible amount of studying. I really shouldn't even be out of Boston," she continued wearily, "because I have so much lab work. . . . I'm sorry . . . I'm rambling," she apologized with a thin, formal smile.

"Don't apologize, Cindy; I'm taking classes part-time and I know how you feel. Of course," she added self-deprecatingly, "mine aren't in pre-med. . . ." Immediately she bit the sentence off in the middle, too late.

"How could you tell I was in pre-med?" Cindy asked, suspiciously aloof once more.

"Your . . . book bag is filled with medical texts," Katie improvised, pointing to the hardback books in the unclosed knapsack. Actually, for all she knew they could be books on hot-air ballooning.

Hostility wavered uncertainly on Cindy's brow before she rubbed it away impatiently with her artist's—surgeon's—hand. Her nails were unpolished and evenly clipped; the hand, not of a young girl, but of one who has a calling. Everything about Cindy Ramsey seemed subject to her vocation: the practical, shoulder-length hair that fell in random waves; the slightly freckled face, completely free from the time-consuming frivolity of cosmetics; the restless eyes, almost too alert, searching and observing. The effect was of wholesome obsession.

Cindy nodded toward the cork bulletin board, where the word "Messages" was pinned in colorful cartoon lettering. "Can I leave a note for my father there? In case he 'passes through' again?"

"Definitely," Katie answered briskly. "I'll see to it that he gets it." Not that he was likely ever to stop by again.

Tearing out a sheet of spiral-bound paper from a composition tablet, Cindy scrawled a short message that looked, from Katie's position on the other side of the desk, like a doctor's illegible prescription.

"I hate to bother you like this, but would you have an envelope, Ms. Bright?"

"Call me Katie," she answered, feeling suddenly elderly. "Sure. Will this do?"

Cindy took the business envelope from Katie and stared absently at the words "Shape-Up" which were featured in a stylized echo across one end. Then she scribbled a name across the front and hastily enclosed her note. Handing it to Katie unsealed, Cindy glanced at her watch, a no-nonsense, stainless-steel affair, and said in a low cry, "I've got to be on that plane! If you could see that he gets it . . ."

The unsealed envelope prompted Katie suddenly to ask, "If he calls? Do you want me to read it aloud to him?"

"No! I mean I hadn't planned . . . I don't know. Whatever. Really, I have to leave," Cindy said in a distressed, urgent tone.

She left, and Katie was left alone and staring, a bit openmouthed, at the envelope in her hand. It read, "2 Durnsl." "2 Durnsl?" Katie squinted; could that possibly be "F. Ramsey?" Good grief; she might as well try to read the Dead Sea Scrolls over the phone as this gibberish.

She turned the envelope over in her hand. Normally Katie had a tremendous respect for other people's privacy.

But this was a special case. First of all, she dreaded
sounding like a fool, unable to read the note, if Fletch *did*
call. Not that he would, but if he did. Then too, she had
Cindy's permission, more or less, to read it. And finally—
oh, the hell with it; she was plain curious.

Katie sat back down, laid the envelope, flap open, on the
desk top in front of her and assembled her tools for the job.
By an extraordinary leap of logic, she'd convinced herself
that if she left no fingerprints, she wouldn't be doing
wrong. Holding down one edge of the envelope with the
blunt tips of a pair of scissors, she grasped the folded sheet
with a pair of eyebrow tweezers and slid it carefully,
slowly, out of the envelope. Bitterly ashamed of her lack of
self-control, she was struck nonetheless by the thought that
she'd make a very passable thief if she ever decided to
pursue that line of work. With the scissors she flipped the
top fold, and with the tweezers the lower fold, of Cindy's
letter.

Daddy—

   I can't make Thanksgiving. Mother's going through a
stage again. Much worse than usual. But I'm holding up,
I really am. Maybe Christmas. I'm sorry.

C.

   P.S. Why aren't you ever around? You're *never*
around.

The note, as it turned out, was perfectly legible, and
Katie felt as though each and every word of it had been
branded on her soul with a hot iron. Feeling very, very
small, Katie folded the letter without playing games with
scissors or tweezers, and replaced it in its envelope. She
had peeked into the very personal domain of three people's
lives, two of them complete strangers to her; it was
inexcusable.

It was also ironic. Had she really complained to Fletcher Ramsey, in her most self-righteous voice, that he didn't respect other people's privacy? At least *his* motive was essentially decent—concern for another's welfare. What had motivated her during that little bit of light-hearted espionage just now? Titillation, she supposed; everything that involved Fletcher Ramsey was a source of fascination for her.

And nosiness. That was the other motive. Katrina Bright had abandoned her attitude of uninvolvement and had become nosy. Next would come meddling, no doubt. She looked up from her desk at the mirrored wall and watched a rather red face lick and seal the gummed flap of an envelope. If only it were as easy to seal off that part of her memory as well.

Traffic going east on the Connecticut Turnpike was about what Katie had expected on the evening before Thanksgiving—hopeless. She was intensely grateful to Marcia for the use of her Mustang. It had a radio (her Volkswagen had none); a working heater (the VW's was frozen in the "Off" position); and—oh, bliss—a functioning muffler. All in all, Katie's spirits were high. Maybe it was the adrenaline, maybe it was the novelty of a job interview, but for the first time in nearly three years she felt as though she were on the verge of Making It Big.

Katie was not an optimist by nature. Nonetheless, she could not shake herself of the feeling that she had a good chance to achieve stardom, riches—and a rough parity with Fletcher Ramsey. Because men like Fletch, whether they admitted it or not, measured your worth in dollars and cents. And while Katie told herself that she cared nothing for car radios and asphalt driveways, she admitted freely that she wanted to be accepted as an equal on Fletcher Ramsey's terms, no matter how stupid they were. His gentle condescension that first night came back, as it had often since then, to prick at her self-esteem: *Financially you were living in a fantasy world . . . you were both children, and this building was your playground.*

"Oh, yeah?" she said aloud, as though Fletch were on the seat next to her. "Just you wait, Fletcher Ramsey. Just you wait." By the time Katie pulled into the nearly empty parking lot of station WTAT, she was absolutely convinced that she would get the job—and determined to run Marcia's Mustang off the nearest cliff, if she didn't.

The station was housed in a small concrete-block building situated by itself on a quiet road and notable mostly for the huge antenna structure that grew out of it. Katie stood nervously under the red neon call letters WTAT that glowered over the entrance and rang the bell, feeling very much alone. She supposed it was nice of Mr. Wyatt to agree to interview her after business hours; and she had every confidence in anyone who was a cousin to Jessica Wyatt; but still, she felt awfully alone.

"Hey, babe. C'mon in." Mr. Wyatt—if it was Mr. Wyatt—held the door open with one hand and used the other, which was clamped around the butt of a burned-out cigar, to wave Katie inside. He was fiftyish, a little paunchy—especially for someone directing an exercise program—wore a heavy gold chain around his open throat and was as near to the stereotype of the Hollywood mogul as Katie could wish.

She moved cautiously past him into what served as a reception area. "Mr. Wyatt?" she asked unnecessarily.

"It's Max, kid."

That, too, seemed to fit. Every story of every casting director and every young ingenue that she'd ever heard trotted across her memory, and Katie looked around, past the iron gray desk and battered filing cabinets, for the notorious "casting couch."

Her furtive glance did not escape him. "You were expecting maybe Hollywood?" he asked with unintended irony. He had a way of chuckling—a kind of hawr-hawr sound—that grated instantly on Katie's nerves, and she hoped that he wouldn't indulge his sense of humor any more than he had to.

"Not Hollywood, no," she answered carefully, "but I thought a studio would be . . . larger, somehow."

"And glitzier? Something more in the line of potted plants, chrome and glass? Uh-uh, babe. You want limos, you want glamor, you go to L.A. *This* is a workshop. Five days a week, flu season or not. What I'm lookin' for is a good face, good bod, and grit."

He reached a hand toward her angora cloche and said cursorily, "Y'mind?" before sliding the hat rather gently off her head. Kate's hair slipped down over the collar of her gray woolen coat. "Long. Good. A perm would be better," he grunted. "O.k., the face is right; let's check out the bod. Bernie!" he yelled up to a glassed-in control room high above them. "Gimme some lights."

Bernie complied and immediately the stage—if that was what they called it—was washed with bright light. Katie winced, her pupils contracting with painful suddenness. She felt slightly ridiculous, standing center stage in a wool coat and suede knee-high boots. And very warm. The interview wasn't going at all the way she'd assumed, and as a result she was showing little of the starlet's eagerness or even nervousness, but only a vague, puzzled reserve.

"O.k. . . . uh . . . Katie, is it? You got your 'skins' with you?"

Skins. Leotards? "Yes," she answered, clutching her leather carry-all as though he might possibly mug her to get at them.

"Good. There's a dressing room back to the right. Put 'em on—skip the leggin's—and let's get on with this; my old lady'll be here any minute to pick me up. I didn't think you'd be so late," he added reproachfully. "How's traffic, by the way? No, never mind. Miserable, naturally. Okay, kid, step on it. Bernie! Come down and take the camera.''

Katie swallowed a grimace and headed for the dressing room. So this was the price of fame. You were hustled through an audition like a pony at auction: check your teeth; slap your rump; *next*. It was demeaning and dispiriting. Halfway to the dressing room she paused, turned on her booted heel and opened her mouth to protest.

But she knew, already, what Max would say—''If you can't stand the heat, kid, stay outta the kitchen.'' And he'd be right. No one had forced her to come. After all, Fletcher Ramsey's brand of success didn't just fall into your lap; you had to scramble for it. She could take a stand right here and argue with the program director about how indelicate he was being or she could . . . go for it.

She went for it. Spinning on her heel the rest of the way around, Katie marched resolutely toward the dressing room. On the door someone had stuck a little green paper star; the kind you got in grade school when your composition wasn't really gold-star quality, but only so-so. A green star never said to Katie, ''Congratulations! You've done better than sixty percent of the class!'' No, a green star only jeered, ''Dummy! Five percent got gold; fifteen percent, silver. *You* got green.'' Tonight Katie Bright was determined to get a gold star, even if it were only for effort.

The dressing room was a grim little closet. Its only furnishings were a chair, a small table and a makeup mirror haloed in light bulbs. The room had an evacuated look—a compact of blusher and a lip-liner lay unclaimed on the table—and Katie wondered, not for the first time, why they needed someone else.

''Hey, kid!''

''Coming!'' Katie answered in her brightest starlet's voice and bounced out on stage, where Max was waiting impatiently. His arm was wrapped comfortably around a petite gray-haired woman with round blue eyes and an Abraham and Straus shopping bag in one hand. He introduced her as Ellie, his wife.

Ellie smiled benignly. "You just go right ahead with the audition, dear, and don't let this silly old bear frighten you."

A flood of warmth poured out from Katie for the mild, reassuring woman. Ellie was the soft, feminine touch that the harshly lit studio, with its impersonal clutter of camera equipment, desperately needed. Once Ellie settled in a nearby chair it became possible for Katie to stand alone, barefoot and bare-legged, the object of cool scrutiny. The goose bumps on her thighs receded; she took a deep breath, exhaled and waited.

"Okay, kid. Let's see what you got."

Music drifted down to her: not the driving beat of a disco tune, which she found worked best for the rhythm of exercise, but a slow, sensuous song by Roberta Flack. A moment of blinding panic gripped Katie. The mood was wrong, the song was wrong, the whole dream was wrong.

Then from somewhere the everyday sound of crinkling wrapping paper penetrated Katie's stagefright. Ellie Wyatt was poking through her shopping bag, admiring the day's treasures. While Katie was focusing intently on the sheer normalcy of Ellie and her parcels, the music slipped in through the back door of her mind. Unconsciously Katie eased into a series of stretches, sliding one arm, then the other, high above her head, feeling the stretch along the side of her body, feeling tension ripple away muscle by muscle. From there she slipped naturally into side-bends.

Katie was used to performing in front of an audience, after all, and before long her attention was completely absorbed by the need to make her transitions between exercises smooth and logical. Feet on the floor, she was bent forward at a right angle, gently bouncing and stretching the small of her back, when Max's voice rolled down over her.

"Katie . . . look, kid, you're not defending your doctoral thesis down there; you're getting an audience fired up about exercising. How about a smile?"

Ellie leaned over conspiratorially and muttered, "Tell him you will if he will. Hasn't had his supper yet. Old sour puss."

Which brought a big, wide, down-to-earth grin to Katie's face; and that, apparently, brought one to Max's face, because he boomed out, "Way to go, kid! O.k., Bernie, zoom in. Tighter . . . tighter. Good. Pull out. . . ."

The tempo of the music changed, and Katie moved into a sequence of aerobic exercises—jumping jacks, side-kicks, waist-kicks. And then it was over. The stagelights were shut down, and Bernie, the quiet, self-effacing technician, removed his headset and went into a back room without ever having said a word to Katie.

Max remained in the control booth. "O.k., Katie. Now before you go—a coupla questions."

At last. The interview part. Katie realized that, conversationally, she had not exactly distinguished herself, so far.

"First. What kinda bra you wearin'?"

Her head shot up toward the booth, but her eyes had not yet readjusted to the dimmed light of the studio.

"A black one," she snapped to the disembodied voice above. "Why? Is it relevant?"

"I mean, it's not one of those elastic jogging things, is it?"

The implication of his question sank in soon enough. Apparently Katie did not have enough bounce to the ounce for her auditioner. Red-hot flames licked her cheeks and the bridge of her nose. "I'm a little confused," she said with caustic sweetness. "Am I auditioning for 'Morning Workout' or for 'Charlie's Angels'?"

"All right, all right. Never mind," he cut in peremptorily. "O.k., kid, that's it. Please don't take this in any way as encouragement," he droned routinely, "but we'd like you to fill out an application for our records—Ellie, find her one, will you? I'll shut down up here. The job starts January first; we'll let you know by December fifteenth. And kid—"

"Yes?" she replied coolly.

"—You got a nice tush."

Chapter Seven

Fortunately for Katie, she'd been raised in a house without fireplaces. The woodsy fragrance of the Thanksgiving fire that warmed her feet held no bittersweet associations with lost youth and Thanksgivings past. It was simply, pleasurably, a blazing fire in an enchanted house. Katie was hunkered down low in a wing-backed loveseat, hiding from the cold draft, her stockinged feet high on a hassock and perilously close to the leaping, crackling flames. Lazily untroubled by the clutter that surrounded her—muffin crumbs, eggshells, scattered sections of the *New York Times*—Katie stroked the furry, purring throat of her curled-up cat and tried to predict where she'd be on January first.

The television interview had been a fiasco, that she knew. But if all else failed—and it would—she'd be right here. Because her absolute last-resort plan was to move the Shape-Up Room into the living room. Where the furniture would go, she had no idea; and of course she'd lose some of her clients, but the plan did have a kind of funky appeal. She pictured a dozen and a half women doing sit-ups before a low-burning fire. Funky, but definitely marketable.

The fireplace, after all, was the focal point of the house—an enormous, brick-lined open hearth that spanned half the width of the room. Thousands of loaves of bread had been baked in the Dutch oven so cunningly built into one side of the fireplace. Hundreds of babies had been delivered with water boiled in the battered copper kettle that still hung on the wrought-iron arm, ready for service. And generations of scratches and distress marks had been accidentally inflicted on the humble pine mantelpiece by mothers, fathers, children—and not by the well-aimed hammer of some modern reproducer of the antique look. All of it was genuine, all of it she loved, but could she possibly take this emotional experience and try to wring a profit from it?

Katie rose and stretched, then took up the crowbar that served as a poker and began banking the still-blazing fire. Helen Ritter's vegetarian Thanksgiving was only an hour away; Katie had definitely miscalculated the length of the day when she built the fire earlier.

The sounds of a car in the driveway made Katie screw up her face in an unsociable grimace. No doubt it was another tourist, wanting to know whether the house was part of the Huguenot Street walking tour. The fact that Katie did not live on that famous street meant nothing; a stone house, to a visiting tourist, was a stone house.

Katie peeked through the lace curtains in the foyer. Red Chevy, white door. Her heart gave a wild, irregular knock in her chest, and the wave of pleasure that washed over her made her earlobes tingle—until she remembered the rollers in her hair: she had decided, in a morning flight of fancy, to pull out all the stops for Helen's socialite event; for the first time in two years, she'd set her hair.

So *now* he has to show up, she thought distractedly, tearing the rollers from her hair and hurling them into an empty wide-mouth vase on the drum table. Didn't the man know how to use the telephone? She raked her fingers through her hair; by the time the brass door knocker whack-whacked, Katie had reduced riotous curls to random zigzags.

Majestically she swung open the door to greet him. But the chipper "Well-look-who's-here" that was poised on her lips died away when she saw his face. His usual exuberance, cockiness, puckish humor—all gone. What was left behind were darkened hollows under his gray-cloud eyes and faint lines from his nose to the corners of his sensitive, well-formed mouth. "Hi, Fletch," she whispered.

His smile was forlorn. Barely nodding toward the Mustang which was parked in front of his Chevrolet, he murmured, "Company? Am I interrupting?" He swept her with a quizzing look, pausing to take in the odd arrangement of her hair. The tumbled curls, as well as her bralessness under the soft cotton sweater and her indoor-use-only patched denims, must have suggested to him that Katie had been dragged out of bed by his knock. The Mustang must have suggested that she'd been dragged out of someone's arms as well, because he turned to leave with a hasty apology for not having called first.

"No, really; don't go. That's Marcia's car; my bug's getting tuned and mufflered this weekend. And speaking of cars," she threw out inanely, "how's . . . Charlotte?" She had to keep him here; if he left, her heart might go with him—she didn't know—and then how would she go on living? It was better not to take the chance.

He turned back to her with a whimsical shrug. "Charlotte? Oh, as well as can be expected. Whimpers about the dampness. Wants a garage."

"And you, Fletch?" she asked, her voice soft with unspoken, pent-up apology. "How're you?"

Again he shrugged. "Oh, as well as can be expected. Kate . . . how would you feel about taking in a waif for Thanksgiving?" He was wearing a light plaid jacket, his collar turned up against the raw November afternoon, his gloveless hands stuffed into his jacket pockets. He was Tiny Tim, the Little Matchstick Girl and Oliver Twist, all rolled into one irresistibly appealing orphan.

Her smile was tender as she held the door open wide. "You bring out the Dickens in me, there's no denying. Come on in and I'll fix us some hot rum toddies."

Fletch passed close to her with a look of—gratitude? She couldn't tell. Automatically he glanced up at the burglar alarm control panel, which of course was turned off—it was always turned off—but, amazingly, he said nothing.

"Go sit in front of the fire," she urged. "I'll only be a minute." She'd do anything, absolutely anything, to see his face light up with that infuriating grin.

"Do you have any aspirin?"

"Yes, sure, in the medicine cabinet," she answered. "That's the bathroom; you can't miss it." The bathroom, which had been carved out of the foyer, back whenever plumbing had been invented, was the same length as the foyer—twenty-five feet. The huge footed bathtub at one end was quite a hop away from the metal shower stall at the other, and someone had considerately placed an overstuffed armchair between them, so that one could stop and catch one's breath enroute. Katie heard Fletch's startled chuckle as he walked in; people always reacted that way.

By the time Katie brought in the steaming toddies, Fletch had settled in pensively before the glowing embers of the banked fire. His hands were still buried in the pockets of his jacket as though he'd caught an irreversible chill. His long legs stretched out forever in front of him, and his gaze seemed to be focused on a point between his knees. "I've been stood up," he said sulkily. In the blurring glow of the dying fire, he really did look to Katie like a junior-high student who'd been left crushed and alone in a Baskin-Robbins. "Cindy was supposed to take me out to Thanksgiving dinner in New York, but she never showed."

Oh, my God. Cindy. "Oh, my God! Cindy! Of course she never showed; but she did try to reach you—I have a note. In my desk." She jumped up to fetch it for him.

"I know; Cindy said she'd stopped by the Shape-Up Room looking for me. Nifty toddy," he added, raising the cut-crystal mug to Katie in polite acknowledgment. "Thanks."

"Oh. You knew. Well . . . here," she said, poking the envelope into his free hand. A little hammer of guilt began banging away at her chest.

Fletch laid the envelope on the small butler's table next to the loveseat. "Don't you want to read it?" she demanded.

"Why?" he asked her softly. "I know what it says. I'm drinking *this*"—he gestured in another toast—"to try to forget what it says. At least for now."

"I read it, you know," Katie admitted defiantly.

Unconsciously he glanced at the still-sealed envelope.

"—And then I sealed it." She took a great gulp of the rum and tea, averting her eyes from his. "—Because I was so ashamed of what I'd done. I feel terrible about it," she whispered, mortified beyond her wildest fears. She was perched on the edge of the loveseat, her face soft with repentance.

"Hey, forget it." He shrugged, reaching over for the envelope and tearing it open. He scanned its contents and sighed. "Kate, if you'd like to listen, I'd like to talk. I told myself I was driving up to New Paltz to work up some sketches on the new location. But what I really wanted," he said, folding the note and turning to her, "was your shoulder to cry on."

"But . . . for heaven's sake, Fletch, don't you understand? I read your *mail*."

"Big deal. I wired your house. Now we're even. Kate

. . . come sit closer to me. Your shoulder's so damn far away," he said wistfully.

Katie allowed herself to sink into the high-backed sofa, mollified by the thought that they were "even," whatever that meant. They sat comfortably side by side, their feet propped up on the hassock, sipping their hot drinks silently. Her shoulder was crackling-close to his, but Fletch wasn't crying on it, and Katie was oddly disappointed. She leaned two or three millimeters nearer to him—she could almost see the electrons jumping from her orbit to his—but Fletch continued to sit motionless and preoccupied.

With an effort she forced herself to break through his absorption. "Psst. Hey, mister," she said with a sensual smile, catching her lower lip softly between her teeth. She pointed shyly. "Shoulder. Cry. Remember?"

It surprised a laugh from him. "Kate . . . you sweet witch." He slipped lower into the sofa, taking both her hands in his, burrowing into her shoulder with comic exaggeration. He drew a deep, contented breath. "God, you smell good."

It occurred to Katie, too late, that Fletch was in a perfect position to monitor the aroused progress of her heart as it thumped arbitrarily under her nubby cotton sweater. Lost in a pleasurable, rum-sweetened haze, she stole a slow, gradual whiff of his flame-warmed hair and realized, without forming the thought, that Thanksgiving would never be the same.

Fletch's fingers were threaded through hers; now he withdrew one hand and trailed a forefinger idly back and forth across her palm. "Kate," he began hesitantly. "When you were nineteen, did you . . . hate your father?"

The question had come at her so obliquely that she turned her body and lowered her face toward his, questioning, before settling back thoughtfully. "Not at nineteen, no," she answered. "But I thought I did, when I was sixteen—I was absolutely the last pubescent girl in Oswego to be allowed to single-date, and I resented that. My dad said I'd thank him for it some day, but so far," she added wryly, "I'm still waiting."

"Yeah, sixteen can be hell," he said reminiscently. "But at sixteen Cindy adored me. It's only since she entered Boston University that she's . . . I don't know, *turned* on me." The sadness in his voice seemed to baffle him; obviously he looked on sadness as something that struck down other people, like a rare skin allergy, or lightning.

"Turned on you? Oh, I don't think so, Fletch," she said quietly as he raised his face to hers, lifting his left arm behind her head. He began teasing a black wisp of her hair through his fingers with soothing monotony, and Katie's sense of compassion, along with her ability to form complete sentences, disappeared in the rush of her accelerating pulse. "If anything . . . she's . . . frantic . . . at the thought of missing you."

"Frantic," he repeated thoughtfully. "That's a good word for her. Everything she does lately is frantic. She always runs, never walks . . . always looking at her watch. . . ."

"Golly. I wonder where she gets it from." Fletch was outlining the curve of her ear with his feather touch; Katie's note of irony came out a little husky.

"Well, that's it, that's what I ask myself. She's not the least like her mother. Her mother," he said dryly, "was *not* a mover, nor was she a shaker. So I guess that leaves me as the role model. But I *have* to hustle to get on in the world. Cindy, on the other hand, is just so brilliant—there's no need for her to drive herself so hard. She can afford to slow down."

"Can she? I thought pre-med was a pretty cutthroat affair."

"Nah. Not for Cindy."

"She's doing well at B.U., then?"

"Extremely well—straight A's in her second semester.

Actually, this year I think she's running into a little trouble with Comparative Anatomy. But that's nothing. Obviously the professor's a noodlehead; Cindy's bound to run up against one every now and then.''

His confidence in his daughter was sublime. Having struggled to the top of his Everest, Fletcher Ramsey seemed to expect Cindy to trot up the east face of the mountain in her sneakers to meet him there. It didn't seem fair to Cindy; but then, Katie didn't know what Cindy was like. "Maybe the problem isn't with school at all. Maybe Cindy's worried about . . . her mother." There. She was doing it again, being nosy, using the information she'd stolen to glean yet more information.

"Ah, yes. My ex-wife." His voice had an acid quality mingled with dry regret.

Katie wanted to say, "Listen, I know your ex-wife tried to jump off a bridge, so why don't we just take it from there?" But she had promised Fletch a shoulder, not a third degree.

"I hate to talk about Dolores," he said quietly, "because I'm a biased witness. But believe me, there's nothing wrong with Dolores—at least, nothing that Cindy can heal. You have to understand that my wife deeply resented becoming pregnant. She'd been accepted at a nursing school in Brooklyn. But instead of moving her bedding into a freshman dorm the Tuesday after Labor Day, she found herself on an army base in Germany, four months pregnant. She's never forgiven me—or Cindy either, for that matter. What Dolores hates more than anything is anyone else's success. She was a tough act to come home to."

Katie stole the briefest possible glance at his face. He was staring at her hand in his, watching himself hold it tightly, watching the vein in his forearm tauten with the effort. A little sound escaped from the back of her throat, a fusion of pain and sympathy. To hide it, Katie said quickly, "Your . . . wife didn't ever go back to a career?"

"Didn't go back. Didn't do anything," he said tiredly. "Just resented. Still resents, especially around the holidays, when there's a possibility that Cindy might be spending some time with me," he added dryly. "Ah, hell . . . Dolores isn't even here to defend herself." His eyebrows contracted in a look of self-contempt. "I'm sure her version would be very different from mine. Forget I said anything."

He lifted Katie's hand to his, turned it palm upward and dropped a long, gentle kiss on it, breathing her scent in deeply. "I wish I could draw a happy ending around this, Katie. But that will depend on Cindy. The poor kid has never known whether to try to succeed, to please me—or not, to satisfy her mother." Fletch looked up and stared vaguely into the embers a moment, then roused himself. "Hey, we're going to lose that fire if we're not careful."

"No, no; I banked it deliberately because . . ." And then she remembered. "Because, oh, my . . . I'm supposed to be at Helen's for a vegetarian Thanksgiving right now!"

A look of disappointment crossed Fletch's brow. "Tell Helen you're sick," he demanded instantly.

"I can't; I spoke with her this morning." She jumped up and ran for the phone.

"Tell Helen your favorite raccoon's broken his ankle." He jumped up and ran after her. "Tell her the pheasant suffered a concussion flying into your kitchen window . . . the mouse has developed a phobia for cats and has to go for therapy . . . the possum sprained a wrist jumping from branch to branch. Tell her . . . I need you," he said softly, cradling her neck and cheek in one hand and turning her face slightly to plant a soft, slow kiss on her mouth.

She pulled away dizzily. "Shhh, let me think," she said through an almost doting smile. It was inconceivable to Katie that she could live through the next four hours without him at her side. She dialed Helen's number. "Helen? Hi, it's Katie. I know; I'm on my way. But I have a horrendous favor to ask. I have a cousin who's just dropped in from—'' She looked up at Fletch for help.

"Minneapolis," he whispered.

"Minneapolis, and I was wondering, if it isn't horribly inconvenient, whether I could . . . that'd be super." Katie eyed Fletcher up, then down. "Oh, he's . . . nice," she said noncommittally. "Six-one, I'd say . . . maybe one hundred eighty pounds?"

"One seven eight." His look was indignant.

"Fine; so we'll see you in a little while." Katie hung up, breathing a sigh of relief. "What do you know about Minneapolis?"

"Not a damn thing; I've always wanted to visit, though. Does Helen plan to fit me out in a dinner jacket?" he asked, amused.

"Don't laugh; it *is* jacket-and-tie." She looked over his open-throated polo shirt. "So now what're we gonna do?" she asked wistfully. Actually, she had a pretty good idea of what they were going to do—eventually.

"Never fear. I have—ahem—a weekend bag in my car." He threw up his hands in a palms-forward gesture of reassurance. "Packed without malice aforethought," he said firmly. And she believed him.

Katie allowed herself exactly ninety seconds for a shower. Soap and lather on the neck, underarms, around the front, down the sides, forget the back, no time, hurry up. She'd pinned her hair on top of her head hastily. The curls drooped in the steam, got wet and straight. Too bad. Out of the shower, grab a towel . . .

"Fletch!"

He was standing before the half-steamed mirror, matter-of-factly knotting his tie. He turned to her with a pleasant smile, eyebrows lifted in polite acknowledgment of his name.

Katie threw the towel up in front of her like an armored

breastplate, then blushed at her provincialism and made a great show of wrapping the towel with careless sophistication around her. One end slipped down. Nonchalantly she dragged it back up. "What're you doing in here, anyway?" She bundled the whole mess into a knot between her breasts, took one step—it all fell down. She grabbed what she could, collapsed in the easy chair, and stared fixedly at the dripping faucet.

"Come along, come along. We're late, you know," he chided in a passable British accent. "Won't do to keep everyone waitin'. Bad form, don't y'know."

"I'll stand up if you turn around first and let me regroup," she said, pouting. "This towel's alive, and I've got to beat it into submission."

He did. She did. He turned back around. It fell down. And then she was in his arms, giggling helplessly, aware of what a bashful idiot she was being. And Fletch was laughing too. He knew, they both knew, that they were starving for one another; that before the night was over they'd be in one another's arms, enjoying deep, long kisses and electric sensations.

And then . . . somehow she wasn't giggling and he wasn't laughing any longer, and the deep, long kisses that were implicitly promised for later were being collected right now. Fletch was sliding his hands up, down, across the curve of her bare back and behind, tracing fire along the hollows and over the bumps of her vertebrae, until slippery dampness turned to white-hot friction.

"Katie . . . oh, love . . . oh, sweet, sweet witch . . ." came in a low murmur from him as he buried his lips in the hollow of her throat, kissing away the sheen of untoweled water that lay in the curve of her neck. "I came in here to wash up," he whispered in a half groan. "Honest."

"I believe you . . . honest," she gasped, hardly able to understand him over the hot pounding in her head. She was still clinging moronically to a corner of the towel, fully

intending to do . . . something with it, she'd forgotten
what. When she lifted her arms up around his neck, the
towel dragged along too.

She drank in the hot wet sweetness of his open kisses as
his hand orbited in a slow-motion ellipse from her buttock,
around her thigh, to the soft, still-damp fuzziness of her
lower abdomen. Eyes shut, her upper body swaying slightly, Katie teetered on the edge of erotic oblivion.

The small part of her mind that was still operational
continued to record sensory input: tweed and linen pressed
to aching, bare breasts; soft wool gabardine rubbing quiver-
ing bare thighs; smooth, cool leather nudging tiptoed bare
feet. Out came the brilliant analysis of all that input: *He's
completely dressed, and you are not.*

Abruptly she pulled away from him, dizzily vulnerable,
unsure of whether she was even breathing or not. Her hands
lay defensively against his chest—how did that towel get
there?—and she murmured weakly, "I don't have any
clothes on," as though that were a logical explanation of
something.

His look was amused and kind. "That," he said,
wrapping the towel tenderly around her shoulders, "I can
see for myself."

"What I mean is, I have to get dressed and . . . we don't
have time." That didn't come out right, either. At all.
Abandoning all attempts at dignity and logic, Katie mumbled, "'Scuse me, please," and escaped to her room.

Closing the bedroom door behind her, Katie turned and
caught a glimpse of herself in the full-length mirror—Lady
Godiva, in a terrycloth shawl. Really, it was getting
ridiculous. Katie was a modern young woman; a product of
the sexual revolution; a *divorcée*, when you came right
down to it. Her days of being a dewy-eyed virgin were
definitely over; so why was she acting like one?

In a determined frenzy Katie slipped The Dress from its
hanger: a black knee-length affair with nice flow, a coral

sash, and what she liked to call her Elizabeth Taylor neckline. She threw it on and studied the deep V-neckline with a dissatisfied sigh; the suggestion of cleavage was anything but Elizabethan. If Fletch wanted a voluptuary, he was wiring the wrong house.

Katie glanced at the watch on her dresser. Dear lord, she was disgracing herself; they were nearly an hour late. Pantyhose, underpants—no, wait. She slithered out of the pantyhose and into the underpants, then back into the pantyhose, then ran down the stairs. Then back up again, for her black sling-back heels.

Fletch was waiting for her at the door, holding her wool coat by its shoulders so she could slip into it, a black folding umbrella tucked under his arm. His lingering look did much to raise her level of confidence.

"Darling, you look absolutely wonderful." His voice was warm, but it also had the lilting, bantering quality she associated so much with him. "It's a fascinating look . . . New York *chic*, and . . . New Wave, would that be?" he ventured, dropping a kiss on the wild zigs and zags of her still uncombed hair.

"I'll do my hair on the way. Right now we're late, and it's *your* fault," she said loftily, and cuffed him lightly on the head with her elegant silk bag. Their wide, silly grins suggested that neither one particularly cared, just then, how late they were.

A soft November drizzle had begun to fall, and as Fletch held the umbrella over her head on the way to the car he quipped, "Just our luck it's the chauffeur's night off. I wouldn't mind so much, but does he have to keep taking the Rolls with him?"

She loved him for that; for understanding her occasional need to make an impression. *He* had no such need, but he was self-conscious about Charlotte the Chevrolet for Katie's sake. It made Katie think more of him, less of Helen Ritter and her stuck-up crowd, and more of Charlotte.

Chapter Eight

*H*elen's modern, brilliantly lit house was only a ten-minute drive away. Fletch hid Charlotte behind a clump of brush close to the house. When Katie got out he handed her the opened umbrella, lifted her in his arms, and carried her across the grassy ditch to the main road.

By any standards of logic, Katie should have felt absurd being cradled in someone's arms in the dark in a drizzling rain, wearing a dress coat—and holding an umbrella. Instead, she nestled closer to him and murmured happily, "Back in Oswego we wouldn't have done it this way."

"Oswego! What does Oswego know about *le bon ton*? Back home you'd probably have arrived in a car with matching doors. No imagination," he said, lowering her slowly to the road. "No sense of *savoir faire*. No . . . time like the present to tell you I adore you," he said in a half whisper, and lowered his face to hers, searching for her mouth and running his tongue lightly over her lower lip, tasting and teasing, before claiming her tongue in a kiss almost bittersweet with yearning.

Fletch released her with a melodramatic sigh. "I wanted that kiss to hold me through dinner," he said, walking with his arm around her toward the house. "But something tells me I'll be dragging you out for another one right after they serve the carrot sticks."

"I adore you." Wherever that happened to rank on the one-to-ten scale of love, Katie was transported. Her head was still ringing with the phrase as the door was opened and their coats were taken by a bored attendant.

"Nice digs," Fletch said dryly, glancing around at the spectacular architecture.

"So this is Helen's idea of a 'little cottage.' It looks like something out of *Star Wars*," Katie said, slightly awestruck by the exotic, indirect lighting. They were standing in a kind of moat that ran on all four sides around a broad expanse of varnished deck which was raised a few steps above the moat. Ten feet above the varnished floor more guests stood in small groups on a banistered walkaround. "Helen always complains that there isn't room to swing a cat."

"A Bengal tiger, maybe." His look was keenly apprecia- tive as he escorted Katie to the main level, where Helen's idea of a few close friends—thirty or so—were gathered. "What does this Helen do for a living? Forge stock certificates?"

"I really don't think she does much of anything." Katie shrugged. "Her father was extremely clever about playing the video-game craze, and the money's just . . . there." It was hard not to make comparisons with Cindy Ramsey, and Katie changed the subject. "I have to admit, I'm limp with hunger."

"What in the love of all that's caloric *is* a vegetarian Thanksgiving, anyway?" Fletch asked.

Katie was searching through the guests for her hostess. "I don't know. I picture sweet potatoes, dressing, cranberries, hot rolls, and an empty platter that says, 'Ha ha. Eat your heart out.'" She made a comically sadistic face, and they were both laughing wickedly when Helen Ritter tapped Katie on the shoulder from behind. "Here at last."

Katie whipped around guiltily. "Helen! I'm *so* sorry we're late," she said, straightening her mouth as best she could. "This is Fletcher Cousin, my Ramsey from Minneapolis." There was a pause. "I mean . . . Ramsey . . . cousin." Katie made a vague motion with her hands, as though she were switching the words in midair.

Helen—tall, severe, a champagne-goddess on ice—looked from one to the other and with a smile of coolly correct skepticism, asked, "A kissing cousin, by any chance?"

Fletch rose instantly to the bait. "Absolutely," he said. "Second cousin, once removed. Watch." He leaned over and kissed Katie lightly on her cheek, then her lips. His voice was bland but edged with defiance as he said, "We in the Minneapolis branch take our family obligations seriously."

"More than your social ones, apparently." Helen's smile was almost an afterthought. "Have you been in New York long, Fletcher? Or are you just passing through?"

"Actually, I'm starting up a new line of business in the area." Fletch lifted two glasses of champagne from a passing tray and handed one to Katie.

"What line of business is that?" Helen looked frankly curious.

"Electronic surveillance," Fletch answered promptly. "My rates are real reasonable by the way," he said in the eager tones of a cut-rate gumshoe. He was very careful not to look at Katie.

Which was just as well. She'd have burst out laughing— or maybe crying. Once again Fletch had put her mind on hold and had invited her to romp with him through the present moment. Katie stared with giddy apprehension at the bubbles in her champagne—little effervescent time-bombs, just like Fletch.

Helen was almost, but not quite, convinced. "But you *are* teasing, aren't you? Yes. You are." She looked more intrigued than annoyed.

Fletch shrugged and tossed off a half smile. It was not a smile Katie liked to see him use in public.

Katie had already noticed that the more flimsily dressed women were staying close to the gas-fueled fireplace in the center of the room. The adventurous guests—and those in wool knits—lounged on the walkaround, leaning on the banister and watching the proceedings below. One of those guests, a dazzling redhead in peacock blue, leaned over the banister and called down to them.

"Helen! Come up here right now! Jerry's telling the funniest joke about a supertanker and a sperm whale. It's a scream." She was just a little too loud to be sober, although the flush on her cheeks heightened her undeniable beauty. Katie decided that overall the woman carried her champagne well.

Helen made her apologies to Katie and Fletch. "I really can't afford to ignore her; she'll walk barefoot on the banister to get attention. Please help yourself to the raw bar." She left them to carry on alone.

"Raw bar? Did that woman say there's a raw bar? Where I come from, that means crustaceans, not cauliflower. Oh, heavenly days; come with me, mam'selle."

The hors d'oeuvres selection was elegance itself: enormous shrimp, and raw oysters and cherrystone clams on the half shell, all arranged on a bed of ice with twists of lemon and cocktail sauce. In a state approaching bliss, Katie nibbled her way through tasty pink shrimpmeats while Fletch downed oysters in between raising and lowering his eyebrows in comic lechery.

"Stop that," she said with a self-conscious giggle. "You know darn well that oysters aren't aphrodisiacs." On the other hand, he was looking so mischievously desirable . . . could it be that the shrimp were?

"Tell me why you told Helen that nonsense about your line of business," she demanded suddenly.

"Damned if I know. She annoyed me, I guess. I had the distinct feeling that if I passed her money test, she was going to suggest a marriage of convenience."

"And we couldn't have that, could we?" Katie said, too lightly.

"Nope; any way you arrange it, marriage is an inconvenience." He eyed another oyster, then glanced at the stiff-lipped attendant standing behind the raw bar, ready to shuck more oysters if necessary. "I don't think he wants me to eat any more," Fletch said ruefully.

"Well, we should be saving room for dinner, which undoubtedly will be delicious, whatever it . . ."

Out of midair a string with a note attached appeared between them, dangling in front of their noses. With one mind Katie and Fletch followed the line of the string up, up to its owner, who was leaning over the banister, forearms resting on the bar, manipulating the string with the skill of a marionette master. Her lazy, come-hither smile went very well with the clingy knit she was modeling.

"Oh, my. The lady with the red hair and the blue dress." Turning over various felonies in her mind, Katie smiled and waved prettily. "Something tells me, Fletch, that the note is for you."

"Who knows? Maybe it's a stickup; you open it, Katie," he ordered.

She did. "Mr. Ramsey—We're still telling dirty jokes up here. Won't you join us? The night is very, very young. Yours, Miranda. P.S. Bring shrimp."

"I was right," Katie said, and handed the note over to Fletch. So this was what it was like to be seen in public with

Fletcher Ramsey. Next time, she'd bring along a can of bug spray.

Katie was not prepared for the scowl that transformed Fletch's pleasant features. "I'm sorry about this, Kate."

"Not at all. Just tell me one thing—does Miss Randy have her shoes on?"

He glanced up, then took a pen from his pocket. "No."

"Uh-oh. Maybe you'd better do as she says, then. We don't want her walking on the banister." It was amazing how flippant one could be when one had the prize—at least for the moment—under lock and key.

Fletch scribbled a reply on the note, tied the string back around it, tied the loose end around the tail of a shrimp and gave Randy the thumbs-up signal to hoist away. Offering Katie a mock-formal elbow, he said, "Dance, shall we?"

She had to ask. "What did you tell her?"

"Very politely that I was otherwise engaged for what I hope is a long, long evening." He took Katie in his arms and embraced rather than led her through the soft slow sounds of a black-tie combo. "Listen. Our song," he murmured into the smooth coil of braid that she had pinned at the base of her neck during the drive over. With both his arms around Katie's waist, he applied subtle, demonic pressure on either side of the base of her spine. She drank in the maddening scent of his aftershave, which acted on her senses like . . . oysters. They weren't really dancing in the traditional sense of the word; but then, neither was anybody else.

The song was "I Can't Give You Anything But Love," and like everything Fletch had ever had to say on the subject, its meaning was ambiguous. For example, did love mean sex or did love mean love? And if love meant . . . love, then why couldn't he give her anything else but? No, he must mean love to be just sex. Actually, at the moment simple sex didn't sound half bad. But where did "adore" fit in? Adore was probably more than sex but less than love.

Katie's response was a confused sigh of almost feline contentment, and a sad, wistful yearning for more. Her mind struggled half-heartedly with the problem of categorizing his feelings for her.

His feelings for her. She wanted so much to give them significance. But that was only half the problem. What about hers for him? *Was* she in love with him? On the whole, she thought . . . yes. But just now it was hard to judge. Her arms were inside his jacket, around his waist, and she decided, again, that he was unbelievably fit for someone who didn't seem to exercise and probably ate his own fast food. He was so lean, so lithe, so physically attractive. Any woman who happened to find herself caught between puberty and senility would want him. And if the truth were to be told, there was nothing in the least soulful about Katie's feelings for him just now.

Abruptly the band ended the song, the drummer beat a little tattoo, and Helen Ritter appeared in front of them, elegant in a white chemise, the picture of the perfect hostess.

"Everyone . . . you all know that I can't bear the thought of yet another turkey in my life"—there was general laughter; Helen had just got divorced, again—"and as a result, I've come up with a better and far healthier idea for this Thanksgiving. Now, I want everyone to know that even though I wasn't up at dawn chopping giblets for stuffing, I was still up very early, creating. I've always felt that the way food looks is just as important as the way it tastes. With that in mind, please . . . enjoy."

The band struck up a rendition of "Take Good Care of Yourself," and a serving dolly bearing Helen's Thanksgiving creation was rolled across the varnished floor to applause and mostly kind laughter.

Fletch turned to Katie with a genuinely baffled look. "You tell *me*. What is it?"

"It's . . . a vegetable turkey, I think."

Not entirely. The "body" of the turkey-object was actually several loaves of crusty bread skewered together. Into these were stuck, as artfully as such things could be arranged, a selection of raw vegetables. The long neck was an unpeeled, carefully fitted zucchini. The head was fashioned from a very small chestnut squash. The breast was made up entirely of radishes; the back, of lettuce, cauliflower, and broccoli florets. Cucumbers sliced lengthwise suggested wings, at least to Helen. The tail, Katie and Fletch both admitted, was outstanding: celery sticks (some curled), carrot sticks and green scallions; blades of wheat, rye and oats. A peacock would have been proud to own it.

Fletch plucked off a radish. "Ah, the idle rich," he murmured, and popped it into his mouth.

"Be fair, Fletch; it must have been a lot of work."

"Exactly. A plain old turkey would've been far easier—just not as chic."

"But that's not the point."

"What *is* the point?" he interrupted. "Surely not to save a few calories. After all, there's some real food around—luckily. Look at those cheeses . . . shishkebabs . . . smoked salmon. No, the point, if there is one, is simply to be different from you and me and every other American."

"Well, what's wrong with *that*, for goodness' sake?" It puzzled her that he was being so intolerant; somehow she thought that he, of all people, would appreciate the off-beat touch.

"I don't know what's wrong with it," he grumbled. "It annoys me. She annoys me. Probably because she doesn't have to work for a living, like you and me and every other American."

"That's not fair, either. Look at your daughter Cindy." It was out before Katie knew it, and she buried her embarrassment in a smudge of Brie, which she spread with extra care on a toasted round.

"Cindy?" he repeated with a blank look. "There's no

comparison. Cindy is working her tail off in pre-med, intent on becoming a surgeon. She has very little time for designing turkeys," he added contemptuously.

Katie, of course, understood that very well. But she was also very aware of her own slow, painful efforts to get a college degree. Ten years ago Katie's parents could not have afforded to send her to college. Now, when they could, she had refused all offers of help, determined to make it on her own. Despite her fierce independence—or perhaps because of it—she resented the silver-spoon set. Still, she understood the obvious difference between Helen's lack of ambition and Cindy's intensely goal-oriented struggle, and her apology was quick and gracious.

His look and tone softened at once. "Hey, I didn't mean to go to battle over Cindy. You're right, to some extent; she'll never have to worry about her next tuition bill." He tilted a bamboo skewer toward Katie's mouth. "How about sharing a piece of kebab—such as it is—to make up?"

Katie bit gently on the tiny piece of lamb on the tip of the skewer, and Fletch pulled the bamboo stick away from her lips. "Did you know your eyes cross when you focus on something in front of you?" His voice was absurdly sensual as he said it.

"They do not!" she said, aghast.

"Yes, they do, a little," he insisted. "You look like a blue-eyed Siamese Cindy once had. It was a beautiful, beautiful cat," he said softly, tucking a tiny wisp of curl back behind her ear. "Aloof and proud . . . but stunningly beautiful."

"The cat?" Katie needed clarification; she didn't want him to mean the cat.

"Of course, the cat," he answered irrepressibly. "C'mon, babe, let's ditch this joint. I know where we can get a good square meal."

"We can't arrive late and leave early!"

"Why not? It's better than arriving early and leaving

late. Besides, if you've been to one vegetarian Thanksgiving, you've been to them all.''

So they said good-night. Katie was never quite sure how he managed it, but Helen ended up holding Fletch's hand much longer than she ought to have and looking far more warmly into his eyes than was strictly necessary as she said, ''But wait until Christmas! My Santa Claus will be a carnivore's delight—barbequed beef and pork and chicken, with a toasted marshmallow beard. You will come, won't you?''

Twenty minutes later Katie and Fletch were sitting, just the two of them, at the Formica counter of Al's Thruway Diner, demolishing two $5.95 Turkey Specials.

''Miserable night, Al. The rain's changed over to sleet.''

''Rotten. Business is off.''

''This is really delicious, Mr. . . . Al.''

''Yeah. My wife does all the cookin'.''

''I'll really have to come here more often.''

''Yeah.''

Katie polished off the last of her cranberry sauce. One tablespoon, zillions of calories. It didn't seem possible. In the blink of an eye she seemed to be tossing three years of denial and discipline to the winds. All that time, she'd been starving for food, starving for love. Minutes later, Katie pushed away the empty dessert plate, the taste of warm, delicious pumpkin pie still lingering in her mouth.

''I am . . . *stuffed*,'' she moaned contentedly.

Fletch leaned back in his vinyl seat, looking entirely serene and American. ''Darlin', welcome to the club.''

Chapter Nine

*T*he weather was having a little identity crisis: From rain it had changed to sleet and then to snow and back to sleet again. Fletcher drove with cautious concentration on the icy road and said little.

Katie's sigh was sympathetic. "Just think; last Thanksgiving the temperature reached seventy degrees."

"Yup. Only in New England." He turned into Katie's driveway; the wheels spun uselessly as he accelerated. "This driveway is a joke, Kate," he said. "I'm sure if I talk to your landlord . . ."

"Oh, no you don't! Don't even think of it," she warned. "If I awake to the sound of a jackhammer next week, Mr. Ramsey, I'll have you drawn and quartered and your head put on a pike for all the world to see."

He grinned at that. "You're a pretty tough lady. How about if I just provide helicopter service from the road to the house?"

"You wouldn't dare," she said, suppressing a smile. Would he?

They pulled up to the house, got out and Katie handed Fletch her keys. Fletch opened the door—*TUH-WEET*—and flipped off the alarm. Katie hadn't seen him turn it on earlier, and naturally she jumped at the sound.

"Not used to it, are you?" he said dryly.

"Sure I am. It's just loud."

"Baloney. That control panel looks untouched and brand new." He was more distressed than annoyed. "How do I convince you that you're in very real danger living alone here?"

"And how do I convince *you* that your fears are those of a born and bred city-brat? You're so exasperating."

"You're so stubborn!"

"You're so right! And now that we've worked all that out," she said more softly, "let's have a fire. I'm freezing in this; let me change into something else. Can you build a fire, Fletch?"

"Can I build a fire. Can a duck swim? I was in the Scouts. I was in the *army*."

"But can you build a fire?" she repeated with friendly persistence.

"I haven't ever tried, actually. But leave it to me."

Shaking her head over his I-can-do-it arrogance, Katie went up to her room to change. It must be inherited, she decided; no longer did she believe that Fletch's formidable confidence was simply a male trait. It must have been taught to him by his parents, whoever they were. All Katie knew about Fletch's parents was that they had owned a station wagon when Fletch was in high school. She had a sudden longing to know more—about them, about him. She wanted to spend the whole night talking to him, asking questions.

Well—some of the night, anyway. With an accelerating pulse Katie pulled off the black dress and her lacy bra and dropped them on a chair, then went on a quick and frantic search through her closet. *Some*thing in there must be warm as well as sexy. Probably it was her mood, but everything seemed inappropriate—either too dressy, or too scratchy, or too constrictive for . . . for watching a fire.

More than anything else Katie wanted softness; so she settled on a white cotton-knit warm-up suit. The pants were baggy and the top was loose, and probably nothing she owned was less provocative, but it felt right, and so she left it on.

The roar of the fire reached Katie before she was halfway down the stairs. She hadn't heard its equal in all the fires she'd made in the stone house so far. Hurrying into the living room, still pulling hairpins from her loosening hair, she stopped in wide-eyed amazement. A solid sheet of flame rose up through the five-foot wide chimney opening. The fire didn't leap or flicker—there was no room for that. It *flamed*. And it didn't crackle; it thundered.

"Fletch! That's not what I meant! That's not a fire, it's an inferno!"

Fletch stood staring at the flames, awestruck. "Yeah. That's what I was thinking."

"The whole chimney could collapse!"

"I know; the same thought occurred to me."

"But I've only been gone a little while; how did you get it to catch so quickly?"

"Kerosene. Newspaper didn't work." Mesmerized, he continued to watch the fire as if it were a tiger in an unlocked cage. "Boy. That's one of the dumber things I've done."

Katie's laugh was a rich, slow peal; he looked so boyishly contrite. This man, she realized suddenly, would stay young forever. "If that's the worst blot on your record," she said softly, "you're in better shape than most Boy Scouts."

"But dammit, I wanted to show you that I could handle a stone house too. *You* look so natural here; a living extension of its history. I'd . . ."

He turned, then, and the gray-eyed intensity shifted from the fire to Katie in her warm-up suit. A tender, surprised smile played on his face. "Look at you," he said, moving closer to her. "One minute you're a bewitching seductress in black; the next, a little lamb in fleecy white. You make it awfully hard for a man."

"Hard for a man to do . . . what?" she challenged, not very defiantly.

"Hard for a man to decide whether to make love to you with wild abandon, or to rock you to sleep in his arms, singing lullabyes in your ear."

"Would a man ever do . . . both?" she whispered.

"I think a man could be persuaded to," he answered in a low, tender voice. He cupped her face in one hand, skimming and exploring her features with the fingertips of the other. "I do love this face . . . this nose . . . this ear . . . this other ear, too," he added with whimsical impartiality. "But especially I love this mouth. . . . It was made to be molested. . . ." He lowered his face to hers, then in one fluid motion straightened up again. "Or better yet . . . wait right here. I've got an idea."

Katie was left standing alone and unmolested in front of the blaze, which had died down to a mere bonfire, while he went upstairs into her bedroom, then into the guest room. He returned with six pillows, her patchwork quilt, and a broad grin on his face. "I couldn't find any bearskin rugs."

Arranging the pillows on the carpet before the fire, he surveyed the work with satisfaction. "One cloud. One goddess. All we need now is the ambrosia."

"I'm afraid I'm all out of ambrosia," she said.

"By some coincidence, I have a bottle of champagne in the car. I'll brave the sleet if you get the glasses."

In her kitchen Katie took out two heavy ironstone mugs from an oak china closet and set them on the counter, then stared blankly at them. Mugs. For champagne? Why was she being so antiromantic all of a sudden? For weeks she had been dancing on the edge of intimacy with Fletch. He was her landlord, her friend and—whether she liked it or not—her protector. Was she ready to accept him tonight for her lover as well? Or was she subconsciously sabotaging the mood, forcing it to stay on a light and friendly plane? Mugs. Really.

Fletch had returned and was brushing away icy sleet from his jacket. "It's crazy out—pouring little balls of ice." He hung up the jacket, removed the foil and the basket from the bottle, and carefully worked out the cork. "Stand by, ready to toast." The cork hurtled straight into the fire. "Looks like we'll have to drink it all in one whack," he grinned. It didn't seem to bother him that he was pouring Dom Perignon into humble containers more suitable for instant coffee.

Fletch clunked his mug against hers. "To Katrina. You've made forty worth waiting for."

"Forty what?" she asked, without thinking.

"Today's my birthday; and it didn't hurt a bit."

"You're kidding!"

"Would I kid about something like that?" He pulled her down with him on the quilt-covered pillows. "Anyway, I've loved every minute of it."

"But you should've told me," she protested. "We could've done something special to celebrate."

"It's not too late, ma'am," he drawled, glancing at his watch. "I still have one hour and . . . twenty-one minutes."

Katie sipped her champagne in mischievous concentration. "Gee . . . that's more than enough time to . . . bake and frost a cake." She made a motion to rise. Ah, champagne. The bubbles were floating straight to her brain, and for the second time that evening she felt giddy and unsteady. "Well, c'mon. Let's get cookin'. I have a fantastic recipe for a double dutch chocolate layer cake."

But he caught her legs like a middle linebacker and held on. "Hold it right there, miss. I was promised a celebration, not a page out of Julia Child. You're going to stay right here and . . ."

He was on his knees now; his arms were around her waist, his face buried in the soft white folds of her pullover. "And . . . what?" she whispered, weak-kneed from his delicious nearness.

"And . . . oh, I don't know," he said in a muffled voice. "Maybe teach me a few exercises to combat middle-age spread. Or whatever."

That—or maybe the way his hands had slid under her knit top—brought a slow, knowing smile to Katie's lips. Eyes closed, her mouth slightly parted with pleasure, she gave herself up to the effects of the champagne and Fletch's wizard touch. Suddenly it was blindingly obvious to her that she had been waiting for weeks for him to touch her again.

The depth of her pleasure amazed her, as he held her soft breasts cupped gently in his hands, his fingers lightly teasing and caressing her nipples. It was a maddening, overwhelming form of arousal. How had she lived so long without reacting like this before?

Katie must have made it blindingly obvious to Fletch that she was melting into a puddle of warm syrup, because he whispered, "More, Kate?" in a way that suggested he knew the answer to the question.

"Oh, please . . . yes."

Fletch was still on his knees and Katie was still standing. He lifted her top up above her breasts and began with exquisite artistry to create music with his tongue there. That did it. The erotic warmth of the fire—and his fiery assault

on her bare flesh—was simply too much for her. Katie had
been resting her hands lightly on his shoulders; now she
leaned heavily into him, her legs having suddenly failed
her.

"Zowie," she gasped.

He chuckled. "Zowie . . . does that mean . . . it's good
. . . or bad?" he murmured between teasing flicks of his
tongue. "I'm too old for Valley talk."

She slid down in his arms onto the pillows beside him.
"Loosely translated," she whispered, skimming his mouth
with tender, light kisses, "zowie means I love what you're
doing, Fletch." And she lay back on Fletch's patchwork
cloud, her breasts bare, her eyes bright with yearning, a
sheen of moisture on her smiling lips. There was sweet,
aroused wonder in her voice. "First, cranberry sauce; now
this. Whatever are you doing to me, Mr. Ramsey?"

"Whatever you want, Katrina. The sky's the limit, on
Cloud Nine." With an easy motion he slid her loose-fitting
top up over her head, most of the way off her arms, as far as
he could reach. With her wrists still caught over her head in
the soft cuffs of her pullover, Katie had the lazy, sexy
feeling that she was his captive, bound to accept the
pleasure he was offering her. Relishing, for the moment,
her passive role, she closed her eyes and in a state of near
bliss absorbed the hot moist trail of his tongue over her
nipples, in the soft valley between her breasts, over her flat
stomach. "I love this cloud . . . the pillows make it soft,
and the champagne makes it . . . float," she said dreamily.

"Are you warm enough, darling?" he murmured. His
voice was genuinely solicitous.

"Hmmmmn . . . getting there," she answered with co-
lossal understatement.

His mouth searched the contours of her face, then found
her mouth and hungrily probed its hot, sweet interior.
"Kate . . . darling . . . does the younger set still say 'I

want you'?'' His hand slipped inside the elastic waist-band of her warm-up pants, rubbing the inside of her thigh to a tingling pitch before coming to rest at the apex of all sensation.

"I think the younger set . . . says something . . . ohh . . . like 'let's get it . . . on,' " she gasped as he worked some incredibly devilish magic at that apex. She slipped her hands out from the sleeves of her pullover, then laced her fingers in his hair. "But I think . . . 'I want you' . . . has a nice ring to it. Oh, Fletch, I *want* you." It was the first time her lips had ever formed the words, the first time she could have possibly felt natural saying them aloud.

"Kate, sweet darling, you've got me," he answered softly. "Or at least, you could have me, if I were un-dressed." He leaned away from her and lay on his back, melting Katie's insides with a smile of breathtaking charm. He was waiting.

But waiting for what? Surely not for her to take off his clothes? When she was married, she and Peter had usually met in bed, conveniently undressed. With a vague gesture toward his belt she murmured, "I don't . . . you're not . . . waiting for me, are you?"

"Who else?"

God, he was being hard on her. Since she'd met him, he'd got her to relax every habit she'd ever formed—got her to eat; got her to admit she wanted him, and to tell him so; got her to admit her needs, every step of the way. And now he wanted her to take him besides. She resisted. "But that's the husb— the man's part," she said weakly.

"In this post-Aquarian age? Not necessarily."

So this too had become a contest of wills. "You want me? Take me." But that was supposed to be *her* line!

He brought his palms up behind his head and crossed his ankles in a deliberately casual pose. Pinpoints of flame— and good humor—danced in his eyes, but she thought there was a soft urgency, almost a pleading, in them as well. "You want me? *Please*, come and take me," his eyes seemed to say.

And did it matter, really, who undressed whom? And which of them wanted the other first, or more? Or even whether he loved her or not? *She* loved *him;* for now, that was enough. He wanted her, and she needed him. The ingredients for rapture were all there; she would sort them all out some other time. Surely for now all that mattered was release from this intolerable agony of yearning.

"Kate," he said softly, "I'll help." He undid the brass buckle of his belt.

And she unzipped his trousers. Fletch unfastened the second button of his shirt, Katie the third and fourth, and both of them, somehow, the fifth through seventh. And then his slacks and underwear were off, and hers, and they were lying in one another's arms, bare and flame-warmed, hungry for one another's kisses, their bodies curved to the contours of the lumpy cloud underneath them.

With unerring accuracy Fletch sought out every flash-point on her body, some places so unexplored that she had never even suspected their existence. With his tongue he seared magical mystery tours on the underside of her breasts, the curve of her armpit, the flare in and then out of her waist and hips. Unpredictably he took tiny, gentle nips in her flesh, and the flashpoints would erupt into sudden, bright flame. His sensitive fingers danced with erotic precision on the softness between her thighs, and Katie decided, almost in despair, that no man should understand a woman so well.

"Yes . . . yes . . . yes," she repeated, assuming that the word resolved all differences, encompassed all meanings, and that he would understand. After a while she thought that the simple repetition wasn't even her voice, but simply the soft hiss of air as she released it from a hot-air balloon, tweaking and adjusting it in her flight to sky blue ecstasy. Her breath collapsed in a series of quick, tense sighs and with a sense of urgency she dragged his face to hers, covering his mouth with deep, bruising kisses.

"Now, please . . . now," she said in a husky, pleading voice, her lips moving against the smooth straight line of his jaw. "Oh, please, Fletch, *now*." With one foot pressing into the floor she lifted herself toward him in an unmistakable invitation.

"Dear love . . ." Fletch brought one leg inside her raised knee, and Katie moved her other leg aside, pleasure-hazy and dizzy with hunger for him. With her help his entry was smooth and swift, a sliding rush that was more wondrous than familiar. It had been so long.

And then she was in the balloon again, floating higher and higher away from the earth, out of range of the sound of Fletch's throaty endearments, rising, rising above the little green patches below her. Whether the patches were fields of clover, or squares on the quilt, she wasn't sure, and she didn't care. All that mattered was the sensation of rising blissfully, breathlessly higher.

She held Fletch tightly in her arms, because she wanted him to come too, higher and higher in her pretty balloon. The colors of the earth so far below her were wrenchingly vivid, lush and fertile and suffused with green light. How beautiful it all was, how very . . . very beautiful. She tried to point out the green translucence to Fletch, to share it with him, but all she could say was his name, once, and then again. And suddenly she heard a long, shuddering sigh—had the balloon been torn, or was that her own voice—and she came wafting gently back down to earth, exhausted and happy and somehow disappointed that the balloon ride was over.

But Fletch wouldn't allow her to descend back to earth, not yet. "Katrina . . . don't . . . stop now," he whispered with electrifying urgency. His elbows were resting on the pillows underneath her, and his tongue seared the inside curves of her ear with hot, wet persuasion as he moved with compelling rhythm inside her.

Katie found her downward drift into serenity abruptly reversed as she soared, like a rocket this time, into the outer perimeters of space. In shockingly few seconds she was gasping for breath; and then all the stars of all the nights in all the universes exploded in a shimmering cascade inside her head, filling her with light and fire.

When she opened her eyes again, dreamily, it was to see pinpoints of flame reflected in Fletch's golden hair as his face lay contentedly in the curve of her shoulder. "That was fun," she murmured serenely, catching a few of the golden hairs between her teeth and tugging lightly. "Let's do it again."

"I thought you did do it again," he said in a hoarse chuckle, without moving. "Are you going to be one of those insatiable types?"

"Why? Do you come across the type often?" Instantly, jealous.

He lifted his head at that and smoothed her straying hair with short, tender pats. The fire was bright, his face was so near; Katie could see the tiny toboggan-scar she'd noticed that first night on the side of his nose.

"There is no one like you, Kate," he said gravely. "No one."

Her heart swelled with love for him; for his tenderness, his cleverness, for the child's scar on his nose. "You're just saying that because shy nymphomaniacs are hard to find," she quipped, partly to beat back the irrational tears that had sprung up. The tears were spillover from her heart, she knew; but how could she explain that?

"A shy nymphomaniac!" he objected indignantly. "Who says you're shy?"

They both laughed and then lay quietly for a long while, breathing in one another's nearness. Outside the night was turning wild. Sleet rapped insistently at the ancient windows, and a low branch began to thump with ominous heaviness on one of the thin, warped panes. Earlier Katie had lit a Victorian hanging kerosene lamp; now the flame leaped and flattened repeatedly, and the elaborately painted flowers on the white bowl seemed to dance with demonic fury around the flickering wick. Fletch's Great Colonial Fire had finally settled down to a crackling blaze, but even so, frequent gusts of wind caused the flames to leap high and little puffs of smoke to backdraft into the room.

"Nuts," Katie said lazily. It was the first spoken word in many minutes. "I'd better close the damper before we choke to death."

"I'll do it. Let me do it." Fletch was on his feet instantly, eager to play with Katie's working museum.

"The iron handle on the left," Katie instructed, shifting her position so that she lay on her side, elbow on the floor, cheek on the palm of her hand. She was still undressed; but more to the point, so was Fletch. With sleepily awakening interest she watched him move unself-consciously in front of the fire. He was not massively built, but there was a lean energy in his movements which greatly appealed to her. He belonged to an age before megavitamins, bulk-up diets and Nautilus equipment, a time when only the quick-witted and the fit could hope to survive.

"Don't damp it down too much," she warned him, her voice breathless with love.

He turned the handle with probing, surgical precision. "How will I know if it's too much?"

"Trial and error." Black sooty smoke poofed back into the room. "Not enough," she added sagely.

"Thanks for the tip," he said, coughing. "This is dangerous, Kate. We could burn the house down. We could die in our sleep of monoxide poisoning. I'm putting on the smoke alarm," he said as he turned away from the fire and looked down at her. "But first," he said, crouching down before her, "I need a kiss."

Katie raised herself up on her hands, her unbound hair falling freely over her breasts and shoulders, and pressed her mouth to his with exquisite familiarity.

"Mmmn-hmmn. Better," he said, and stood up.

"Fletch, what's that aftershave you wear? It drives me," she added candidly, "a little crazy."

"*Topaz*. Cindy's bought it for me ever since she was a kid. The topaz is November's birthstone, you see. Cindy's very organized about such things; it's just lucky for me that *Topaz* doesn't smell like lilies of the valley," he said over his shoulder as he switched the alarm on.

Something vaguely illogical was bumping into the back of Katie's pleasure-sated mind. She flopped over onto her stomach and rested her chin thoughtfully on her crossed knuckles. "Cindy never mentioned that it was your birthday in her note to you," she said shyly. That damn note. Why this need to remind Fletch that she'd been a snoop?

Fletch returned with her hairbrush in his hand. "That's a long story," he said. "First, watch this trick; I learned it when I worked summers as a caddy at my parents' golf club." He flipped the brush backward in the air and caught it—by the bristles. "Hmmmph. That's not right." He tried it again, caught it by the handle properly, grinned and knelt down over Katie's legs, supported by his knees on either side of her.

With long, slow strokes he began to brush her hair. "When Cindy was barely more than a toddler," he explained, "my birthday fell, as it does this year, on Thanksgiving Day. She considered *that* arrangement a big gyp," he chuckled.

"You mean, that Thanksgiving might outrival your birthday?"

"Oh, no; she was mad that my birthday might outrival her Thanksgiving. So she came up with a compromise: when Dolores lit the candles on my cake Cindy made everyone sing 'Happy Thanksgiving to You' instead of the usual number. Naturally, when she grew older and we teased her about her selfishness, she was mortified. And now, of course, it's become our little joke. But this year . . . well, this year it was different," he said softly. His voice trailed off thoughtfully as he drew Katie's brush through her long, thick hair.

"Tell me about your parents," Katie said, relaxing with catlike contentment under his fluid, soothing strokes.

"My father died a couple of years ago," he said, quietly. "He was a surgeon and wanted me to be one. My mother still lives in Brooklyn with my younger sister, who's been smarter than I have about not marrying."

"Your father was in medicine? Really? Then that explains . . ."

"Cindy? Yes and no. It's true that she had to listen to her grandfather complain for years that I never went to med school. I guess a man's medical practice is a little like an acquired fortune; he wants to be able to pass it on to the next in line. But I just never really had the calling. Dolores wanted to be a nurse a hell of a lot more than I wanted to be a doctor—and Cindy wants to be a surgeon more than either one of us wanted to be anything."

"Was Cindy trying to please your father, do you think?"

"That may have been a factor at first, but certainly not now," Fletch answered ironically. "This doesn't hurt, does it? There's an unbelievable tangle back here," he grumbled, gently separating some snarled strands. "Dad would've loved your hair," he mused. "He had a theory that eating a raw egg every day kept the coat smooth and glossy."

"Was your dad a veterinarian, then?" she asked, surprised.

"Orthopedics. But he did keep our Springer Spaniel incredibly well groomed."

She could hear the smile in his voice as he resumed his long, smooth strokes. He was so very methodical, beginning at the forehead and dragging the bristles in one fluid motion to mid-back; not an inch was left unbrushed. "How did your father feel about . . . Dolores?" Katie ventured. What a dumb question. How would any father feel about his eighteen-year-old son having to get married?

Fletch was patiently polite. "About what you'd expect. He resented Dolores for taking away my opportunity to shine in med school. Ironic, isn't it? Dolores, of course, resented *me* for being the cause of her giving up a similar opportunity. Maybe that's why I'd move heaven and earth to make sure Cindy gets *her* opportunity." He tossed the brush aside and began a slow, heat-filled neck rub. She marveled at his energy; she herself had none just now.

"Fletch, there's something I have to know," she began softly. "But don't answer if you don't want to. It's just that I've wondered . . . but it's none of my business, really. . . . Anyway I'd still . . ." Her brain reeled from the sound of her own babbling. She took a deep breath. "Did Dolores try to jump off a bridge in Germany?"

The brush stopped in mid-stroke. "No. Why?" He sounded puzzled. Not surprisingly.

"Jimmy didn't talk her out of it? Jumping, I mean? Off the bridge?" Oh, she was making a grand mess of it.

"Jimmy did talk someone away from a bridge railing once. I've forgotten her name—Maryanne, Marlene? Jimmy was far more shaken by the experience than the woman was, apparently. She worked as a waitress in a bar, and whenever I saw her afterward, she seemed perfectly cheerful. Personally, I think Jimmy overreacted. He was like that. . . ."

Katie half turned to Fletch. "Then what was the 'big favor' you said you owed Jimmy?"

He kissed the top of her hair. "I blush to say it. I lost heavily once in a poker game. I was young. I was stupid. No excuse. Jimmy, who barely knew me then, gave me his winnings, his watch, and—when it looked as if things might get rough—his right arm. I never forgot it.''

"Ah." Katie felt pretty silly. This was what came of an overactive imagination, she told herself. She was as bad as Jimmy. Life wasn't really like "Dallas." People didn't jump off bridges to get out of bad marriages. They just . . . walked away. Sometimes with skinny models.

Fletch sensed her faltering mood and tried to steer her out of it. "Damn it, Kate. No more about me or my family. Tell me about yours.''

"Mmmn . . . a little to the right," she pleaded sleepily. "There's so little to tell. Two older brothers . . . both married . . . one happily. One sells computers and the other's in a religious ashram in India. Do you want more?''

"'Course I do. Which one is in the ashram?''

"Which do you think?" she said with a yawn.

"The unhappy one.''

"Nope; the other one. My brother and sister-in-law plan to celebrate their twentieth anniversary there. They've been kicking around the world for the last two or three years.''

"No kidding? How can they afford it?''

How Fletch could keep up such a lively interest in her family and such a slow, sensual neck rub at the same darn time . . . "Oh—they get by. They live extremely simply. For example, they've never owned a stereo speaker the size of a small hotel.'' She grinned.

Fletch was more amused than offended. Bending over Katie, he buried his face in the thick black folds of her newly brushed hair. "Why is it that you hold my hard-earned money against me?" he murmured.

"Oh, pooh," Katie said in a pleasurable haze as she filled their mugs with flat champagne. "I'm not holding anything against you. In fact," she said into her pillow with a wicked smile, "it seems to me, it's the other way around.''

"Witch! You've put a spell on me," he said in a husky whisper into her hair. Sliding his hands underneath her, he caressed the tips of her breasts to a state of fierce excitement while he dropped tender nips and kisses on her shoulder and the back of her neck. "Kate . . . lift up . . . yes . . . more . . . ah, love . . ."

The champagne got even flatter.

Chapter Ten

$\mathscr{K}$atie was sleepily aware that her shoulder was cold, and she pulled up the . . . what? The afghan? Yes . . . Fletch had dragged it from the kitchen sofa to cover them, before they fell asleep in front of the fire. A band of warmth—Fletch's arm—encircled her waist, and his warm breath fell in a regular pattern on the back of her neck. The ice storm was lashing the stone house with its full fury; but the house had stood through far worse in centuries gone by, as it would stand for centuries to come. Feeling snug and secure, Kate burrowed into the curve of Fletch's body, and drifted cozily back to sleep.

TUH-WEET! TUH-WEET! TUH-WEET!

Fletch threw off the afghan and sat bolt upright. "My God, the house is on fire!"

TUH-WEET! TUH-WEET! TUH-WEET!

Roused from a deep sleep, Katie was only half-conscious. "Wha . . . it can't be. The fire's gone out. . . ."

TUH-WEET! TUH-WEET! TUH-WEET!

Simultaneously they jumped up from their quilted nest, and promptly whacked their heads together.

TUH-WEET! TUH-WEET! TUH-WEET!

"Yow!" The knock made Katie's teeth rattle, and she rubbed her forehead furiously as she dashed still half-asleep from room to room, searching for a fire. "Turn it off, Fletch! There's no fire!"

"There must be!" he yelled back. "Keep looking!" But he shut down the alarm, and the hideous noise stopped. Katie tore her bathrobe from the hook on her bedroom door and returned downstairs, her adrenaline slowly receding, a dull, throbbing headache slowly advancing. Fletch was standing next to the control box, looking surprisingly warm-blooded for a naked man in November. Suddenly he flipped off the dim light.

"Kate," he whispered in a deadly serious voice. "Come here."

Something in his tone caused her adrenaline to begin pumping anew. "What is it?" she whispered, groping toward him.

"If the alarm wasn't for fire, then it must be for . . ."

"Burglars! Oh, my God, Fletch!"

"Shh! Just stand still. Get behind me and don't move." His whisper sounded like a shout in the pitch-black foyer.

It was the first time in her life that Katie had experienced total, abject fear. Her heart rioted in her chest, and she was distinctly aware of a rushing pressure in her head. She was going to faint. Oh God, she was going to . . . Something appallingly cold and wet brushed Katie's leg and she screamed. Instantly Fletch turned on the light: It was Moose, settled back on his hindquarters, licking his sleet-dampened fur.

"He must have been outside," she said, still in a whisper. "I thought he was in an upstairs bedroom."

"How the hell did he get in?" Fletch asked in a normal voice.

"Shh. Through his little exit-door, of course."

"Kate." Fletch's look was exasperated, even angry. *"He* set off the alarm."

"Oh. *Oh*. Uh-oh." She winced. It was now pretty obvious to everyone in the room that the alarm had never been tested before today. Immediately deciding that the best defense was a good offense, Katie said, "You're completely overplaying the importance of this gadget, Fletch. And anyway, *you're* here. Why should I worry?" Her voice had become soft with reconciliation and tender irony as she slipped one arm around his waist and led him back to the living room. "You must be freezing to death. I'll light the kerosene heaters."

Earlier Fletch had insisted that they turn off the space heaters for the night. With sublime confidence he'd said, "This fire will last until morning. Then I'll get up, like the early settlers, and throw a log or two on it to freshen it up." At the moment, a small handful of embers were all that remained.

If Katie had been very, very nice, she'd have let the matter lie. But she was feeling, still, a tad defensive. "You'll notice, great Eagle Scout, that your fire's dead."

"I said I was a Scout, not a Green Beret."

"You should've used oak."

"Pine smells better."

"Pine burns out faster."

"So who cares?" he sulked. "It was nice while it lasted."

It was typical of his short-term attitudes. Nice while it lasted. *Us, too?* she wanted to ask. *Will that be what you say about us, too?* Katie threw another match—her fifth—

into the growing pool of kerosene at the bottom of the space heater. The tiny flame-tips kept going out, drowned in too much fuel. "Damn!" she muttered, lighting number six. Her fingers shivered; number six went out too.

And then they heard the *big* siren. No little tuh-weet this time. The siren was deafening, urgent and coming closer. A blue light flashed through the darkened room, throwing Fletch and Katie into wild disco relief. Tires crunched to a halt in front of the house, doors opened and slammed. Microphoned voices droned from a radio-telephone.

Police. Fletch was scrambling into his pants as Katie stood frozen to the spot, clutching the box of matches like a trapped arsonist. "Dear God in heaven—what are *they* doing here?" she wailed.

The door knocker pounded loudly—or was that her heart?—and Fletch hurried to answer it, muttering something about "automatic call-through." He had just enough time to pull on a t-shirt before he answered the door. *She* hadn't even thought of dressing, and stood behind him, gripping the lapels of her robe up near her throat in a panic of modesty.

The policeman was big. His hat was big, his oilskins were big, his boots were big. Something about him reminded Katie of Darth Vader. Standing in the driving sleet, he looked official, skeptical and not very happy to be dragged out of a warm police station into an ice storm.

"We got a call that there's been a break-in? Mr. . . . er . . . Bright, is it?"

"Ramsey. Fletcher Ramsey. Come in, officer." Fletch's voice, Katie noted automatically, was courteous, business-like and surprisingly unmortified. How did the man do it? The policeman stepped inside the foyer; instantly the room shrank. He looked expectantly at Fletch.

"Recently I had a combination burglar and fire alarm installed," Fletch began succinctly. "It had an automaticdialer option, which of course you're familiar with. When the alarm first sounded we thought it was a—"

"—fire," Katie interjected. Surely she should be explaining all of this.

"—But it wasn't, of course. Next we assumed that it had to be a—"

"—burglar." Dammit. It was her house.

"But what actually happened was—"

"—the cat," Katie concluded. "The cat did it."

"Did . . . what, Mrs. Ramsey?" the officer asked. His head had been moving back and forth between them like a spectator at a tennis match; now he settled his look on Katie, and she flinched at his reference to her as Fletch's wife.

"My name is Katrina Bright," she said with wounded dignity.

"Ms. Bright is divorced, officer," Fletch explained.

"I see. Ms. Bright is living here with you, Mr. Ramsey? Because the recorded message did mention her name."

"No," she objected quickly. "It's Mr. Ramsey who's living with . . . well, staying with . . . who's visiting," she finished lamely. Then she rallied. "It's *my* house."

The policeman turned to Fletch. "But it's *your* burglar alarm?"

"My alarm, and my fault," Fletch added generously. "I had the unit installed professionally, of course; but I didn't realize the cat has his own entrance. The microwave sensors picked up the animal's motion, and . . . off it went," he explained with an apologetic smile. "I'm very sorry for the inconvenience, officer. It won't happen again, I assure you."

The policeman was not amused. "Were you aware that there's an ordinance against automatic dialers in this town?"

Fletch stared at him blankly. "As a matter of fact . . . no," he answered quietly.

"There is. You'll have to make arrangements with a monitoring service if you want to keep the automatic dialing feature. They would double check with you before routing any emergency call to us. Until then, I suggest that you leave the alarm disabled." He touched his hat in a polite, old-fashioned way. "Good-night, Mr. Ramsey . . . Ms. . . . Bright." And he let himself out.

"Oh, nuts. Oh, *damn*." Katie stormed back to the living room and with one well-aimed match lit the balky kerosene heater. Then she stood up and turned on Fletch. "Do you have *any* idea how humiliated I feel just now?"

"Of course I do, Kate. I . . ."

"Oh, no you don't. No you *don't!*" Her voice cracked with fury. "Embarrassment is beneath you, isn't it? It's too . . . *ordinary* for you to bother with, isn't it?"

"I admit, it was an awkward situation."

"Awkward? *Awk*ward! I feel like jumping off the Kingston Bridge and *you* call it awkward! Don't you understand? I *live* here; I have to face these people every day."

"What're you talking about?" he objected. "You didn't know that cop."

"It doesn't *mat*-ter," she seethed, clenching her fists and bringing them down in midair. "Every time I drive past the police station I'll remember tonight. I'll remember that I ran around like a chicken without a head, terrified of fire and burglars and who knows what else—things I'd never even thought about before I met you. I'll remember that a cop mistook me for your . . . score. In *your* house, no less." Her lower lip trembled, and that fueled her anger. "But most of all I'll remember that you just marched into my life . . . overran it . . . forced me out of my . . . *lair,* as you put it . . . made me . . . respond to you . . ." She couldn't go on.

"Was that so bad?" he asked with infuriating tenderness.

"Yes! Before I met you I didn't believe in men; but I did

believe in . . . myself, my job. . . ." She made a motion that encompassed her surroundings. "All this. But you've turned my whole life upside-down and inside-out." Her bafflement softened the hard edges of her voice, and she finished on a note almost of despair. "Now I don't know *what* I want."

"You want what I want, Kate," Fletch said softly. "What everyone wants. Happiness. Pleasure."

He lifted the afghan from the floor and wrapped it around Katie's shoulders, and his closeness made her heart pound. Her reactions were becoming almost Pavlovian; one deep breath near him, and desire came automatically. It angered her. She threw down the afghan petulantly and collapsed into the loveseat, crossing her legs underneath her, rubbing her cold bare feet with her hands. "I want more than pleasure, Fletch," she said quietly, without looking up at him.

He sat beside her and dragged the patchwork quilt up over her lap. "What *do* you want, then, Kate?" The question was forthright, almost puzzled.

And she didn't blame him. All this time she had been portraying herself as fiercely independent. Then they'd made love, and, son of a gun, it turned out that Katie Bright liked the idea of a permanent relationship after all. How predictable. How . . . *ordinary*. Well, she would never admit it. Not in a million years.

"Katie?" he repeated. "Tell me what you want. Please."

And that was all it took to drag it out of her. "I want . . . an oak fire, Fletch, not a pine one," she said almost plaintively.

"Ah." It was all he said. Ah.

Katie's heart plummeted; she had hoped for so much more. She had told him as plainly as she could that she wanted long-lasting love, and all she'd got in return was one single syllable. A kind of numb quietness settled over her, and she stared emptily at the burned-out ashes in the fireplace.

Fletch made a small sound in the back of his throat. "Kate . . . I've never built an oak fire before. All the women I've ever known . . . well, the flames didn't last. How will I know if this is an oak fire?"

She looked at him then and saw that his eyes were bright with—she didn't know what. Apprehension? Taking his hand in her own, Katie laid it over her heart, her gaze never leaving him as she whispered, "Can you feel it? The heat? It's an oak fire, Fletch."

"You could never burn with less," he answered tenderly, lifting her hand to his lips. "It's not in your nature. But if you knew *my* track record . . ." He trailed off, his voice filled with self-contempt.

"Why is that?" she asked, more sadly than curiously. "Why do you back away from committing yourself to people?"

"But I don't! Just because I haven't remarried . . . My wife, my daughter, surely those are commitments?"

He was hurt, perhaps even shocked, but Katie plowed on anyway, not at all sure of her motives. "You gave Dolores your name and Cindy her tuition and me the most sophisticated protection that money can buy. But . . ."

"I'm trying to buy you all off—is that it?" he interrupted, his quick intelligence leaping ahead of her carefully chosen words. Now there was no doubt of his hurt. His voice dropped to a low, ominous register. "I'm impressed. Apparently you know me far better than I know myself."

And then the anger came, as he lashed out against the accusation. "Look, Dr. Freud—I don't *know* what kind of wood is fueling my fire. Pine, oak, charcoal briquets—who the hell cares? All I know is that the fire is burning hot—*hot,* you noodlehead!" He gripped her shoulders hard and pinned her to the back of the sofa. "This fire is *consuming* me. You want to know how much sleep I've had the last few nights? *Zip.* I don't like tossing, lady, and I don't like turning. My idea of a good night's rest does not include counting up either your irresistible charms or your very resistible faults—one of which is an irritating habit of analyzing every goddamned thing to death.''

He was nose to nose with her as he pounded home his challenge. ''Look. As far as I'm concerned, you, for the moment, are *it*. Nothing's come even close. Now—is that good enough for you, or not?''

''I guess it's . . . good enough—for the mo——''

And that was as much as Katie got to say. But later, much later, she managed to finish the sentence. ''For the moment, Ramsey. Only for the moment.''

Chapter Eleven

$\mathcal{W}$ ell, that's it. Now we've had it all.'' Marcia was standing at the window in the Shape-Up Room, hands on her hips, gazing philosophically at the last of the falling snowflakes. ''An ice storm, a record cold-wave and now a ten-inch snowfall. And it's only December tenth, mind you. Is it possible that someone up there doesn't like us?''

''If so, he's voicing his displeasure by kicking the jet stream around.'' Katie shook the snow from her hat and stomped her boots into the mat. ''I heard it on the radio as I came in—the jet stream has moved north from its usual position. Or maybe it was south. Anyway, it's not where it's supposed to be.''

She glanced around. The next scheduled session was due to begin in ten minutes, but the room was virtually empty. Six o'clock; Friday night; a heavy snowfall. The wonder was that anyone had shown up at all.

''It's kind of pretty, though, isn't it?'' Marcia mused.

"Still so clean and fresh. It makes me want to use it somehow." She turned around; inspiration was written all over her grinning, freckled face. "Let's go skiing! Call up Ski-Shawnga; see if they're open. Never mind; I'll do it."

"Uh . . . Marcia?" Katie inclined her head in the direction of the two women warming up. "Haven't you forgotten something?" she asked dryly.

Marcia looked up from the phone book. "Ruth! Chrissie! Come on over for a minute." She punched out the phone number.

"Marcia . . ."

"You're open? Great! Is the rental shop open too? Thanks." Down went the receiver; out came the grin.

"Marcia . . ."

"Ladies—the first white snow falls but once a year. Are you going to hide inside on a glorious evening like this? Or would you rather go skiing? Say yes!"

Ruth looked at Chrissie; Chrissie looked at Ruth. "No. We don't think so." Ruth and Chrissie were dorm-mates at the college. Both were a little overweight, but neither was really uncomfortable about it. They seemed, in fact, remarkably at ease about everything. "But don't let us keep you here," Ruth said.

"Actually, we hate it when we're the only ones in class," Chrissie added.

"Besides, we were thinking of skipping tonight anyway; the Caboose is having live reggae."

"But thanks for asking," Chrissie said politely.

Chrissie looked at Ruth; Ruth looked at Chrissie. "Well. Bye." Chrissie fluttered a hand at them.

"See you Monday," said Ruth smiling. And they left.

"Not the most dedicated souls," Marcia said with a shrug.

"Look who's talking. Marcia, we have regular hours posted on the door. I'd like to stick to them." *Here I go again*, Katie thought. *Always the voice of reason.*

Not that Marcia's feelings were hurt by the mild reprimand. "Honestly, Kate! Half the shops in New Paltz closed down early today—if they even opened in the first place. Your loyalty is touching, but misplaced. And anyway, where's your holiday spirit?"

Katie tried another tack. "I'm not dressed for skiing."

"We'll wear our leotards under our jeans; that'll be warm enough."

Another tack. "How much are lift tickets this year?"

"At Ski-Shawnga? It's not exactly St. Moritz," Marcia retorted. "You can afford it."

Ski-Shawnga was a friendly, charming, but very, very small ski slope, perfect for beginners. Katie had skied there two or three times before, and that was the sum total of her experience. Marcia, on the other hand, really *had* been to St. Moritz.

Katie was forced to confess the real reason for her reluctance to leave. "I'm expecting Fletch to meet me here tonight," she said offhandedly.

Marcia's look was depressingly sympathetic. "His track record's a little spotty, isn't it? You waited for him *last* Friday, and he never showed."

"But he did show up on Saturday morning."

"When you were off shopping somewhere. And then he was too busy to hang around for the weekend. And—that's right—he also stood you up the Wednesday before that."

"I wasn't . . . 'stood up,'" Katie answered loftily. Really, such bluntness. "He called and left a message with Jessica that time."

"Some romance," Marcia answered. Bluntly.

The funny thing was, Katie had been thinking along the same lines herself. It seemed to her that a romance less than three weeks old ought to have more urgency to it. They'd managed to get together twice on his mad dashes up and down the Thruway between his restaurants, but . . . only twice? Was that any way for someone consumed by fire—pine *or* oak—to act? Granted, both times were unbelievably exciting and tender. They hadn't bothered going out to dinner as planned; they had hardly left the vicinity of the fireplace, except for the long, long bath. . . .

"It's such a perfect evening to spend in front of the fire, Marsh. Maybe I'll pass on skiing." The Thruway had been shut down for a few hours that morning, but it was open for traffic again. Tonight he would surely come.

"You can leave a note for him to join us, Katie," Marcia urged. "There'll be a fire in the main lounge. *Please*."

Marcia? Pleading? Katie sighed. "Chuck's still in Long Island, I take it?"

"Yes. Three broken toes, Katie. Is that so many? I can understand his mother wanting him to visit her over the weekend; but to allow him to miss a week of classes, just to give her moral support . . . am I being cruel and heartless?" Marcia seemed genuinely frightened by the possibility.

"I suppose that depends. Can his mother get around on the crutches?"

"He says she can. She's only forty-five, you know, and reasonably athletic. And Chuck's sister and brother are still living at home. So—am I heartless or not?" she repeated.

"Oh, Marsh—how can I answer that? You and Chuck will have to work his mother out between you. You know what I think? I think maybe we both need to work out our frustration on the slopes. Let's go skiing."

"Will you? Great! I'll get my things. Oh—and check your messages before we leave," Marcia said, pointing to two or three pink slips on Katie's desk.

Katie shuffled through them. The burglar alarm people had returned her call, finally. Humph. Mr. Barker, the real-estate agent, had no more leads for the moment. Humph. And Jessica would like her to call.

She rang up the number. Jessie had had to quit the Shape-Up Room almost immediately; her husband did not approve. Maybe he'd had a change of heart. "Jessica? Katie. What's up?"

"Katie! You'll never guess! Never! My cousin Max told his wife—and she told me—that you're one of his top contenders for the 'Morning Workout.' Can you believe it? I'm so excited I could die. I'll want your autograph, of course," she tittered.

It was a bolt of lightning, dropped right in Katie's lap. Naturally she had never thought for a moment that she'd make it into any final running. But on the other hand, there was something about Max's oddly benign farewell—"You got a nice tush"—that had stayed with her. Infuriated her, but stayed with her.

"Jessica, for Pete's sake. Just because I'm a contender . . . it means nothing. Don't mention it to anyone, please. It'll just be more embarrassing when I'm not chosen. Promise?"

"Well . . . o.k. But I've already told my husband." Jessica was deflated and defiant.

"But thanks for tipping me off, Jess. Now I won't be caught speechless when and if the call comes." Katie's voice was filled with wry kindliness. Jessica was so naive.

She hung up just as Marcia returned. "Did you write your note?" Marcia reminded her.

"Did I write? . . . Oh, not yet." Katie scribbled directions to Fletch and taped them to the door. "Marcia, Jessica just passed on the silliest little rumor. . . ."

The rum toddies tasted surprisingly like her own, and the fire—pine—was cheerful enough, surrounded as it was by laughing, merry skiers and snow bunnies. Katie's skis and boots stood propped up against the wall, ready to go, but still she lingered. The roads were clear, even up here. So what was his excuse? Katie resolved not to look at the door again. She looked at the door again.

So this was what it meant to be in love with a builder of

empires. Well, if Fletch wanted to roam the earth in search of wealth and adventure, let him, damn him. *She* would not play Penelope to his Ulysses, sitting at home all day, patiently weaving her cloth. Oh, no. Katie ordered another round of rum toddies for Marcia and herself.

"He's going to England, you know. That's what all the running around is for. To arrange meetings and such. He flies out Sunday for two weeks. Or so. It depends. He says." Katie propped her chin on her fist and couldn't help looking wistful.

"England? What for?"

"He wants to open up a chain of Fletcher's Fish and Chips there," she sighed. Up came the other fist; now she looked more glum than wistful.

"You're kidding. Fish and Chips in England! Isn't that a little like bringing coals to Newcastle?"

"He says his are better. He says, what do the English know. Anyway, what Flesher Ramsey wants, Flesher Ramsey gets." Katie slurred the last in a sad, singsong contralto.

"Hi, beautiful. You live around here?"

He was strongly built, brown-haired, raspy-voiced, the first man Katie had ever seen who wore his gold chains on the outside of his turtleneck, and Katie—well, she stared. It did look odd.

"Who, me?" she murmured reluctantly. "Oh, no, I'm from . . . Gary, Indiana. Just here for the weekend, visiting my, um, sister-in-law. My husband's sister, that is. We're related by marriage. Mine, I mean."

"Right, right. I get it." He turned to the woman on his other side.

Marcia leaned toward Katie and said in a confidential whisper, "I don't know who to give the prize to—him, for his brilliant come-on; or you, for your sophisticated brush-off."

"I'm out of practice," Katie said dryly. "And what's

more, I don't want to be *in* practice. We came here to ski, didn't we?" She stood up and was surprised to see that someone had moved the floor. It was much farther from her feet than it used to be. "Darn bartender," she muttered. "Spiking those toddies."

Marcia stood up and agreed. "Whooh! I'll say. But it's also 112° in here. We need some fresh air."

The two women hoisted their skis over their shoulders and headed for the door.

"Kate! What's your hurry?" came Fletch's voice behind her. Katie swung around to face him, her skis nearly beheading him in the process. "Careful," he said quickly. "Don't you know those are lethal?"

"Of course I do. They are not," she huffed. And then she saw Cindy. "Oh, Cindy, hello. Cindy Ramsey, this is Marcia Welkins. Marcia, you know Fletch," she said with fierce concentration. There. Had she got them all?

"What a fan*tas*tic idea, to go skiing," Cindy said with almost unnerving exuberance. "I would've made daddy come even if he didn't want to. It's such a beautiful night . . . crisp, cold, moon, stars . . . and snow. . . ." She drummed her fingers on the shoulder strap of her handbag, eager to get going. "Daddy, I'll meet you at the rental shop. Hurry. This is going to be so fan*tas*tic."

"It's only a J-bar, Cindy," Marcia said laconically. "I'm not even sure they have all the trails groomed yet. Don't get your hopes too high; the trails certainly aren't."

Cindy laughed almost shrilly at the weak joke and left them. Katie's responses were, if anything, a little slowed by the toddies, and as a result Cindy struck her as being a bit manic. *Poor kid. She's so happy to be with her dad.*

Marcia, no doubt remembering Katie's mood earlier, walked tactfully ahead of Fletch and her.

"Here, Kate. I'll take those," Fletch said, gesturing toward her skis.

"No you won't," Katie answered regally.

"Yes, I . . . *will*." He wrested them from her shoulder. "What's wrong with you, anyway? I've been on a marathon drive for the last seven hours, and this is the thanks I get?" His smile was lopsidedly wounded. "I thought we were going out—at last—to dinner," he added with tender slyness.

"This was an impomptru decision."

"Im . . . promptu?" he corrected politely.

"Whatever."

He leaned over and stole a light kiss as they walked. "Uh-huh. As I suspected, rum breath." Katie's complete inability to tolerate alcohol in any amount had become a standing joke between them. "Are you sure you're fit to ski?"

"I'm fit." To be tied, she wanted to shout. "However, if you think *you* can't manage it . . ."

"I think I can manage it," he answered with an amused look.

"Oh? I suppose you learned to ski at St. Moritz?" Everyone else she knew seemed to have.

"Hardly. But my parents had a winter home in Lake Placid."

"Oh, of course; *hardly* the same," she answered ironically. Winter homes; country clubs. The more she learned about him, the less she sympathized with his desperate crawl up the ladder of success.

They were at the rental shop and he handed her her skis. "Darling, if you'll stop sticking pins in me just long enough for me to get outfitted," he teased, "I'll have some good news for you."

She glared at him. On the whole, there was very little difference between a pleased face and a smug face, she decided. He went in and Katie stepped into her bindings and very, very cautiously practiced moving around over the hostile surface of the snow. She slid her left ski forward; then her right. And then, not according to plan, both skis went forward, and Katie was dumped on her bottom.

Unfortunately, she was still there when Fletch and Cindy came out looking relaxed and very continental, somehow. Maybe it was Cindy's short fur jacket. Who but a jet-setter could afford to risk tearing apart blue fox on the slopes?

"Cindy, you go on ahead. I'll catch up with you."

"O.k., daddy." Cindy threw Katie a bright, merry look. "Don't be long."

Fletch stood over Katie, offhandedly elegant in a heavy teal-colored sweater under a silvery tweed jacket. *"No* one skis in tweed," Katie objected, trying to disentangle skis from poles and arms.

"Don't worry, I won't fall. Can I take your hand and help you up?"

"If I can find it." She extended her mittened hand, still wrapped in a pole strap, to him. "It seems to me that if God had intended for man to ski, he'd have given us a lot longer feet."

Fletch maneuvered his skis closer to hers. "If he *hadn't* intended us to ski, he wouldn't have put in hills and mountains. O.k., now, alley—whoa!" Down he came, his skis trapped under hers, his knee near her chin.

"You have snow on your tweeds." Her grin was broad; suddenly he was looking so much less jet-setty. More . . . approachable.

"Witch."

His face was very near to hers, and even in the outdoor lights she could see and admire the ruddy healthiness of him. Sprinkled all over with snow crystals, he seemed to her magically, overwhelmingly handsome. *Why* couldn't she make him love her? Why?

"Kate . . . when you look at me like that . . ." he murmured, bringing his mouth close to hers. His tongue played over her night-chilled lips before entering her mouth, warm on warm, in a tonguing kiss of hypnotizing intoxication. Between them they were separated by at least six layers of clothing, and mittens, hats, scarves, gloves . . . but for the space of one crystalline kiss, they were together again in front of the fire, bodies glistening with flamed heat, locked in love.

Dizzy, Katie drew away from him. This wouldn't do; she was becoming a thrall to passion. Her need for him was far outstripping her need for all other things in life. How else to explain the unbearable tedium of days spent away from him? She might just as well be weaving—weaving an endless, borderless, colorless shawl.

"This isn't the right place," she gasped, rising and brushing herself off.

"Let's go home, then," he answered huskily as he followed her example.

Home. How easily he'd said the word. For the first time Katie wondered whether he had any other such "homes" scattered up and down the Thruway. Obviously the agony of waiting for him was making her paranoid.

And then there was Cindy. "Where will we put your daughter? In the guest room?" she asked, aware that the question sounded somehow churlish.

"Cindy's booked into a motel for the night," he answered, moving toward the ski lift. "But you're right; I don't have any place to put her when she visits me away from the city. That's the bad news. The good news is that after February first, she'll have a place to stay—and so will the Shape-Up Room."

His little bombshell had all the effect he could have hoped for. Katie rammed her poles into the snow ahead of her, bringing her slow forward progress to an abrupt stop. "What did you say?"

"Just this: I've found a great property east of New Paltz on Ledge Road. The second floor is an apartment with good potential—and a great view of the mountains. I can have it worked over to suit me. After all, I can't count on crashing at the stone house whenever I pass through," he added.

Why couldn't he? With fine illogic Katie instantly reversed herself and decided that the only thing worse than just waiting for him, would be not waiting for him.

"The downstairs," he continued, "will make an attractive business rental. I . . . ah, had in mind a certain fitness club," he added coyly.

"Oh, really?" Her mind ran over the available rentals. She'd looked at nothing on Ledge Road. "What sort of business is in there now?" she asked suspiciously.

Fletch looked uncomfortable. "It's a . . . sort of a . . . laundromat."

They were sidestepping up a small hill on their way to the J-bar lift. Katie was positioned above Fletch; when she stopped again abruptly, he nearly lost his balance. "What —now what?"

"A laundromat wouldn't be suitable, not without expensive modifications," she said firmly. "Why are they going out of business, anyway?"

"Why? Because I'm buying the damn place and *taking* them out of business, that's why," he said in irritation.

"That's crazy," she breathed. "That's really crazy."

"It's a nice view," he said stubbornly. "And I don't want to have to listen to the thunk of agitators and tumblers all evening."

"Fletch—you know that's not the reason you're considering it." He was buying her off, making her a gift of the laundromat. Part of her conceded that it was a fascinating move. It relieved him of any guilt he might feel at evicting her, and it let him stay close to her—but not too close. His nights would be his own, to spend as he liked. Katie felt deeply hurt and yet deeply flattered; confused, she said nothing.

"Hey—there goes Cindy. Watch that kid go!" It wasn't

an attempt to distract Katie; Fletch was simply being a proud and enthusiastic father.

Cindy shot past them like a fur-clad bullet, taking the last mogul with a flourish, using it to catapult herself in a free-fall through the air, landing neatly on both skis, and coming up to them in a wave of snow. Katie was no judge, of course, but it seemed to her that Cindy would feel perfectly at home in the Winter Olympics.

"Daddy, it's just perfect conditions. Not challenging, but really fun! Come on. It's just like old times." And she beckoned him to take the next ride up the lift behind her.

Fletch turned to Katie. "What do y' say, love? Ready? Or should we . . ."

"No, no, no. You just go right up. I'll pass on this first run and catch you the next time. Really. Go." And she shooed him away in her most beguiling manner.

She needed time to think. Desperately she wanted a moment away from his magnetic presence to sort things out. Fletch was right; she was obsessed with analyzing other people's motives. And obsessed with making them seem more complex than they really were. After all, wasn't it possible that Fletch was simply being nice?

No. It was not. Of that she was convinced. It was so frustrating; she needed time to sort out the tangle of emotional and practical considerations. His business proposal had thrown Katie, quite simply, for a loop.

Not to mention that she had to recover the knack of moving around on skis without making a fool of herself. Katie sidestepped furiously up her little slope, pointed her skis in a V-shape in front of her, and snowplowed her way cautiously down the short hill. By the end of the previous winter she had entertained thoughts of mastering the stem Christie, a simple maneuver which at least would lift her from the ranks of the crass beginner.

But not tonight. This was awful. She should be focusing

every atom of intellectual energy on Fletch's proposal. But she needed every atom to make her body stand upright, turn on command and—oh!—pick herself up after a fall. She brushed off her bottom, her sleeves, her increasingly wet denims, and sidestepped up the hill again. By the time Fletch and Cindy flew past—didn't anyone ever ski at a dignified pace anymore?—Katie had reacquainted herself with basic survival techniques.

"Hey, sweet pickle, ready?" He was friendly, loose, exhilarated.

"As I'll ever be." She was hostile, tense, exhausted.

Katie eyed the J-bar balefully. If only she could nonchalantly slip into place without forcing the attendant to stop the whole lift while she organized her skis, her poles and the limbs that were attached to them.

Cindy virtually skied into position. Naturally. The J-bar caught her just below her bottom and lifted her smoothly forward and up the slope. Ignoring the obvious need to hold on, Cindy used both hands to tuck her hair back under her bright red cap. She would.

Fletch also went ahead of Katie, and she liked him for that. He seemed to know instinctively that she preferred not to be watched. Then it was her turn. The J-bar rumbled around the U-turn. Katie stepped hastily, too hastily, into place, wobbling but not falling. The bar made contact with the top of her thighs; she grabbed the vertical support, clutching her ski poles with a deathlike grip in the other hand, and—ta-dah!—she also was carried forward and up. She felt joyous relief; the rest was all downhill. So to speak.

Getting off the lift was easier than getting on. The three of them paused a moment at the top of the slope, each feeling light-hearted for an obviously different reason, and exchanged pleasantries about the fine night. Cindy dropped down the slope, and then Fletch. Katie took a deep breath, pointed her skis into a V, and began slowly plowing downward. It was not a graceful maneuver, but provided no one fell in front of her, she'd get by. At the moment survival meant more to her than style.

But where were Fletch and Cindy? She looked around quickly. Was that the two of them, halfway down the slope already? And looking up in her direction like two patient ski instructors? A cheek-reddening sense of underprivilege seized her as she snowplowed toward them. She felt insufferably childish and untutored. Incomprehensibly, long-forgotten memories flashed across her mind—the time when she was six and her best friend got a pair of white majorette boots with tassels; the day her brother was accepted into the University of Chicago. She had been pleased for her friend, excited for her brother and eager for the day when *her* turn would come to enjoy the finer things in life. Suddenly, she felt as though she'd never had her turn.

"Whew! Sorry I held you two up," she said breathlessly. "Why don't you go on ahead without me?"

"We wouldn't think of it," Cindy answered politely, stealing a glance at her father.

"I was watching your moves, Kate, and . . . look, once you get your skis parallel, just lean on the inside edges. . . ."

"Oh, I know that," she lied. Actually, she'd forgotten that business about the inside edges. "I was just warming up. Professionally, it wouldn't do for me to break a leg." Her smile was brisk. "Please. Go on ahead." It was practically a command, and Fletch, with something like a sigh, fell in behind Cindy and whooshed effortlessly downward.

You're being an ass, Katie told herself. *Grow up, will you? Stop feeling sorry for yourself and get on with your life.* She found herself gritting her teeth in fierce resolve. In self-directed anger she forced herself out of her snowplow and gradually lined up her skis parallel as she traversed the slope. All well and good, she realized, but in a few more

yards she would have to reverse direction and traverse the
slope toward the other side.

Her skis veed out for the turn in the inevitable snowplow.
No. Not this time. *Pick up that ski, pick it up*, she told
herself. It only weighed a million pounds; but she lifted
it—not high—and placed it neatly alongside the other.
Direction reversed, mission accomplished. Oh, golly. Oh,
boy. It was her first stem-Christie ever. All she'd had to do
was . . . *do* it. After that, each turn got easier, smoother;
her speed improved, moderately, and by the time she
reached the bottom of the slope, Katie no longer felt like a
spectacle. She felt . . . good about herself. Felt great about
herself.

Fletch was there under the lights, waiting. "So you were
holding back, after all," he greeted her.

"Sure. What'd you think?" she said, flushed with
triumph. Her jaw hurt from gritting her teeth so hard, she
realized; that made her grin.

"I thought you were too proud to accept any help,
naturally."

"Who, me?" she asked innocently, and they both
laughed. "Where's Cindy?"

"Cindy left; she's on her way back to the motel in
Charlotte," Fletch said briefly.

"So soon?" Katie had the uncomfortable feeling that
Cindy had left because of her. And then: "She took
Charlotte? Then how will *you?* . . ."

"With you, of course." His look was a tender grimace.
"Or is that being presumptuous?"

"But I came in Marcia's car." Whoops. Marcia. Katie
had forgotten all about her. "Have you seen her, by the
way?" Katie asked, looking over the people standing in the
lift line. "I didn't mean to abandon her."

"She'll turn up. Well, Kate—have you thought about
it?" Fletch moved his skis perpendicular to hers, blocking
her way forward. He wanted an answer. Now, as usual.

Again the white majorette boots flashed through her consciousness. Katie had always dreamed of having a fairy godmother. Well, here he was, standing in front of her, waiting to sprinkle stardust and presents over her. All she had to say was a simple yes, and the Shape-Up Room would be out of trouble. Just as soon as Fletch had all the washing machines and dryers torn out of the laundromat, and all the plumbing, and had new floors laid in, and carpeting and air conditioning and . . .

"No, Fletch," she said gently. "How can I possibly?" The question hung in the air between them; Katie's anguish was almost palpable.

"I *knew* it," he said in almost triumphant exasperation. "It's the old pride again, isn't it?"

He lifted one ski pole and brought it down across hers; metal clinked against metal, and Katie had the odd impression that he'd challenged her to a duel and that they were locked, sword to sword, in combat. "It is not pride," she said stiffly. It was; but it was so many other things too.

"Ah, but it *is*. Pride and insecurity—they seem to go together. Once again you're worried about appearances. How would it look," he said in mocking anger, "if Katie Bright were to get a rent-free ride for a while? Terrible. Just terrible."

"That's not it!" she cried, pushing her skis back from his with her poles. "I just haven't had a chance to tell you. I've been offered the lead role on a television show," she blurted, in the most blatant lie she'd ever told.

Chapter Twelve

Since when?'' He wasn't openmouthed, exactly. But he was caught completely off guard, and his astonished face looked endearingly childish.

Katie cleared her throat and fussed unnecessarily with her ski-pole straps. ''I auditioned before Thanksgiving, but it didn't seem worth mentioning because I assumed I didn't have a chance.''

''That sounds like you,'' he said, a little dryly. ''What TV show? Tell me about it.'' The pained look of surprise was not enthusiastic.

''It's called the 'Morning Workout,' a half-hour exercise show put on the air by WTAT outside of New Haven. They're looking for someone new to do the show. The job starts in January and . . . that's basically it.'' She watched him carefully as she stammered out her fabrication. Would he see through it?

''But . . . Kate, that's . . . phenomenal. Just like that?

No television experience, and you walk into a lead role? Darling, that's just an incredible success story,'' he said warmly, and somehow managed to give her a squeeze without either of them falling.

"It's a very small station," she demurred, as the full significance of her lie began sinking in. What on earth had she done just now? "Really, Fletch, you're making too much of it."

"Kate, will you stop selling yourself short? You should be delighted with yourself; I am."

Whatever enthusiasm he had lacked initially was more than made up for by his eager questions and repeated compliments. Katie gave him scanty answers, and turned away the compliments. She tried desperately to change the subject. "Fletch . . . I haven't seen Marcia since you arrived. She may assume that I'm going back in your car; we'd better find her."

And she hurried ahead of him toward the lodge. Oblivious to her discomfort, Fletch continued to heap praise on Katie for her great beauty, her great talent, her great charm, her great everything. He was dismayingly supportive, considering that it would mean moving from New Paltz if she took the job. If she got *offered* the job, she corrected ruefully. Wouldn't he have any regrets? After all, she'd no longer be a pit stop on the Thruway. Katie had a moment of panic and desolation. Then she remembered that the job offer was a myth, and merely felt panic.

They found Marcia seated alone at a table, elbows resting on the arms of her chair, fingertips of both hands touching contemplatively. With a jolt Katie saw that Marcia's right ankle was taped and bandaged and propped up on a chair, pillowed by her down parka.

"Hi, kiddos. The ski patrol found you, then? I figured they couldn't miss Cindy's fur jacket."

"No one found us; what's happened?!"

"It's too quaint for words. I was headed for the lift-line when some good-looking hot-dog type shot past me, clipping my ski and knocking me down. My binding didn't release, and I sprained my ankle. The jerk didn't even look back. End of romance," she said dryly.

"That's horrible! Does it hurt much? Can you walk? Have you been waiting long?"

"Yes; no; with help; no." Marcia's smile was a bit grim, but she had never, as long as Katie had known her, completely lost her sense of humor. "So what do you think, Katie? Will one sprained ankle beat three broken toes?"

Katie grinned at her. "I dunno, Marsh. That's a tough call. Come on, let's see if you can stand."

Marcia motioned to Fletch with a snap of her fingers. "Jarvis . . . my cane, please," she said loftily. She winked at Katie and said, "The rental shop is really quite well stocked. They tried to unload a pair of fancy aluminum crutches on me; but I've never been much of an impulse buyer. Besides, it's hardly a sprain at all."

Marcia's breezy bravado was nowhere in evidence on the short walk to her Mustang—the sprain really was painful—but her spirits improved again once she was settled in the front seat. Katie sat behind her; Fletch drove.

"They said I'd be fine in a week, Katie; but we'd better try drafting Jessie for the next few days or you'll work yourself into the ground by then. We're always so damn short-handed, aren't we?"

Fletch had been very quiet, but now he joined in. "In a couple of weeks that won't be a problem anymore, will it?"

"Why? What happens then?" Marcia asked blankly.

Katie poked her a little viciously between the shoulder blades as Fletch went on to say, "Katie's fantastic new job, of course. The 'Morning Workout.'"

"Oh *that* job," Marcia mumbled in some confusion.

It was impossible for Katie to tell, without seeing his

eyes, if Fletch's enthusiasm was still unqualified. He sounded to her a little more subdued than before, but that might just be wishful thinking.

"But I'm being tactless, Marcia," Fletch continued. "Katie's new career means you'll be out of a job, doesn't it? What will *you* be doing after the first of the month?" he asked politely.

"I suppose I'll get by," Marcia answered cautiously. "I graduate in June, anyway. Maybe I'll just take over the Shape-Up Room," she added impishly, turning her head slightly in Katie's direction.

Another poke in the shoulder blades. "*So,* Fletch," Katie interrupted briskly, "you must have your plans and your workmen all lined up by now. What sort of architectural style have you decided on for the New Paltz Fish and Chips?" Fletch had told her almost nothing about the proposed renovation. She knew that he'd felt more and more uncomfortable about evicting her. Both of them had been avoiding the subject altogether.

"That's a funny thing, the question of a style." His voice was thoughtful and directed obviously to Katie alone. "I had in mind something low with a mansard roof. Unobtrusive. But after experiencing the stone house—you know, the intensity of it—the proposed plans look insipid to me. My architect is going stark crazy, of course. She's had to tear up three designs in three weeks and may leave the project altogether. I'm pretty sure she hates me," he added with comic sorrow.

"I doubt it," Katie answered softly. It was the first mention of the architect's sex, and it had been made so casually that Katie almost missed it. So much for small talk. Katie wished she'd never brought the subject up. The last thing she needed was to imagine Fletch spending long evenings poring over proposed renovation sketches with a female architect.

The conversation petered out after that. Fletch seemed troubled; Katie *was* troubled; and Marcia's sprain had begun throbbing in earnest. When they reached the Shape-Up Room Katie reclaimed her VW, then followed behind Fletch and Marcia to Marcia's apartment. Before long Marcia was safely deposited at home, Katie and Fletch were in the VW, and Katie found herself asking Fletch, with idiotic self-consciousness, where he wanted to go.

In the darkened parked car Fletch turned to Katie and slipped his hand behind her head, automatically searching for and finding a hairpin. He slid the pin from her coiled hair; before long the rest would follow. It had become a game between them; he hated her hair to be bound up and as a result her car and her house were filled with cast-off hairpins.

"You seem awfully standoffish tonight, Kate," he said softly. "Now that you're on the brink of fame, have you begun already to cast off your friends?" She could hear the gentle irony in his voice, feel it in his touch as he pulled another hairpin halfway out, then stuck it back in, as though he'd been taking a liberty with her.

"Is that what you think?" Her bare hands were resting on the leather cover of the steering wheel. She'd lost her mittens again. "You think that I'm standoffish?"

"What else?"

"Maybe . . . that *you* are. After all, I've been home every night for the past couple of weeks—wondering, usually, whether you've been avoiding me."

To her utter dismay, he didn't protest. He was supposed to say, "Nonsense, you silly thing; I've just been reroofing the house of an elderly aunt after it collapsed in a storm." Or: "I fell down a mineshaft and only just crawled out this morning." *Anything* but what he did say, which was, "You're right; I've been avoiding you. Maybe we should talk about it over a fire."

How she drove home she never knew. Her hands shook

the whole time, that she remembered. But shifting gears, stopping at lights—did she ever use a turn signal?—those things she didn't remember. By sheer luck Katie had managed to get her infamous driveway plowed. One of the services had hired a new man, and he didn't realize that the stone house driveway had been blackballed by his company. In an agony of anticipation she parked the car in front of the house.

Inside she changed into dry clothes and busied herself brewing hot cocoa while Fletch built the fire. He'd become comically possessive about the fireplace. Her father had been that way about one corner of the basement family room, and Katie responded with nostalgic affection to Fletch's proprietary ways.

They were comfortably settled in the high-backed love-seat, sipping carefully from steaming mugs, when Fletch murmured wistfully, "You'll be moving from the stone house, of course? No more fires?"

"It would seem that way," she answered ambiguously.

Fletch was thoughtful a moment, and then he unleashed a barrage of objections. "But what'll happen to your lease?"

"I suppose I'll break it and pay the penalty."

"But where will you live?"

"I'll look for an apartment the first chance I get."

"But won't Durette object to your moving out at the beginning of winter?"

"He's talked about selling the place, anyway." She shrugged. How long before she tripped herself up in a lie? she wondered. Once Fletch flew to England, she could make up a brand new lie about something happening to change her mind. But for now Katie felt as though she were tiptoeing through a minefield.

Almost clairvoyantly, Fletch brought up his trip to London. "I'm flying out tomorrow instead of Sunday," he said without preamble.

Stunned, she turned to him. "Oh? When are all your London meetings?"

"Monday."

"See?" she said lightly. "Didn't I say you were avoiding me?" But her voice shook just a little as she said it.

Fletch put his mug down and leaned toward the fire, forearms resting on his thighs, hands laced loosely through one another. "Obviously I could say that I've been hopelessly preoccupied with setting up the London trip," he said quietly.

"Obviously."

"And I could add that renovation of the New Paltz building is eating up huge chunks of my time."

"I'm sure it is."

"But you want me to cut through all that bull, don't you?"

"That'd be nice," she said evenly, gathering all her self-control like a mantle around her.

"O.k., then, here it is." He drew a deep breath, held it, then let it come flying out. "You ruin my concentration."

"I what?"

"I can't think clearly around you. Not only that," he said, turning his head around to face her, "but you . . . sap all my energy."

His explanation was so unlike what she had been preparing for that she let out a startled whistle. "My goodness. Sap all your energy? It sounds vaguely indecent."

His scowl wasn't entirely good-natured as he stood up and began pacing, caged and hungry, in front of the fire. "Dammit, I'm serious, Kate. I've worked for years to get myself positioned where I am."

"And where are you?" she asked cogently.

"If this London deal goes through, Fletcher's Fish and Chips will have gone international. Wall Street likes that; New York'll fall like a ripe apple into my lap."

He turned and leaned into the mantelpiece, his face

hidden from view between his arms. "Don't you see?" he asked quietly.

Yes. She saw. She saw it in the glittering intensity of his eyes; in the hunched determination of his shoulders. He was going to resist, with all his formidable energy, the attraction she held for him. If Katie were less proud, or more confident, she might have chosen just then to fight for his love. But as it was she watched paralyzed as the skyscrapers of Wall Street blocked out the sun for her.

"Give me . . . a little more time, Kate. Let me put this dream in order."

How desperately he wanted to keep his freedom, she thought sadly. Earlier he'd tried to buy it, and now he was pleading for it. Did he really think she'd force him into a commitment? How? With a shotgun? Suddenly she felt embarrassed, she didn't know why.

She decided to play it light and breezy. Groping for an argument that would appeal to him, she said, "You've got it all wrong, pal. You don't owe me. Heck, if it weren't for you I'd never have had the gumption to go after the television job. I'd be stuck in a rut, running a nowhere business. If anything, I owe *you*."

She rose from the sofa and said in a softer, truer voice, "You're the best thing that's ever happened to me, Fletch."

When she placed her hand lightly on his shoulder he whirled around on her. "That's a perfect example of what I mean!" he snapped, and Katie withdrew her hand in confusion. "You touch me, and suddenly my mind turns to peanut butter. I can't tie my own shoelaces, much less organize a takeover strategy for the British Isles."

He paused and she thought maybe she'd get in a word or two edgewise. But no, he wasn't finished. "Look at the expression on your face," he fumed. "Aren't you supposed to look crushed or hurt or something? Look at your eyes," he said, cradling her face in his hands, touching his thumbs to the corners of her eyes, ". . . dancing with bright light . . . almost amused . . . so filled with wisdom and compassion. What do you know that I don't, Kate? Tell me, witch," he murmured. "Tell me how this story will end."

How strange that he saw answers in her eyes when really she was looking questions at him. "All right," she said lightly, "since you persist in this whimsy that I'm a witch. I predict that like Colonel Sanders, you'll travel around the world until you're in your eighties, promoting your restaurants."

"Not only a witch, but a *mean* witch," he cried, and lifted her in his arms. "For that rotten prophecy you're going to burn at the stake, my love."

"Oh, yeah? Sez who?" she whispered, burying her nose in the soft wool of his sweater.

"Sez me. In fact, I am personally going to light the fire under you." His voice was a low, rumbling threat.

"You be careful, mister," Katie answered, nose still buried, "or I'll turn you into a frog."

Laughing huskily, he said, *"That* does it. We're going upstairs. We'll see about frogs." His arms, taut and sinewy under the wool sweater, shifted her weight slightly for the haul upstairs. He leaned over her hair and grasped a hairpin between his teeth, easing it out from her bun and then dropping it to the floor. "Two down, six to go," he predicted as he carried her out of the room.

The living room doorway was a heavy, massive affair that had stood as an outside entrance before the second portion of the house was built. Still feeling devilish, Katie grabbed hold of both sides of the doorway and cried, "Wait a minute!"

Fletch did—he had no choice—and she said innocently, "Did I ever explain that the living-room part was originally a country tavern? Look at this door," she commanded. "See this? And that? Knife marks," she explained airily from the cradle of his arms. "I have it on excellent authority. Also—I don't remember quite where—there's still a bullet lodged in the door someplace,'' she added enticingly.

He shifted her weight again, this time so that he could press his finger to one of the knife slits. "Honest?"

"Yup."

He scanned the door wistfully; and then the corners of his mouth lifted in a slow, vague smile. "Later." And he carried his perfectly willing but increasingly diabolical victim up the stairs.

At the top of the stairway Katie nodded toward the locked-up part of the house, the rooms which stood above the living room and the foyer. "I have a key, you know," she whispered conspiratorially in his ear. "They used to conduct cockfights in there. And during Prohibition, well you can imagine how perfect this place was for business. There are still some ancient bottles of liquor under the cobwebs. I think they're *mostly* empty, but still . . .''

"Kate," he groaned. "Why are you doing this to me?" His voice was thick with conflicting desires.

"Just testing," she answered blithely. She would have liked to add, *to see how deep your love is,* but . . . "Well, Fletch, which will it be? History, or romance?"

For an answer he pressed his lips to her brow in a kiss of sweet-tempered longing, carried her into the bedroom and dropped her on the bed with a bounce. He lay down next to her, sliding his hand down the outer seam of her worn and faded at-home jeans. His voice had a sexy softness in it as he said, "I don't see any burning stake up here, my bewitching friend. Maybe I should just tie you to the bedposts.''

The sound that left Katie's throat as a chuckle ended up a tight, breathless moan as his hand wandered from the outside seam of her jeans and began a lazy perusal of the inside seam. "You may have to tie me to the bedposts just . . . to keep me from climbing up them," she said in a pleasure-murmur.

Fletch's laugh was low and deep as he shifted his attention, almost predictably, to her bound-up hair. He hunted down and removed the remaining hairpins and loosened her hair into a free-fall over her shoulders. "Better," he said simply.

"Much," she agreed, her scalp still tingling with pleasure from his curiously comforting touch.

With shameless forethought Katie had turned the electric blanket to "high" earlier; now the heat filtered cozily through the patchwork quilt to surround them like a warm bath. "But even so," she said with a wistful sigh, "I wish I'd met you in warmer weather."

"Darling, I'm warm; aren't you warm?" he asked with a smile. He pulled his sweater over his head and tossed it on the floor, and then his t-shirt; and she marveled, again, at the compact, sinewy strength of his lean torso.

"Overall, in fact, I think we manage very well," he murmured into her ear. His touch, his smell, the timbre of his voice—she had become addicted to them all. He hooked his thumbs under her jersey and eased it upward. "The important thing," he murmured between quick, branding-iron kisses to her ear, her cheek, the underside of her jaw, "is to stay . . . close to . . . a source of heat."

Katie's hands roamed freely, possessively, over the taut muscle lines of his back and slipped tentatively under his form-fitting denims—so much better tailored than hers— tracing a path inside the waistband as far as they could, then tugged impatiently at the snap. His voice dropped to a knowing, husky register as he reached down to unsnap and unzip his denims. "I was saying . . . we're—oh, lord, Katie—we're fine as long as we stay close to a source of heat. Fireplace . . . bathtub . . . electric blanket. . . ."

". . . Fletcher Ramsey," she added in a long, drawn-out sigh, her increasingly confident hands moving over his increasingly responsive form.

"Yes? Love?" he whispered, dragging his mouth across

her lower belly as he slid her jeans, and the bikinis underneath, farther and farther down.

"I mean . . . *you're* a pretty fair source of heat yourself," she explained breathlessly.

"Ah, no, love . . . just a reflection . . . of a bright, bright fire."

She dragged his face to hers, pressing wet kisses to his eyelids, his nose, and his mouth—again and again, to his mouth. Heartachingly in love with him, she could not taste him enough.

With a groan he pulled his mouth away from her kisses, returning to tease her sensitive breasts with skilled fluency. She lifted her body to meet his tonguing touch and wound her hands through the thick silkiness of his hair, pressing his mouth to her aching breasts until the two of them formed a perfect circle of desire.

It seemed inconceivable that he could make love to her like this without being in love with her. The thought drifted in, then out, of her brain, a random particle floating in the highly charged atmosphere of their loveplay. Other bits and pieces of thought pierced the thick mist of her desire: gone for the next two weeks . . . missing for most of the last two . . . his architect, a woman . . . more time for his dream.

It was unbearable. She felt she was losing him, and yet she'd never really *had* him. A kind of fierce possessiveness streamed through her, and she said with a low cry, "Fletch . . . love me!"

"Sweetheart . . . I will," he answered in a voice heavy with passion.

In perfect, urgent harmony they cast off the rest of their clothes, and Katie, still seeking blindly to possess, lifted herself on top of him, fitting herself to the form she had learned so well. Her arms were braced on either side of his pillowed head, her long black hair grazed the light golden hairs of his chest.

"How can you live without . . . *us?*" she asked, her voice low with wonder and despair.

His hands were fitted around her thighs and hips as he held her fast, and his laugh was weak as he guided her hips. "Cold showers help a little, and . . . oh, Kate, Kate . . . and thousands of . . . of push-ups . . . push . . ."

She leaned over—almost fell—into his kiss, limp with yearning, filled with him, filled with love. Her breath dissolved in a series of quick, sharp gasps, and from the back of her consciousness a slow echoing refrain came rumbling forward, rolling, rolling like a train, louder and louder, nearer and nearer, until she cried, "Fletch, I love you . . . love you!"

And then the train passed; but whether Katie was on the train, or under it, she could not have said. Nor could she have said whether her exhaustion was from loving, or from her futile effort not to love him too much. All she knew for certain was that she was at peace; blissful, radiant peace.

She lay half on top, half alongside of Fletch, curled in his arms, listening to the reassurance of his soft regular breathing. Her legs were entwined in his, and she was cozily aware of the paths of heat that his body traced on hers. With gossamer tenderness Fletch began trailing a finger through the black strands of her hair, smoothing and straightening. She heard the thoughtful hesitation in his voice as he murmured in her ear, "Kate . . . would it complicate your life hopelessly . . . if I said I loved you?"

Chapter Thirteen

*I*t would and it did. On Sunday morning Katie sat alone at the oversized mahogany table, poking unhungrily at two chopped and mashed boiled eggs. Salt, pepper and butter had done nothing to give them flavor, and she pushed her bowl away listlessly. Complicated her life! You might say that.

It was one thing to love a man who didn't love you back. That wasn't terribly complicated. Eventually Katie would have got it through her lovestruck head that Fletch had nothing to give her, and she'd have just . . . given up. It might take years, but if she shut her eyes and gritted her teeth, she could do it. But this! To have him in love with her; in love, but still not willing to commit himself to a permanent relationship. It was . . . complicated. Aaagh. Too complicated.

She rubbed idly at a small spot in the bright red tablecloth. Coffee? No, a teardrop. Oh, no. No tears. Katie stood up, briskly brushed aside a matching tear from her other eye, and cleared away the dishes. There was simply no time in her life for moping. She'd know by Tuesday whether she was leaving for a new career, or moving the Shape-Up Room into the stone house. In the meantime, with Marcia laid up, it would be double shifts for a while.

Katie crumbled her untouched muffin onto a cookie sheet already laden with sunflower seeds and bits of suet. The ground was still buried under melting snow, and Katie's little smorgasbord was intended to help tide over the cardinals, bluejays and sparrows that visited by the dozens every day.

Outside the morning was brilliant and surprisingly warm; at this rate the snow couldn't possibly last until Christmas. Katie trudged through the sloppy snow to a spot about ten yards from the house near a magnolia tree, which by common consent had been designated the local snack bar, and set the tray down. Retracing her steps in the sinkholes she'd created, she stood a moment in front of the house, letting the warmth of the sun fall full on her face, telling herself against all the evidence that spring would not be long now.

The front of the stone house faced a slate-encrusted ledge topped by a grove of pines and firs, which added to Katie's sense of peaceful isolation. There was no wind, and no sound of civilization—only the cheeps of the brawling sparrows, and the occasional shrill cry of a bluejay as it swept low, warning the smaller birds to clear out because the next time, it meant to land.

In the skyscraping oak tree above her Katie heard the soft flutter of wings as a starling shifted restlessly from one branch to another, unable to decide whether to fight the crowds at the snack tray, or to dine alone on ordinary seed at the hanging feeder. Aloof and indifferent to *haute cuisine*, the starling settled on the feeder. No one bothered at all about Katie; everyone was used to the tall black-crested creature who often stood for long moments, watching and wondering.

The brief sunny intermission was interrupted by the sound of an engine that Katie knew well: Charlotte was returning. The car—and Cindy—had checked out of their motel sometime yesterday without letting Fletch know. Fletch had acted nonchalant about Cindy's sudden disappearance, explaining that Cindy had several friends in the area, but it was obvious that he was troubled by his daughter's unpredictable behavior. Katie had assumed that Cindy was upset by Fletch's attention to her on the ski slope. Apparently all the women in Fletch's life were rather fierce about one another. Cindy, Katie, his ex-wife Dolores —maybe they should band together and form an Association of Neglected Women.

Cindy pulled up in front of Katie and rolled the window down. Katie was shocked at the girl's haggard, drawn face. "Hello. Is my father here?" Again, it was more accusation than question.

"I'm afraid you're too late, Cindy. He decided to try to fly out yesterday. He chartered a plane to New York and caught an overseas flight from there."

The look on Cindy's face was compounded of so many emotions that Katie could only guess at some. Surprise, hurt, anger, guilt—and something indefinable. What was it?

"We were supposed to drive together to Boston today," she said dully.

"Right. He said that. But since he couldn't get a Saturday flight out of Logan—and since he couldn't get in touch with you—he switched to JFK." Katie hated mediating. She was too fair-minded to give either side all of her sympathy.

So, Cindy thought, Katie hated her, obviously. "Well how was *I* supposed to know he'd leave yesterday?" she sulked. "What was his all-fired hurry, anyway? And what'm I supposed to do with Charlotte? Is he flying back to Boston or to New York? God, if this isn't the absolute bottom. The pits." Cindy folded her arms over the steering wheel and dropped her forehead onto the sleeve of her blue fox jacket.

It occurred to Katie that despite Cindy's very practical calling to the medical profession, she had a real flair for the dramatic. "Cindy, it's not worth getting upset over," Katie said gently. "Your father did say he was coming back to New Paltz through New York, but whether you leave the car in town or take it back to Boston, I'm sure it'll be fine with him."

Cindy raised her head and looked wearily at Katie. "Can I use your phone?"

"Sure. Come on in," Katie answered, absurdly pleased that the girl had made the simple request. It was the first sign of familiarity that Cindy had allowed herself with Katie.

Inside Cindy sat on the telephone bench under the sunny foyer window and punched out her number. She had her father's trick of looking completely at home in the stone house, and her golden hair had her father's trick of catching and bouncing back sunbeams. She was a lovely girl, filled with natural grace despite the edgy, raw quality so much in evidence just now.

"Cindy, can I get you some coffee?" She looked as though she could certainly use a cup.

"I suppose," Cindy answered absently. She took out a small phone directory from her bag, then tried another number. When there was no answer at that one either, she dragged into the kitchen and fell into the rocking chair near the heater. "I don't know why I expected any answers. On a Sunday morning most of my friends couldn't hear a bomb if it exploded in their beds."

Moose, who had been curled up on the kitchen sofa, lifted his head regally. Normally he held humans in low esteem; but a blue fox—ah, that was something else again.

He trotted over to Cindy and leaped up onto her lap, fairly gracefully for a sixteen-pound cat, and began a thorough sniffing-over of Cindy's jacket.

Cindy chuckled softly—her father's sound—and suddenly Katie's heart thundered in her chest. Briefly she considered chaining the girl to the rocking chair and feeding her treats just to hear that laugh while Fletch was away.

"Nice cat," Cindy commented. *"Big* cat." Moose's purring roar could be heard across the room. "What kind is he?"

"Alley, I'm afraid," Katie answered.

"Oh, I'm sure not," Cindy protested. "He looks like an Odd-Eyed British Shorthair, actually. They're a special breed, you know."

Her voice had all the arrogant authority of a twelve-year-old—just like her father. It was obvious to Katie that she was going to be extremely fond of this girl, no matter how spoiled she was. Aloud Katie said, "The cat may have a touch of blue blood in him, but I knew his mother, and she was a tramp. Not to mention," she added with a whimsical smile, "she was also a calico."

Cindy grinned then, Fletch all over again, and Katie found herself wondering which, if any, features were inherited from the mysterious and moody Dolores. "Cream? Sugar?"

"Black."

Cindy leaned back in the rocker, her hands sliding through Moose's fur with a languid, almost theatrically graceful motion. Fletch again, dammit. The cat seemed to act as a talisman for Cindy, drawing away her tense, brittle impatience, and even the dark shadows from under her eyes. It was a remarkable transformation: from blasé sophisticate to normal nineteen-year-old.

"Aren't you warm in that jacket?" Katie asked, for something to say. "Would you like me to hang it up for you?"

"Oh, no, I'm fine; it's just a chill," Cindy answered quickly, and Katie thought she saw some of the sharp edginess return to the girl's face. "Y'know, I'm glad daddy's not here, actually," Cindy continued with a brave defiance. "It gives me a chance to look you over."

"Gracious," Katie answered on a slightly mocking note. "You make me feel a bit like a used desk for sale. What exactly do you look for when you look one over?" she added, intrigued.

"Integrity, for one thing," Cindy answered promptly. "Daddy's very big on that. Daddy seems to think you have it, and it *looks* like you have it," she said tentatively.

Katie's smile was startled. "How can you tell?"

"By the look on your face when . . . it's just a certain . . . look," Cindy said evasively. "And of course for daddy you'd have to have a certain beauty," she continued, struggling for the words. "Not just a *pretty* beauty, if you know what I mean. But a . . . a beauty like this house has, an interesting beauty. Daddy's crazy about this house, you know," she added. "In fact, I was more jealous about *it* than *you*. Because daddy hardly ever talks about you." Cindy stood up and dumped the still-purring cat on the floor. "But now I'm much more jealous of you than the house. Can I use your bathroom?"

For sheer candor, it was a bravura performance. Lots of people, including Katie, would have needed more than thirty seconds to pour out their souls to a stranger. Not Cindy. Completely bemused, Katie indicated the bathroom, then tried to regather her wits. What could she possibly say to reassure this . . . urchin, that wouldn't sound glib? Katie couldn't deny that Fletch cared for her—Cindy would see through that—or even that she loved Fletch. Cindy would see through that, too. And yet Cindy seemed, in her flippant way, desperate for comfort of some kind.

Katie sat on the telephone bench, pinching dried leaves off the geranium, waiting to accost Cindy with reassurances when she came out of the bathroom. But when Cindy did come out, about to hook up her fur jacket, the words died in Katie's throat. She could see that every button, top to bottom on Cindy's blouse, had been torn away; the blouse was held together with two large safety pins. A wave of something like nausea passed over Katie, and she said, "Cindy?" It was all that came out.

But Cindy understood her well enough. "I suppose you mean this?" she said, flicking her fingers toward the safety pins. "It was nothing, really," she said lightly. "The party got a little out of hand, that's all. I suppose you never had a 'lost weekend' of your own?" The belligerence was painful to see; it gave the girl a furtive look.

"No-o . . . not 'lost' in the way you mean," Katie said hesitantly. "I've had weekends I've regretted; but none that I couldn't . . . remember."

"I remember it!" Cindy snapped. "Most of it. Enough of it. Look . . . can you give me a lift to the bus station? I'll leave Charlotte here with you. My dad'll head straight for this place when he gets off the plane; the car may as well be here as anywhere." She dug distractedly through her bag, pulled out a bus schedule and said, "Perfect. The next bus leaves in twenty minutes."

"Cindy, look at me," Katie said. When Cindy wouldn't look up from her schedule, Katie plowed ahead anyway. "Don't do anything silly just to get your father's attention. He's so proud of you . . . of your work at school. He adores you; you must know that. You already *have* his attention, you goose," she said lightly.

"What there is of it," Cindy answered with a defiant lift of her chin. "Well, thanks for the tip. Can we go now? I've really got to get back to Boston."

On Tuesday Marcia hobbled into the Shape-Up Room, vowing that one more day spent on her back would send her right up the wall, ankle or no ankle.

"Not that it's been a *complete* waste of time," she added slyly. "Chuck's been around since Sunday."

"Marcia! How you talk," Katie admonished her in tones of mock scandal. "Is his mother better, then?" Katie sat Marcia down at her desk, conveniently close to a file drawer that needed updating.

"Oh, his mom's well enough, I guess. It's Chuck who's becoming the royal pain. Do you know—he's accused me of spraining my ankle on *purpose?* He says it's a power play; that I can't stand it when his mother has the upper hand. I like that!"

"To be honest, Marsh, the thought occurred to me, too. Not," Katie added hastily, seeing the blood rush to her friend's face, "not that you'd hurt yourself deliberately— obviously it wasn't your fault—but still . . . it was a funny coincidence, that's all."

The indignation left Marcia's face and was replaced by the oddly speculative look that she had had when Katie found her in the ski lodge.

"You want to know something, Kate? I've wondered about it, myself. And . . . wanna know something else? I've broken off the engagement."

Katie swung around. "You're kidding!" Instantly she was aware that she'd said the exact same thing when Marcia had first announced her engagement.

"Yeah. I mean no, I'm not kidding. I never did know why we got engaged in the first place. And now, I'm not quite sure why I broke it off. I just think we were . . . happier . . . the old way. In fact, I don't even think we should live together. I think I'd like more freedom," Marcia said vaguely. "More what you and Fletch have." She skimmed half-heartedly through the files, weeding out the expired memberships.

Katie threw her hands up into the air. "That does it. I'm convinced people always want what they don't have." And then she made herself smile. "I don't know why I'm taking you seriously, anyway. By tomorrow you'll have changed your mind again."

"I don't think so," Marcia said in a voice that was surprisingly subdued.

The news plunged Katie into a vat of depression for the next couple of hours. There wasn't much to rejoice about. She hadn't heard from Fletch since he'd left for England. She was worried, whether or not she was entitled to be, about Cindy. And now Marcia.

And on top of everything else Katie was all too aware that it was Tuesday. Today she should hear from WTAT. Every time the phone rang she had to rein in her galloping pulse. By late afternoon she'd become weary of false alarms, and weary from conducting all the exercise classes. When the phone rang at 4:30 Katie said in a voice still winded from exercise, "Get that, will you, Marsh?"

Marcia did. "Katie, come quick," she squeaked, her hand held tightly over the phone. "It's WTAT. It's Max. Max!" Marcia jumped—hopped—up and down like a contestant on a game show.

"Marcia, will you calm down!" Katie squeaked back. She ripped the phone from Marcia's hand and said, "This is Katie Bright."

"Hey-y, kid. Max here."

"Yes, Max; how are you?" Katie tried very hard to sound like the skinny model that her ex-husband had run off with, but it was no use; the excitement broke through.

"You grew on me, kid," Max said abruptly. She could hear the cigar chomped between his molars. "But I don't mind tellin' you, kid, I'm nervous as hell about your lack of experience. So here's how I'm gonna handle it. The 'Workout' show is gonna have alternating ladies—you and Dee-Dee. Dee-Dee has worked in television before. She's blonde and a little . . . fuller than you are. And perkier.

Between the two of you, I think we can give 'em what they want. And if one of you really takes off with the viewers, well . . . We'll see how it goes. You with me so far?''

"I think so." How dumb. I think so. Where were her wits?

"All right. Now—salary. As I say, I'm a little iffy about you. . . .''

By the time Max finished with her, Katie felt that she should be paying *him* for the privilege of apprenticing in the television trade. Katie was too dazed to take notes and only hazily remembered talk of a contract; talk of a publicity session; talk of apartment rentals in the area. Astoundingly, mention was made of a talk-show hostess; but whether Katie was eventually to become one, or to be interviewed by one, she wasn't sure. The only thing she *was* sure about was the salary, and that was—all things considered—pretty good.

"How good?" Marcia asked flatly after Katie hung up.

"Thirty-five thousand, I think."

"What do you mean, you *think?*"

"Well, he said something about video and royalties and I don't know what all else." Nothing had sunk in yet; absolutely nothing. Katie's thought processes were a fuzzy, excited blur. "Do you think I should get an agent, Marsh?"

"Yes. *No*. It's too late; you'll scare him away. Take it. You can worry about driving a better bargain some other time. Call him back." Marcia handed Katie the phone.

"He said I should let him know in a couple of days. And really, I wish I had even more time," Katie fretted. "It's such a big decision. There are so many . . . ramifications."

"For Pete's sake! You've had weeks to think about this!"

"Yes, but I didn't want to—"

"—be optimistic? God forbid," Marcia said dryly. A thought occurred to her. "You're waiting for Fletch to call, aren't you?" she said bluntly.

"He might," Katie answered offhandedly.

"And what if he does? Will that change anything?"

Katie shrugged. She didn't know.

"What if he wanted to get married?" Marcia asked shrewdly. "Would *that* change anything?"

"Darned if I know," Katie said with an enigmatic smile.

But he didn't call, although Katie rushed home without even stopping for cat food. The hour was much later in Britain, of course; hope for a call disappeared pretty quickly after 7:00 P.M. The cat went to bed hungry, and Katie went to bed dejected. Not only dejected, but angry with herself for being dejected. Because exactly what she'd predicted would happen if she ever let herself get involved with a man *was* happening. Exactly.

While Fletch was off building empires in Europe, Katie was building castles in the air. She had developed her ability to dream and speculate into a fine art. Well, now it was time to act. Katie made herself fall asleep by counting the overhead beams, left to right, right to left, until her eyelids dropped closed from sheer weariness. In the morning she called her landlord to ask him what he thought about her leaving the stone house on January first.

"I think it stinks," was his candid reply.

Nor was he reassured when Katie told him that of course she expected to give up her deposit as a penalty, and that she was almost a hundred percent sure that she could arrange for new tenants. "There are three young women attending the Shape-Up Room who're tired of living in a dorm at the college. I think they'd jump at this chance, Mr. Durette."

"Students. Hah!" he snorted at the other end of the line. "The last students I rented to kept a goat—it chewed the lawn down to stubble. And their May Day bonfire. Petrified the neighborhood. Nope. No college types."

"These girls are nothing like that, Mr. Durette. One is an exchange student from South Korea. One is a music major. She plays the cello. And the third is, I think, the daughter of a minister." Actually, Katie made up the business of the minister out of desperation. She knew the girls; they'd be good tenants.

"I don't like it." There was a pause. "Tell 'em to send references." Another pause. "I don't like it." He hung up.

Katie had little time to agonize over her landlord's reservations. Without hesitating, she rang up station WTAT and was put through to Max. Her acceptance was brief— Max didn't seem surprised—and a day was set during the following week for a rundown and a photo session. She could tie that in with a search for an apartment. That left phasing out the Shape-Up Room.

In a way Fletch had done that for her. Business had been falling off steadily ever since Fletch's announcement that the new building would be converted to a restaurant. Some of the members had already asked for a refund. Others had signed up at a rival fitness salon. Katie's indecisiveness had cost her dearly, and so had her lack of capital. If only she'd been able to reconcile herself to moving the Shape-Up Room into her beloved stone house . . . if only she'd had enough money to afford the one or two suitable locations for a new Shape-Up Room . . . if only she'd been able to swallow her pride and accept Fletch's offer of the revamped laundromat . . .

"If, if, *if!*" she said in exasperation to Marcia. "I blew it; I was a rotten businesswoman, and that's that. Maybe I'll be better as a TV personality," she growled as she rolled another envelope through the typewriter.

"Still no word from Fletch?" Marcia ventured. It was obvious that Katie's tension was not just professional.

"Fletch! Fletch who?" Katie growled again.

Together the two women were plodding through the alphabet and had reached the G's. Katie typed the envelopes, and Marcia stuffed in each an announcement that the Shape-up Room was closing its doors.

"Griswold, Janice." Marcia made a notation on the file folder and handed it to Katie.

"Janice." A pained look crossed Katie's face. Janice was her very first client.

"Don't even think about it," Marcia warned her. "You've made your decision; don't look back."

"But . . ." Katie handed Marcia the typed envelope and bit her lip. "You're right. I'm just going to . . . go for it," she said firmly. And yet, after all this time, she still didn't know what it was she was going for.

Katie didn't get back to the stone house that night until midnight. Exhausted from her heavy workload, she was only droopily aware that something had changed along the route to her front door. Just as she dropped off to sleep, she thought she knew what it was, but with sleep came sweet and easy oblivion.

At seven-thirty the next morning, Katie was awakened from a deep, dreamless state by three things: the bright sun, slanting into her eyes; the phone, ringing in her ears; and another sound, loud and insistent, from outside.

She dragged the receiver from its hook without lifting her head from the pillow and murmured "H'lo" sleepily.

"Hello, sweetheart-eart. How are you-ou?"

"Fletch! Is that you?" she said, instantly, almost violently, awake. "There's something wrong with this connection."

"I can hear you fine-ine," he said, his voice faint and echoing in the overseas transmission.

"There's an echo when you talk," she moaned. For pity's sake—this was supposed to be the age of advanced communication; Alexander Graham Bell had probably done better than this. "It's good to hear your voice, Fletch," she found herself shouting. "Both of them."

"Hey, you don't have to shout-out. You're coming through loud and clear-ear. How's everything going-ing?"

"Right on schedule," she said with feigned cheerfulness. "I've called Durette and . . . oh, I forgot to ask what to do about the alarm. Well, we can talk about that when you get back. When do you think that'll be?"

"I don't know, Kate-ate; things aren't going as well as I thought-ought. With luck I'll be back by Christmas-ess. If I can get a flight-ight."

"Fletch, I can't stand this connection. Can you call me back again?" She was in despair; she could hardly concentrate on what he was saying in that maddening echo.

"I'll try-eye," he said. And then she thought he said, "I've bought a house," or maybe a horse.

"I can barely hear you anymore, Fletch," she wailed, panicky at the thought of losing him. "Call me back."

"I will-ill. I love you-ou."

"I love you too, Fletch. I love . . ." But because of the infuriating time-lapse, he'd already hung up.

"Damn." She stared fixedly at the phone, willing it to ring. But when it didn't after one minute, then two, then three, she gradually shook herself loose from her trance and began responding to the world on her side of the Atlantic. The cat had crawled, reluctantly, out from under the covers, and was testing the morning temperature. He wrinkled his nose with distaste: still December. The sunbeam that played across Katie's rose-printed flannel nightgown was bright, but it was not warm. Still, she was dimly aware that it was a fine morning. The birds . . .

What birds? She couldn't hear any birds. All she could hear was the loud, tat-a-tat din of a . . . jackhammer. It was a jackhammer. Katie jumped out of bed and knelt at the windowseat, her hands on the cold stone sill, and peered out. A workman was doing his level best to remove the biggest of the driveway boulders. The other workman was there for moral support apparently.

It took Katie mere split seconds to get dressed. With one

last glance at the bedroom phone she ran down the stairs. With a second last glance at the phone in the foyer, she charged out the door, intent on stopping the horrendous noise.

Katie loved the peaceful morning sounds of the country. She thought the invention of the clock radio was an abuse of electricity. As for the prebreakfast jackhammer! . . . She approached the two men with her hands clamped over her ears, her face squinched in a universal expression of suffering. The man at the jackhammer—the grumpy-looking one—kept up the hammering. But the other man—the nice one—gave Katie a friendly wink and a smiling nod and poked his partner to stop.

The nice one took off his protective headset and said, "Don't worry, miss. You'll be able to get your car out of here whenever you want."

"That's not what I'm worried about. Why are you here so early? Why are you here at all?" she added, puzzled.

"*I* know, *I* know," he sang sympathetically. "But you know how new owners are. They can't stand to wait for a more logical season. Plus," he added confidentially, "I hear no plowing service'll go near this place. I can see why," he clucked. "The road's a disgrace."

After the tenth word Katie had understood nothing he said. "New owner?" she repeated faintly. "What new owner?"

"Some fast-food tycoon, I hear. I hear he's goin' t' tear the place completely apart and modernize it."

"Thank you. I don't mean to hold you up," she said evenly and indicated to the grumpy one that he could proceed. Which he did.

Her hands were trembling with fury as she dialed Fletch's London hotel. She hadn't wanted to seem to be hunting him down before this; now she couldn't care less. Her house! He'd taken her business; he'd taken *her*. But this was the last straw. He knew that she loved this house, wanted it for her own. "Put me through to Fletcher Ramsey's suite, please," she demanded crisply.

The desk clerk, with cool British reserve, declined. "I'm sorry, madam. Mr. Ramsey is in conference and has left word that we are to hold his calls."

"This is absolutely urgent," she argued, giving him her name. Something in her voice prompted him to put her call through, and the next voice she heard was Fletch's.

"Kate? Is something wrong?" he asked, obviously in alarm.

"You *bet* there's something wrong. Why didn't you *tell* me you'd bought this house out from under me? Do you get some particular thrill from driving impoverished women out into the storm?" She had one hand over her free ear, trying to blot out the jackhammering.

"Kate, I tried to tell you on the phone earlier. . . ."

"I thought you said you'd bought an old horse, not a stone house," she fumed. "You *know* I want this place myself." She sounded to herself like a greedy sibling fighting over an inheritance. She despised herself; but her sense of betrayal was deep.

"And what did you expect to buy it with, Kate? Green Stamps?" He'd lowered his voice; she wondered if the others at the meeting were in earshot of this silly quarrel. "Kate, real estate is hot right now. Durette let my man in New York know that he was tired of renting the house and that it was going on the market. If I hadn't bought it, some complete stranger would have. It was an obvious choice for me. It's a good investment; it's perfectly situated for my business; and this way at least it stays . . . in the family," he said with quiet irony.

She barreled right over his allusion to family. "I never saw anyone so determined to drive me out of the state," she said theatrically.

"*You* took the job in Connecticut, for chrissake!" he answered heatedly.

"You made me do that!" she snuffled, near tears.

"I did *not!*"

"You did *too!* Oh, this is *stupid,*" she said shakily. "I sound stupid. You sound stupid. Enjoy your house, Ramsey. Just don't show up in it before January first." She slammed down the receiver with a bang that could easily be heard over the jackhammers and across the Atlantic.

Chapter Fourteen

$\mathcal{I}$ want to have a party," Katie announced to Marcia over coffee later that day. "I've been in an absolutely vile mood for weeks—tense, exhausted, undecided. I hate myself," she brooded. "If I throw a party I'll have a chance to say good-bye to all my friends and to the stone house, and I won't feel so bad about . . . things," she finished up cryptically. "How does Christmas Eve sound?"

"Fine with me. Chuck and I can easily go to Long Island the next day. Will your parents come down for the party?"

"Come *up*, you mean. They're still in Florida with their friends, so I doubt it. They seem quite happy away from the cold; my dad's discovered deep-sea fishing and loves it."

The extended vacation her parents were enjoying was one reason Katie had decided to have the party. Christmas Eve would seem empty without them. This Christmas, which for a while she'd thought might be the happiest of her life, could very well end up the worst if she didn't do something.

"I think a party would be a master stroke," Marcia said, watching her friend with wry amusement. "Sending invitations; shopping for food; cooking; serving; cleaning up—just the things to fill up all your spare time and cure your exhaustion."

"I suppose I've had more rational ideas, now that you mention it," Katie admitted as she cleared her desk of the coffee cups. The two friends exchanged a look of perfect understanding. "I want to feel good again about life, Marsh. Fletch taught me that, at least. I don't want to hide anymore."

Marcia reached across the desk top and gave Katie a quick squeeze of her hand. "Katie, you insecure dope—I'm going to miss you."

"But I'll only be a ferry ride away from Long Island," Katie protested lightly, though the sadness in her voice was obvious. "So anyway, about my party," she said, forcing herself into an upbeat mode. "You're right. I can't do it alone. Which chores are you signing up for?"

In wordless apology Marcia raised her bandaged leg from the pillow it had been resting on. "Invitations, obviously. I can also trim bread crusts and assemble simple hors d'oeuvres. And I think," she said, staring at her ankle in disgust, "that's about it. Make it a dressy affair, Katie. I want to cover up this mess with a long skirt if possible."

"Oh, don't worry," Katie laughed. "Anyone with any brains'll wear something floor-length—or else put up with a wicked draft around the knees." Suddenly she remembered a lovely skirt she'd seen in a clothing shop in town: slashes of shimmery greens and burgundies in an antique tapestry effect. Would it still be there? "You know, Marsh . . . I think this party just may end up being lots of fun."

For the next week Katie ran a flat-out race with time. Fortunately, Jessica was available to relieve Katie from leading some of the classes. And fortunately the announcement of the party was received with tremendous excitement and offers of help by some of the members of the Shape-Up Room. Many of them were bringing something: casseroles, hors d'oeuvres, punches, liqueurs, low-cal desserts, high-cal desserts—the list was endless, the enthusiasm boundless. Marcia coordinated the menu, discouraging some ideas (bananas flambée was impractical, she said) and encouraging others (tiny hot croissants filled with spinach and cheeses sounded good, she said). It was an astonishing display of loyalty and good spirits, and Katie said so to Marcia.

"It amazes me that so many can spare the time on Christmas Eve from their own families and friends," Katie said as she packed up the last of her files. The office end of the room was looking emptier.

"That's not surprising. A lot of the college women can't afford to fly home," Marcia said practically. "And lots of people have nothing planned for Christmas Eve. It can be a very lonely time," she added. "But the main reason is that everyone wants to say good-bye to *you*. Don't you realize that?"

"I guess now I do," Katie answered softly. "But it's only hit me in the last day or two how important the Shape-Up Room was to a lot of the women. I only wish I'd realized it sooner," she said ruefully. "But I figured if what I was doing had any importance, I'd be . . . rich?" she ventured, her mouth curling upward in a funny little smile. "Or at least solvent?"

"Yeah . . . we were a little naïve there," Marcia said, and they both shared a weary, punchy laugh. "So how's the Great Apartment Hunt coming?" Marcia asked, changing the subject.

"I have five viewings lined up for the weekend. I hope I find something instantly—I could use the extra day to get ready for the party."

"Don't be silly, child," Marcia objected. "You'll still have to do the promotional shots for Max. You'll never get through a photo session *and* find an apartment, all in one day."

"Sure I can," Katie countered. "I'm not in the least fussy about an apartment. Bed, bath and stove; that's all I want. After the stone house . . . And as for the photo session—how long can a couple of publicity shots take?"

Six hours, that's how long. Katie found out very quickly on Saturday that a promotional photo was nothing like, say, a passport photo. First, there was the makeup session. That lasted well over an hour as the makeup man experimented with blushers and shadows on the fine contours of her face.

It was the first time in her life that any but her own hand had touched her face in that way, and the effect on Katie was profound. She found herself almost completely detached, watching her face in the mirror being transformed by a pair of strange hands into a salable, marketable commodity. Where was Katrina Bright?

Buried. Buried under skillful makeup, long lashes and clever highlights. It seemed to Katie that her eyelids rose more slowly under the added weight of her new lashes; that her mouth became afraid to smile for fear of creasing something. And yet when she did try out a shy, tentative grin—on command of the makeup man—she was astounded to see that her teeth looked whiter in contrast to her carefully modulated lip color, and that her eyes looked enormous under the artistic shadows of this stranger's hand. She looked infinitely more sophisticated and, she had to admit, more beautiful than she ever had before. But it was a brittle, sophisticated beauty. She reminded herself of—yes, that was it!—Peter's New York model.

And then her hair. She'd never worn it the way it was arranged in the next half hour: teased and curled and manelike. The effect was undeniably sexy. The effect on *her* was undeniably sexy. She felt . . . different. Seductive, vampish. No—more like a seductive, vampish actress.

She was no longer Katrina Bright; she was this new . . . creature, an exciting, daring woman. Where had the new creature come from? Had she stepped out of Katie Bright; or had Katie Bright stepped into the new creature's shape? She tossed her hair back from her head. It had new weight, new motion. There was so much of it.

"Now that's not bad." It was Max, watching her from the door to the dressing room, a shrewd expression on his round, rather good-humored face. "Nice work, Charley. It's the look I wanted."

The makeup man packed up his kit and left the small room; there wouldn't have been space for three. Katie felt her cheeks warm at Max's detached appraisal, then realized a blush would hardly show through her new face; it was a comforting thought. Without removing the cotton dressing gown she wore over her dance leotards, she reached down for her briefcase.

"I have the signed contract right here," she said formally. "There were three or four questions . . ." she began.

"Sure kid, there's bound to be. We'll get to 'em later. For now, I have a photographer waiting who charges by the hour. How about slipping into these," he said, tossing a leotard on the dressing table, "and hustling out there like a good little girl, hey? Dee-Dee'll be by a little later. You'll like her. By the way, you don't object to 'Trina Bright' in the releases, do you? 'Kate' and 'Katie' are too ordinary. 'Katrina' is too European. 'Trina' is good, though; it goes with Dee-Dee."

She *hated* the nickname Trina. Her older brother's best friend had used it to tease her, calling her Trina-Prima-Donna whenever she'd refuse to fetch something for him, or to run an errand. "If it's all the same to you, I'd prefer any of the other names you mentioned."

"If it's all the same to *you*, kid, I'd prefer 'Trina,'" he replied calmly.

And that was obviously that. She fingered the contract in her hand. Time to tear it up? For what—a tantrum over a stage name? What did she care what some faceless audience knew her by? She bit her tongue and held her peace, watching him watch her in the mirror. Max lifted a curled lock of her hair horizontally, and then let it drop. The spun, blow-dried strands of the lock barely touched the teased strands beneath it. "I like that," he said reflectively. "It's the right look. C'mon kid; you're burnin' daylight." And he left her to change.

A sense of distaste clung to her, like sticky air on a hot, muggy day. It occurred to her that apparently everyone in the studio had the right to touch her—makeup man, wardrobe, set director. She'd met them all and been handled by them all. Like a potted plant. Inevitably she thought of Fletch's electric touch. When *he* lifted and played with her hair, a hot current of pleasure would wash over her from her scalp to her toes. Would that openness to sensation last? Or would she become emotionally calloused, insensitive to these men, to all men? To Fletch.

She held up Max's leotard in front of her. Even in its unstretched state, it was obvious that it would not cover the same amount of her that her own leotard did. The bodice was not, for one thing, sewn into the traditional overlapping V. Both sides of *this* V plunged recklessly to the waist. The bra had not been invented that could co-exist with Max's circus costume and so Katie removed hers.

She pulled the leotard over her. It was black, like her own, but it had a thin half-inch band of sequins sewn around the waist. Far more of her showed than didn't. It would be patently absurd to do anything but stand still in the outfit. Even then, she ran the risk of being arrested for indecent exposure. Katie looked at her reflection with a kind of melancholy awe. On television? With her mother and father still living in the United States?

She changed into her own leotard, but she left out the bra. It was the best she could do. There wasn't a doubt in her mind that she was being a nincompoop. After all, every month some ingenuous young thing was being featured in *Playboy* wearing infinitely less. Often the parents of the young thing were included in a family photo, usually around the barbeque. So why should Katie fuss over a little extra cleavage or a bit more thigh? Was it because her mom and dad hadn't made the leap to the New Morality? Or because *she* hadn't?

The answer was academic. She would *not* allow herself to be recorded in Max's sequin outfit. By any kind of camera. And she told him so.

"It didn't fit. I kept falling out," she said bluntly. If they wanted her to talk show-biz, so be it.

Max scanned her slowly, top to bottom. "Yeah. I can see that. You're a little more . . . muscular than I thought. Okay. We'll shoot you as you are. I'll have the other outfit reworked. Make sure you check in with wardrobe and get measured."

Finally, the photo-shoot began. Katie was shot in various exercise positions, and she was shot in pensive close-ups. At first it went horribly.

"Smile—I need *teeth*," the photographer implored.

"Here. *Teeth*," she answered.

"Not *gritted*, dammit."

Then Max pulled the photographer aside and they had a little conference. After that they pretty much let Katie choose her own expressions, and the session had become remarkably free of acid rain.

When it was over, Max said to her, "Your instincts were right, kid. You're not the bouncy, grinning type. Dee-Dee'll hold that end down. We're going to bill you as the aloof, mysterious one. Arrogant, but not *quite* bitchy," he said with a warning in his voice. He became thoughtful. "I like that. As if you don't really give a . . . hoot, whether they watch you or not. Good."

Trina-Prima-Donna. Had her brother's best friend been right, after all? Katie stumbled through her good-byes and headed for the ladies' room, where she scrubbed her face for longer than she ever had before. By the time she picked up her briefcase and remembered the undiscussed contracts, Max had left. Katie handed them over to the secretary at the desk, too tired to care whether she was signing herself into slavery or not. She spent the evening at a nearby motel, calling up all her potential landlords and rearranging the apartment viewings for the next day.

A good night's sleep rallied her spirits somewhat. She'd gone to the wire over the sequined outfit, and Max had accepted it. For the moment. She'd refused to pretend that she was Farrah Fawcett on camera, and Max had accepted *that*. Sort of. Maybe she'd survive in the TV jungle, after all.

Her little Volkswagen, its clutch slipping ominously, ferried her from one undesirable location to another. What could possibly compare with a 250-year old stone house nestled in the middle of a pine grove and bordered by a slate ledge, a running brook, acres of wilderness and a pheasant farm? Nothing, that's what; everything she looked at seemed cold, small and strange. When Katie finally wrote out her check for the rent deposit, it was to a woman who did not require a lease, liked cats, was from a town even smaller than Oswego—and looked a little like her mother.

"So what does the place look like?" Marcia asked curiously over the phone late that evening.

"Small. The living room and bedroom back-to-back aren't any longer than the stone house bathroom. I may as well take up residence in a bushel basket."

"You'll adjust. Look where Chuck and I are living—our

whole apartment is smaller than your present kitchen. Are there any good fields for Moose to hunt in?''

''I doubt that I'll even let him outside; there's a lot of traffic on my street.''

''Oh, well, cheer up; before long you'll be buying yourself a house in the country.''

''I hope so,'' Katie answered tiredly, and hung up. Immediately the phone rang again.

''Kate? Don't hang up on me,'' Fletch said quickly. As if she would. ''Can you hear me all right this time?''

All too well, she groaned to herself. How she'd missed that voice. ''The connection is fine,'' she said, forcing her voice down to chill level.

''The connection *isn't* fine,'' he complained with a rueful laugh. ''I'm dying by degrees without you, darling. I miss you. God, I hate telephones. They're so inadequate.'' His voice was husky with longing.

''Then come ho—to New Paltz,'' she said unexpectedly. Really, either she was a factor in his life, or she wasn't.

''I'd love to, but . . . how can I? I haven't finished up in London yet.''

Her voice dropped from chill to freeze. ''Ah, that's a pity.'' If she *wasn't* a factor, then why didn't he just . . . leave her alone?

There was a painful pause and then Fletch said quietly, ''What do you want me to do, Kate? Just walk away from London, from my meetings?''

''No.'' *Yes.*

''Would you rather I abandoned the British expansion altogether?''

''Of course not.'' Well *obviously* she would.

''I'll only be a bit longer, love. In fact I'm scheduled to fly back on Christmas Eve. I know you've barred me from the stone house, but would you make an exception? In the spirit of Christmas?'' Despite the orphan tone, there was smiling confidence in his question.

"Oh—didn't I say? I'm having a largish party on Christmas Eve." She tried to make it sound as though he might or might not have been included on her guest list of a thousand.

"A Christmas party! Can I come?"

"If you'd . . . like. You won't know many of the guests, of course."

"No problem; I'll treat all of 'em as future customers. You won't mind if I hand out grand-opening leaflets and Fish and Chips ballpoints?"

"Very funny."

"You're splitting your sides, I know," he said wryly. "Darling—I'll see you Christmas. Don't worry about meeting me at the airport with Charlotte; I'll get there on my own somehow."

Her eyebrows lifted. "Good of you," she intoned.

The last thought that drifted through her mind before sleep came was that he was the most amazingly confident man she'd ever known; it never failed to surprise her.

The alarm went off the next morning just before dawn. With reluctant, sleepy movements Katie pulled on her warmest, wooliest clothes, sipping coffee as she dressed and laced herself into hiking boots. Delicate pink light had begun to filter through the east windows, and by the time Katie hunted down a rusty saw in the cellar, the sun was fully up. It was time to cut down the Christmas tree.

Katie had been waiting for this morning since last spring. She and Jimmy, who was alive then, both had their own favorite trees. Jimmy had said that since he cut down the firewood, *he* should choose the tree. Katie had merely said—"too bad." She tramped through the frozen dry grass of a little-used truck path. The morning had a beautiful, breath-taking stillness; the only sound was the swish of the grass beneath her boots.

A surge of remorse rocketed through her; right now she'd let Jimmy cut down every tree on the property if he were alive to savor the morning. An old tree trunk had been dragged out of the path where it had fallen and lay on the side of the rutted road. Overwhelmed with emotion, Katie sat down on it, and for a brief moment the stillness was complete.

And then a low series of quick dry sobs escaped her, and Katie buried her head in her mittened hands, her body hunched up in a small-child position of grief, and wept openly for a long, long time. She wept tears for Jimmy's old age; tears for Cindy's youth; tears for her too-soon marriage and for Marcia's mixed-up engagement. Tears for all the generations of ghosts in the stone house—babies, children, parents and grandparents, loving and unloved; tears for everyone, for promise unfulfilled.

It was only when Katie dried her face on her parka sleeves, her salty cheeks and nose tingling in the crisp, cold air, that she realized her tears had not been for Fletch. Now why was that? she wondered, renewing her traipse along the road. Had her mind and emotions learned to protect themselves by going on "hold" whenever Fletch became the object of consideration?

Oddly refreshed, and still sniffling occasionally, Katie turned into a grove of pine trees alongside the road. She walked up to Jimmy's tree. It was short and fat, with almost no bad angles. Her choice was taller and more elegant, but the short fat one looked friendlier. Jimmy had felt certain it would have a sense of humor. After Katie cut it down she discovered in its boughs a tiny abandoned bird's nest, a token of good luck; she and Jimmy had chosen well.

The tree was heavier than she imagined, and dragging it back to the house took longer than she thought. Katie barely had time to change and dash off for her first class. Her fingers were sticky with pine resin, and she left them that way. The smell was delightful, the resin a balm on her raw emotions, soothing and cheering.

That evening, holiday anticipation settled over Katie like

a rainbow. She connected all the strings of twinkle lights together and plugged them in to check the bulbs. Every one of the white stars winked—surely another good omen? As she threaded the wires through the branches she decided that life, after all, was good. Her parents were together and happy and in good health. She had—all on her own—made it to first base in a new career. Dozens of people had wished her well in the last week and said how much they'd miss her. She had friends—Marcia and Chuck would be there any minute to help her trim the tree—and she had a lover. A part-time lover.

Then came the sigh. It was obvious to Kate, even if it wasn't to Fletch, that she loved him too much to accept being a part-time pursuit in his life. The only logical thing was to tell him that she couldn't live without him, and then never see him again. Of course, put that way, it sounded a little dumb. But when the time came, she'd express herself differently. She'd make it make sense.

The door knocker thunked and Katie said, "Come in; it's open." She was standing on a chair, barely able to reach the top branches of her short tree.

"Katie! That tree is *huge*. I thought you said . . ."

"It looked a heck of a lot smaller outdoors. Hi, Chuck."

"Hello, Katie; how's it goin'?"

"You can't possibly have enough ornaments."

"Right you are, Marsh. Which means you'll have to string a little extra popcorn. Three and a half miles of it should do nicely. Chuck, see if you can find a chair and a pillow for this lady."

"A chair and a whip, you mean." Chuck threw Marcia a half-friendly, half-despairing look and went upstairs for a pillow.

Katie turned to Marcia. "What's with him?"

"I think he's suggesting that I'm becoming a tiger to live with," Marcia said dryly.

"Are you?"

Marcia shrugged. "I seem to growl a lot. It started when he went home to his mother. I hated that. But now that he's back, I'm not much happier. I feel . . . caged, in fact. You figure it out."

"I think the holidays have everyone on edge. I overflowed myself this morning—although I have to admit, I feel much better for it." The last twinkling light was in place. "There. How's that?"

"Very pretty. Does it bother you that you can't open the front door with the tree in place?"

"Oh. Maybe we should move it a little."

"Not me, thanks. I've got a gimpy leg. Where's Chuck? He's always underfoot when I don't need him, and never around when I do. *Chuck!*"

The hostility in Marcia's voice alarmed Katie. She'd never heard it directed at Chuck before. It broke her heart to think that these two might not make it as a couple.

Just then Chuck appeared, pillow in hand. "Use that tone of voice with me again, young lady, and you'll end up with a mouthful of feathers." He set the pillow on the telephone bench and brought a comfortable chair over. "I'll get the popcorn," he said quietly to Katie.

"Thanks, Chuck. I've got the needles and thread right here." Katie watched his retreating form with fondness. Chuck was—well—Chuck. Tall, a bit gawky, with a nearsighted look that suggested someone had just stepped on his glasses. He had a wonderfully warm smile and a penetrating intelligence. Katie had an impulse to bat her female friend on the head; how could Marcia treat him that way?

When he returned Katie offered to make hot toddies; maybe they would help soften the sharpness in the room. She left the two to themselves while she fixed the drinks and put together a tray of cheese, fruit and crackers. The scene in the foyer when she came back wasn't the least what she'd expected to find: Chuck and Marcia were alternately throwing kernels of popcorn into one another's open, laughing mouths.

The reconciliation that had obviously taken place lasted the rest of the evening. Marcia led the three in singing carols. Their most ambitious effort, "The Twelve Days of Christmas," reduced everyone to comic exhaustion. Chuck strung a crown of white kernels for Marcia's head and assembled and hung garlands around the fireplace and doorway. The tree was hung with dozens of antique and handmade ornaments that Katie had collected over the last several years, almost as though she'd known that one day they would adorn this tree in this house. Marcia had strung what did seem like miles of popcorn, but . . . the tree was very, very large.

"It's no use," Marcia said flatly. "The tree needs more something. The decorations are beautiful as far as they go. . . . Katie, open your present. There's no point in waiting until Christmas."

"Oh, but, Marsh, I haven't wrapped yours yet. . . ."

"Katie," Marcia moaned in exasperation. "Will you stop it? Just open the present."

She did. Marcia had remembered Katie's wild enthusiasm over an ornament they'd seen together in Poughkeepsie: a small, perfectly realistic crystal icicle imported from Belgium. They were outrageously expensive, but Katie had determined to buy three or four the next time she was in Poughkeepsie. There were dozens in the box—fifty, to be precise.

"It seemed like a nice round number," Marcia said matter-of-factly.

Chuck and Katie hung them one by one with much supervision from Marcia. A little rush of Christmas joy washed over Katie as she arranged each icicle to catch and reflect the twinkle of the white lights. When they were finished Katie switched off the overhead light and they stepped back to survey the miracle. The tree shimmered with fairy-tale magic. It was exquisite and charming at the same time, the perfect expression of Christmas in the stone house. No one spoke; no one needed to. It was a moment of sweet, simple pleasure.

Katie carried the moment with her to bed and through the last days before Christmas. Her expectations were rising impossibly high, she reminded herself. But then she'd let herself be lifted even higher on the crest of another wave of pleasure as she sought out and found the exact right present for someone; and higher still, when she wrapped it and added it to the growing pile under the fairy-tale tree.

She was spending a reckless amount of money—indulging in a charge-account frenzy, in fact—but the need to budget a business had suddenly disappeared. Only one rent remained from now on, and no operating expenses. How simple the wage-earner's life must be, she thought naively as she handed over her credit card to the assistant behind the jewelry counter. With a light heart—and an even lighter pocketbook—Katie carried home yet another bundle of holiday bounty.

Chapter Fifteen

One of the best things about the stone house was that a visitor never noticed a bit of unmopped floorboard or a dusty knicknack. The house was simply too big, too interesting, too authentic to be bothered about a white-glove inspection. For her party Katie dutifully dragged out the mop, the vacuum and the can of spray-wax. But no vacuum was powerful enough to suck out hundreds of years of dust from between the wide pine planks. And though there must have been countless fingerprints on the mantel and doorways, who could find them?—all the wood was oiled, not painted. As for the furniture, most of Mr. Durette's pieces were crazed and not polishable.

Still, Katie dusted the spokes of the spinning wheel with care and knocked down a cobweb from a corner of the foyer where it had been brooding for the last month. She wondered, briefly, whether Fletch was buying all the furnishings too, then dismissed the thought. Who cared?

Not she—she told herself. When she was rich she'd buy her own spinning wheel.

It was time for the fire. The Yule log—which had been cut down expressly for Christmas by Jimmy—was a foot in diameter, cut from the base of a lightning-blasted oak tree. Katie had had to roll it up into place over two cookie sheets; she couldn't possibly have lifted it. Where was someone strong when you needed him? Enroute from London, that's where.

The fire was lit; the house was ready. Katie drifted through the downstairs rooms, completely enchanted with the holiday effect she'd achieved. Everywhere there were candles—and of course, candleholders. In the last week Katie had sunk a good portion of her future wages into precious metals: She'd bought candleholders made of brass and pewter, and an exquisite pair made of sterling. She'd convinced herself that a stone house needed lots of candle-holders. What if the power went out?

Every suitable surface held tiered trays and quaint bowls filled with holiday goodies—tiny pastries and cookies and nuts and the most perfect fruit she could find. A white linen tablecloth had bought (MasterCard) to dress up the mahogany dining table. On it a large bowl of cut French crystal (savings account) waited to be filled with the Christmas punch that was still cooling in the fridge. Katie made a tiny adjustment to one of the crystal mugs and moved a stack of gilt-edged china plates (VISA) two inches to the right.

Even the cat, curled into a large white circle of fur on the red cushion of the rocking chair, looked appropriate. All that was missing was snow. No—no snow, she pleaded silently. Forget snow. She wanted that plane *not* to be weatherbound. The sound of an approaching car sent Katie tumbling from her reverie. Fletch! It was Fletch and she looked like a ragamuffin.

But it was a Mustang, thank goodness. Darn it. Katie let

Marcia in with a frantic "Merry Christmas; I'm still not dressed."

Marcia slipped out of her coat almost shyly, the way people do when they are dressed to the nines and no one else is. She wore a long black velvet skirt and a dove gray satin blouse with wide sleeves.

"Marcia, you look stunning. Sensational. How does your ankle feel? Will you be able to stand all evening long?"

Marcia's face was pure mischief as she grabbed her skirt with both hands and lifted it to her knees.

Katie stared at her friend's feet and laughed. "Running shoes? Nice touch."

"Hey—if the shoe fits . . . The only thing is, I have to walk like a geisha or my toes stick out. Hurry up and get ready. I feel sublimely conspicuous."

She needn't have. Guests began arriving early while Katie was upstairs dressing. Each time the door knocker sounded, Katie stopped to listen at the top of the stairs. None of the voices so far was Fletch's; but it was early. Katie stepped into the heavy tapestried folds of the burgundy and forest green skirt she'd coveted earlier. Her blouse —also new, also astronomically priced—was of creamy Irish linen, scooped in front and trimmed in hand-made lace. She'd told herself that the clothes suited the stone house perfectly. They did. She'd told herself that she was on the verge of bankruptcy. She was. And then she'd bought the outfit anyway.

By the time Katie arranged a frame of braided hair around her face and went downstairs, Marcia had lit all the candles, transforming the stone house into a scene of colonial graciousness. It looked more enchanting than ever, a throwback to a simpler, gentler age. The early guests were those who'd promised to bring prepared dishes; they wandered from room to room, whispering excitedly, caught up in the antique charm of the house. They might have been giggling debutantes at a colonial governor's ball.

Several young men were there, husbands and dates, and Katie was introduced to those she didn't know. Before long the stone house had absorbed dozens of laughing, chatting people in festive dress, drinking and eating and exchanging gossip and good wishes. Over and over again Katie was told, graciously, what a wonderful house she lived in—and she was asked, graciously, how she could bear to be leaving it.

At one point Katie paused at the top of the stairs, looking down at the scene of countrified elegance below her. It was a wonderful party, the best she'd ever given. Over the top of the twinkling tree she scanned the assembly of relaxed and friendly guests. She spotted Chuck, putting his arm around Marcia and whispering in her ear. Marcia's smile was broad; she looked, Katie thought, pleasantly shocked. Helen Ritter was there, in a mauve silk jumpsuit, probably acting more like a hostess than Katie. Even Jessica and her husband had stopped by; where had they found a sitter on Christmas Eve?

It was an absolute waste of time, of course, but Katie searched the faces for Fletch, her ears open for the sound of approaching cars. By now she'd been stood up enough times to be used to the feeling of dwindling expectations. Still, the evening wasn't over, not yet. Tentative strains of "Deck the Halls" reached her through the thick stone walls of the living room; someone had organized a caroling party. The phone rang and Katie took it in her bedroom, closing the door on the Christmas merriment.

It was Fletch, and Katie thought he must still be in London, because his voice was low and difficult to understand.

"I'm at the Shape-Up Room. Can you come here, Kate? Now?"

The question was put so abruptly that for a moment she was taken aback. "Are you *serious?*" she answered incredulously. "I have fifty guests downstairs; I can't just tell them to pack it in and go home!" Then: "Fletch . . . what's wrong?" She was convinced that she was imagining the call.

"It's Cindy. She met me at the airport, but something's wrong with her. She's 'on' something, but I don't know what." The words were carefully measured, but jet-lag and alarm hovered around the edges.

"Should we get her to an emergency room?" Katie asked quickly, her mind running through contingency plans.

"I . . . I don't know. I wanted to, but she's completely paranoid about it. She doesn't seem *that* bad, but . . . I don't know. Can you come? You don't have to stay long."

"I'll be there in ten minutes."

Katie sought out Marcia, who had taken charge of the carolers, and pulled her off to one side, explaining what she'd learned.

"Katie, how awful for you—for everyone," Marcia said.

"Can you take over as hostess, Marcia? Everything seems under control, but someone should . . . I won't be long," Katie said, kissing her friend on her cheek. "I hate to ask you."

"Well, if I don't step in, Helen Ritter certainly will," Marcia said grimly. "Wish Fletch a—never mind. Just go."

Katie let herself out the back way with the incoherent excuse that the ginger ale was on the porch. With luck she'd have an hour before they sent out a search party for her. She decided to take Charlotte. The car was parked out of the way on the grass; most of the other cars were hopelessly parked in. No one seemed to have left yet. Katie acknowledged to herself that she was walking out on one hell of a good party and then thought no more about it.

She let herself into the building and walked quickly down the deserted hall between the Shape-Up Room and the closed-down racquetball club. The glass door to the Shape-Up Room was locked, and while Katie fumbled with her key Fletch met her and opened it from inside.

"How is she?" she asked him, throwing down her coat and automatically lowering her voice as though she were in a hospital room.

"The same." Fletch stared in some confusion at Katie, still in her Christmas elegance, and said, "Kate, I'm sorry. You were having a party," as though the thought had occurred to him for the first time.

There it was, that look she loved to distraction: the twelve-year-old who's narrowly missed being hit by a falling brick.

"Da-*dee!*" came a wail on the other side of the louvred screen. "Daddy daddy daddy," in rapid succession and rising panic. "Where are you?"

"Right here, darling," Fletch called. He signaled to Katie to come with him.

They walked around the screen. Cindy had been lying on an exercise mat with Fletch's overcoat on top of her; but this she had thrown off. She was sitting bolt upright.

"Daddy, I'm not tired; why do you want me to sleep? Do you think I still nap? Well, I don't anymore. Even when I was little I didn't have to when I didn't want to. Mother said I didn't. Did you think I did? Well, I didn't. You didn't know that, did you? Because you lived somewhere else, didn't you? Serves you right." And she folded her arms across her chest, a heart-wrenchingly defiant brat.

"She's been going like that, a mile a minute, since she found me at the airport. Her pulse is a little high, but her eyes look all right."

"It looks like amphetamines to me," Katie said quietly. "Once in a while someone on a crash diet will come in high like this—"

"So he's brought you, after all," Cindy interrupted with

shrill loftiness, pointing to Kate. "I knew he would." And she folded her arms across her chest again, this time in smug satisfaction. "You look very pretty, by the way. I'd like to get up now. I'd like a glass of water."

Fletch, looking helpless, seized on this chance to be useful and walked toward the water cooler.

"Yes, very pretty," Cindy repeated. "Do you have any children?" she asked, jumping up and leaving Fletch's coat behind her.

"No."

"Do you want any?"

"Yes, someday."

"It's best not to have them too young. That can be a terrible mistake. Mother told me that. Over and over. I won't have any until I'm thirty-four. I have everything planned. Thank you, daddy." She took the paper cup and emptied it thirstily. "She's prettier than mother, don't you think, daddy?"

"That's like comparing apples and oranges, Cindy," Fletch said gently.

"Apples and lemons," she corrected, and turned back to Katie. "You look exactly the way Christmas ought to look. I'm sorry I'm wearing old things," she said formally, indicating her sweater and jeans. "I was at JFK, on my way to mother. She lives in California. There were *millions* of people at the airport, all pushing and shoving and angry and . . . Merry Christmas. And my flight, wouldn't you know it, was leaving an hour before daddy's arrived. It wasn't fair. All of a sudden it just hit me. It wasn't *fair*. So I called up mother—she wasn't in and I left a message with her boyfriend—and . . . and . . ."

Here Cindy faltered and rubbed her forehead confusedly, looking around the room, trying to orient herself.

"Would you like to walk a bit, up and down?" Katie asked with infinite tenderness.

"Yes. Yes, I'd like that. And I'm sure mother is sad and depressed now and it's all my fault," she went on, regaining the thread she'd lost.

She wrung her hands in a childish gesture of anxiety as she and Katie walked up, then down, the length of the room. Fletch was half seated on the desk top, looking deliberately casual, trying not to frighten his daughter with expressions of alarm. His eyes never left the two women.

"So I signed up to go standby on a later flight, because that way I could see *both* of them for Christmas and wish *both* of them Merry Christmas, but the flight was very late and I knew I'd be tired and so I took another . . ."

"—pill?" Katie volunteered, filling in the sudden guilty silence.

In a childish reflex Cindy looked quickly at her father, still at the far end of the room, and whispered, "You know about that?"

"It was just a guess," Katie answered with a soft, reassuring smile.

"Oh, of course," Cindy said with a giddy, conspiratorial laugh, "you must use them to stay *thin*. All my friends do."

"But I don't, Cindy, because when I did they made me confused and besides . . . they would exhaust me," Katie said, choosing her words carefully.

"Oh, I *know*," Cindy said with a violent nod of her head. "I use them before exams and I'm just a total . . . *loss* after exam week." A thought occurred to her. "How *do* you keep going, then?"

"I have lots of little tricks, Cindy. Tomorrow I'll show them to you."

"Daddy wants me to go to the hospital," Cindy said in a stage whisper that was louder than her normal voice. "But I don't think I'm that bad. Do you?"

"Would you mind just stopping by for a quick check-up to make sure?" Katie ventured.

"I certainly *would,*" Cindy answered instantly, and moved away from Katie suspiciously.

"Then you don't have to," Katie said soothingly. "We'll just . . . walk."

"How does daddy *do* it?" Cindy asked fretfully. "Get his energy, I mean. Always flying or driving or in conference. *Up* and down, *back* and forth, *never* stopping, go, go, go. I can't keep up that kind of pace. I try so hard and I just . . . can't," she said in a small despairing voice.

For the next hour they paced the room almost without pause, as Katie helped Cindy walk off the effects of the drug. Cindy's monologue during that time went nearly uninterrupted; Katie found that if she tried to speak, the girl became confused and disoriented. At one point Fletch walked toward them. Cindy waved him away. "I'm talking such nonsense, daddy. Don't listen."

And she returned to her ramblings about childhood friends and university friends, professors and relatives and every single cat she'd ever owned. Woven in and out of her monologue, like a single dark thread, were frequent references to her mother. Before long it became apparent to Katie that Cindy was carrying a heavy burden of guilt for having been born—as Fletch had once put it—"nine months after prom night." Cindy took her parents' abandoned careers in medicine very seriously. From what Katie could gather, Fletch had never blamed Cindy; but his wife had.

As the two women approached the office end of the room Cindy, reverting to her stage whisper, said suddenly, "I'm tired. Mother couldn't keep up with him either, you know. She said it tired her out just to watch him. Do you know why they got divorced? Mother said he was too perfect. He never hollered at her, I guess. Such a funny reason," Cindy said with a shaky giggle. Then, abruptly, she said, "You don't talk very much."

It brought a startled laugh from Katie; she was encouraged that the girl was acute enough even to notice the silence. "What would you like me to talk about, Cindy?"

"My father. Tell me why you love him. Is it because he's so perfect?" They had come within a few feet of Fletch, who was still leaning against the desk watching them intently. Cindy threw her father a gray-eyed look of antagonistic longing; she got back a gray-eyed look of rueful love.

In an attempt to reassure Cindy, Kate said, "Him? *He's* not perfect." Katie threw Fletch a look similar to Cindy's. The look *she* got back was also of rueful love, but there was something more—a glint of humor, of grown-up understanding between them. It was a look that promised more would come.

"He's *perfect,*" Cindy insisted, and then narrowed her eyes suspiciously at Fletch as though he were a possibly flawed diamond. "Is there really something wrong with him?"

"Well, for one thing," Katie said, speaking directly to Fletch over Cindy's shoulder, "he expects everyone *else* to be perfect. Sometimes we're just not as organized and smart as we should be. But there's nothing wrong with that—as long as we've tried our best." It was a signal aimed straight at Fletch. Would he understand?

"That's right, that's right," Cindy agreed excitedly. "As long as we've *tried.* Even God doesn't expect us to do more than that."

A pained look of comprehension flickered across the tired, drawn features of Fletch's face. He put his arms around Cindy's shoulders and smoothed back her curly bangs. "Is it something to do with school, Cindy?" he urged softly.

"Yes. Yes yes yes."

"You're not doing as well as you'd hoped?"

"I'm *failing,* daddy," she wailed. "Two subjects— Comparative Anatomy and Physics. I didn't take the exam in one, and I just failed the other outright. I've made a real mess of it because . . . because I can't do it. I *tried,* for you and for grandpa, but . . . I don't *want* to be a surgeon. Oh, daddy, I hate it,'' she gasped. And then she broke down in chest-racking sobs on Fletch's shoulder, the little girl who wanted to please all of the people all of the time, and couldn't.

With a heart-robbing look of paternal tenderness, Fletch murmured, "Cindy . . . sweetheart . . . hey . . . don't cry, honey. What a thing to cry about,'' he said soothingly, rocking her back and forth in his arms. "Who cares about pre-med? *I* sure don't. Shhh . . .''

Katie left them alone, then, because the moment belonged to Cindy's tears and her father's soothing whispers.

Completely sapped of energy, Katie wandered down the empty hall, emotionally incapable of making even simple decisions. She stared blankly through the glass wall of one of the racquetball courts, unused now for several weeks. She saw no ghosts; just an empty court. Dimly it occurred to her that she had been interrupted in the middle of something. "Oh, yes . . . the party,'' she whispered dully.

The cold air in the unheated hallway permeated the delicate linen of her blouse. The Shape-Up Room was warm, but that was off limits just now. And her coat was there. Katie hugged herself, consolidating her warmth, and wandered into the women's locker room. Emotional numbness was rapidly being overtaken by physical numbness. In an almost instinctive groping for warmth, Katie turned on the heat in the small steam room which she'd had installed at such great expense and which was so rarely used. She would sit here until the chill passed. Katie stepped inside, closed the door, and sat down on the redwood bench fully dressed, her mind, heart and body frosted over.

Within minutes she felt the edge of a wave of warmth lap at her feet. A violent shiver shook her as her body began to respond. Not long after that the heat became overwhelming, and yet so had her need to stay there. Katie unfastened the waistband of her skirt, the deep reds and greens of the tapestried folds jarring her loose from her daze. *It's Christmas Eve.*

She removed her blouse and stockings and left them with the skirt on the bench outside. Then she settled back in the steam room, clad only in a slip and underthings, wrapped in a warm cocoon of steam. Limb by limb, muscle by muscle, slow, lazy heat penetrated her. What little strength she still had melted away, and with it the anxiety and tension of the last hour—of the last weeks. It seemed incredible to her that she had not taken advantage of the steam room during all that time; but no, like any other fool during the holiday season, Katie had run around instead in a state of near hysteria.

She took a deep, deep breath, filling her lungs with steamy air, and then exhaled slowly and leaned her head on the wall behind her. A sheen of dampness covered her whole body; the lacy slip clung in wet folds to her rising, falling breasts. She'd forgotten to listen to her body during these past two weeks. Like Cindy, she had ignored it, abused it, and now it was taking its revenge: Katie couldn't have lifted a finger, if her life depended on it.

The tapping on the small pane of glass in the heavy door did not surprise her. Languidly, she opened her eyes and turned her head toward the door. Katie could barely make out the shape of a face through the thick mist of steam; she knew him, instead, by the sudden thick pounding of her heart.

"Come in, Fletch." The steam played funny tricks with her voice; it sounded low and sultry and desolate.

Through a haze of steam she watched him come toward her and sit down. He was dressed in a three-piece suit, his tie loosened but still knotted, and she was seized by the odd fancy that he was a businessman being ferried across Long Island Sound on a foggy night.

"Hi."

"Hi," she answered, just as though they were striking up a conversation on the afterdeck of the ferry.

"I was afraid I'd find you huddled in the hallway, frozen solid." The jacket came off; the tie was undone.

"Never underestimate the will to survive. Is Cindy asleep?"

"Yes, thank God. After her 'confession,' " he said with wry emphasis, "exhaustion finally caught up with her. She's asleep under my coat right now. She looks like a kid on a kindergarten mat."

Fletch was quiet for a bit; it didn't take long before he, too, felt the enervating effect of the steam. "I'm exhausted," he said faintly. "Too tired to take off my pants."

She opened her eyes and without lifting her head turned to him. He was in the same position she was, his head resting on the wall behind him, his eyes closed. "You'll ruin your suit," she warned tiredly.

"Who cares," he answered, equally tiredly. "Or . . . did you have something else in mind?" he added, the barest hint of a smile lifting one end of his weary question.

"Not a thing." It was incredible, but true.

"My eyelids weigh a hundred pounds apiece," he sighed. There was another period of silence. "Kate. Is she . . . hooked?" The question was put baldly, almost naively.

"Not in any physical sense," Katie answered carefully. "I gather she was an occasional user, not a habitual one."

" 'Was'?" He sounded hopeful.

"Of course. We can help her through this. And anyway, once she changes to some other major, a lot of the pressure will drop away. She won't need the extra stimulants—coffee and tea should do just fine."

"Poor little Cindy. I didn't give a damn whether she went to med school or not."

"Did you ever tell her that?"

"No, of course not." He sounded shocked. "How can you tell a kid that you don't believe in what she's doing? Naturally I encouraged her, cheered her on. . . ."

"It sounds to me," Katie said thoughtfully, "like a case of crossed signals. Both of you had laudable intentions, but . . ."

"Yowch," he interrupted, "I can't stand it; I'm boiling. I've got to get these pants off." He peeled away the clammy worsted pin-stripes and tossed them, with his jacket, shirt and tie, out the steam room door. "I'm sorry, Kate. Where were we?"

He was standing in the middle of the wood-lined room, looking down at her, his hands resting on his hips. His hair clung to his face in dark curls, wet with steam and sweat; his undershirt and shorts clung to him in a way that . . . that suggested that his exhaustion wasn't total.

"You looked very, very beautiful tonight, Kate," he said softly. "It's not often that I'm forced to watch without touching. Which is wonderful for building character, I might add," he said ironically. "I . . . Kate, I went through an unbelievable array of emotions out there. I can't begin to tell you how frightened I was, and jealous."

"*Jealous?*" Her look was baffled.

He collapsed next to her again, as though the effort to stand and undress had drained him. "Sure, jealous. Out of nowhere my daughter turns to you and spills her soul. At first I thought it was because you were a neutral third party. But after you left the room, you know what she told me? That of everyone she knew, *you* would understand her best. I asked her why, and she said, because you feed the birds when it snows. That's a *reason?* I don't know if I'm in love with Katie Bright or Mary Poppins," he added sulkily, obviously still hurt.

"Fletch, don't take it that way," Katie said quickly. "Cindy was just warming up with me, working up her courage to tell you she wanted to drop the pre-med program. That decision may have seemed insignificant to you, but as you admitted yourself, *she* didn't know that. She loves you so much. You heard her say it to me—I know you did; she was practically shouting.''

"I suppose I did," he admitted, still needing reassurance.

"Well . . . really, Fletch . . . what's the problem, then?"

"The problem is I'm feeling unloved. No, no, let me finish," he said, raising a hand to ward off her protests. "For weeks now I've been reeling under a barrage of on-again, off-again hostilities from Cindy—and from *you*, sweet pickle. No, let me *finish*. Normally I don't worry much about what people think of me—it's a waste of time—but in London, I worried. A lot. The way I figure it—stop me if I'm wrong—I expect absurdly too much of people.''

She didn't stop him.

He grimaced and went on. "It's also possible that occasionally I may have a tendency to . . . well, to manipulate people.''

Here she did stop him. "Not just 'occasionally.' ''

"So all right, most of the time. I vowed I just wouldn't be that way anymore. No pushing, no shoving. I promise. In London I sat down and looked not at where I was going, but at how I was getting there. And the answer was: *alone*. All I could think of was your prediction that I'd be the new Colonel Sanders, white-haired and moving eternally from one location to another. I don't want that. I canceled the London expansion," he said flatly. He then turned to her, as if to ask her the time. "Will you marry me?"

"No," she answered, as promptly as if she'd said "seven thirty-five."

It was a dream, all a dream. Ever since the phone call in the middle of her party earlier, Katie had felt that she had one foot in and one foot out of reality. Certain realities were undeniable: the steamy heat; the trickles of sweat that ran down her back, between her breasts and down the side of her temples; the hard redwood seat underneath her; the feeling of heavy wetness in her lungs.

But Fletch? The dancing gray eyes under drawn-together golden brows—were they real? He hadn't so much as touched her all evening. She might even be hallucinating. For all she knew he could be the devil asking for her soul. She needed—something, she didn't know what—*proof* that he was Fletcher Ramsey.

Oh, God . . . I'm delirious, she thought in despair.

Fletch had been waiting patiently for Katie to elaborate on her one-word refusal. When she said nothing, he asked politely, "Do I get a reason? Or just no?"

Still he didn't touch her. She could not understand it—unless he was a ghost, devil or hallucination. *Definitely delirious,* she repeated to herself. She made a fierce attempt to sound—especially to herself—rational and in control. "I can't marry you," she began carefully, "because I'm about to start a new career. It wouldn't be fair to my career, and it wouldn't be fair to you. I'd like to give it my best shot, now that I've made the decision and signed a contract." There. That had come out logical. *"You,* surely, can understand that," she added.

"No, I can't," he shot back. "I thought tonight's theme was the giving-up of ambition."

Still he hadn't touched her. "And *I* thought it was being true to oneself. If Cindy hates pre-med, fine. If you feel spread too thin, all well and good. I'm really, truly happy that you're both coming to terms with your real needs."

"My real needs are *you,* nimwit. Aren't you listening?" He was becoming testy. So much for his promise not to push or shove.

Still, he hadn't touched her. "I need you too, Fletch," she said, admitting the obvious. "But I may need

. . . something more. I may need to prove to myself that I can afford to live, on my own, above the poverty line. Plus I'd like to find out if I enjoy being . . . you know, being a celebrity,'' she added awkwardly.

He seized on that. ''That's a god-awful reason for doing something.''

''It was good enough for Barbara Walters,'' she flashed. Still he hadn't touched her; it wasn't funny anymore.

''So the answer is no?'' he said quietly.

''Well, no, it's not no, exactly. Can't we just . . . wait on this?'' she asked plaintively.

''How long before I can ask you again?''

''Six months?'' she ventured. ''That's how long my contract is for.''

''It sounds hopelessly Victorian,'' he grumbled. He shifted his weight on the bench, lifting his arm to the other side of her, flattening his palm against the wall, encircling her. ''Even though you won't marry me yet, will you let me make love to you?'' Closing his eyes, he lowered his lips to hers in a kiss that was, in every way, hot and steamy.

''I . . . that . . . seems fair,'' she said breathlessly after he released her.

Two weeks of pent-up passion exploded then; within seconds, fragments of clothing were scattered over the floor, and Fletch was sliding his mouth across Katie's superheated, damp body, pausing to tease the top of one breast, nipping lovingly at the nape of her neck, sliding in a random pattern across her love points, leaving her dazzled from his little erotic surprises.

They were lying on a bed of turkish towels that he'd arranged. ''Kate, Kate,'' he whispered in husky, hypnotic tones, kneading the ultrasensitive flesh on the inside of her thigh. ''I wonder what I *did* before I loved you? What did I think about? How did my days pass? And my nights?'' He ran his tongue across the tiny beads of heat above her upper lip before plunging hungrily into her opened mouth.

Dazed and in love, she pulled away from his kiss and said in a voice throaty with passion, "You were busy building an empire, mister. Only now," she said in a sweet, adoring chuckle, "the emperor has no clothes." And she slid her hands randomly as far as they could reach over his slick torso, relishing the line of muscle and ligament, telling herself over and over again that he was *real*, he was here, he was hers. Their bodies slid effortlessly over one another, thigh across thigh, cheek against cheek, his breast over hers. The gliding ease in the entry of his wet, heated body into hers was unlike anything Katie had ever known, a kind of slow skating through fire.

Lifted on the wing of rapture, Katie was briefly, dizzily aware that it was she who had become the wild card in their relationship. Then the question of her future, like the traumas of her past, dissolved in a pool of love, and she melted along with them, wet and liquid, while part of him melted inside of her, filling the core of her shimmering desire.

When at last they lay quietly, Katie, nestled in the hollow of his shoulder, whispered, "Merry Christmas" sleepily and fell into a doze. It lasted until Fletch shook her gently, and murmured, "It's 2:00 A.M., sweet; let's gather up Cindy and go home. It's been a long, long day."

Chapter Sixteen

$\mathscr{I}$t was early evening.

"Okay, that's a wrap." Max's sigh of relief was audible.

Someone handed Katie a towel. Scattered applause rippled through the tiny studio.

"Great choreography, Miss Bright."

"Very nice. *Very* nice."

"Look out, Jane Fonda!"

It was Katie's television debut, her first performance before a camera. She had been sure she'd be awkward, rattled and amateurish. Instead she was graceful, poised and professional. The taping was done in one take, and as usual Katie gave the credit to everyone else. Having two of WTAT's staff don leotards and work out as her "class" behind the cameras had helped a lot. And so, in her own strange way, had Dee-Dee, Katie's junior colleague. Dee-Dee's debut earlier that day would've made a performing bear look good, Katie told herself wryly.

It was Dee-Dee's job to stretch and warm up the television audience. Katie was to put them through the more rigorous exercises. Katie had choreographed the entire half-hour, and her program was excellent: tight, smooth, intelligent. However, it had taken six disastrous hours to tape Dee-Dee's part of the program. The only stretching anyone had done during that time was in bending over double with laughter.

Dee-Dee forgot, more than once, the order of the exercises. She giggled after every flub. Her leotard split up the back after an especially spellbinding waist-bend. She giggled some more. She pouted prettily when she was criticized. She pouted prettily when she got it right. The program director hated her. Everyone else loved her.

Including Katie. She couldn't help it; there was something irrepressible about Dee-Dee, a kind of high-voltage energy that seeped from every pore. She was not a quick study and even a little silly, but she made you want to jump up and exercise, if only to show her how it should be done. Undoubtedly she had a future in show business.

Katie mopped her damp brow, squeezed hands that were offered in congratulation and escaped to her tiny dressing room, feeling very much like a Broadway Star. Well, a little like one, anyway. She'd already given her first interview— to the *New Haven Weekly Courier*. She'd taped her first show. And she sat surrounded by flowers and congratulatory messages.

There was a basket of fruit from her parents; a pot of happy-looking daisies from Marcia; and a very practical philodendron from a no-nonsense aunt in Oswego. Dozens of cards and Mailgrams had arrived from friends and relatives. And today some of the Shaper-Uppers had sent a poinsettia the size of a small palm tree. Aunt Bernice's philodendron could survive in the windowless dressing room; but the poinsettia would have to go home to the new apartment tonight. Maybe it'd cheer the place up.

Katie released her breath in what sounded—for a Broadway Star—illogically like a sigh. *He could've sent a telegram, at least.*

She told herself that she was bound to have these little sighing spells until she got used to things. It was perfectly natural to be homesick, especially with Fletch finishing up business in London for the next few days.

She picked up and reread Marcia's note.

Katie—

Good luck!
P.S. I think Chuck and I have figured out our problem. We were just too crowded in my place. Being laid up (notice I said *up*) didn't help, either. We're now looking for a bigger place. Keep in touch.

Max popped his head into the opened doorway. "Nice work, kid. You've got the makings of a real trouper. I wish I could say the same for Dee-Dee Dumb-Dumb," he growled. "Still and all," he added resignedly, "one for two ain't bad."

"Don't give up on her, Max. I think with a little practice she'll be terrific." Katie found herself sounding fervent. "She has real charisma."

"We'll see." His voice was grim. "Incidentally, I'm sorry about the latest fiasco with the sequined suit. They're going to make a third one. I seem to be surrounded by . . . ah, forget it. Need a lift?"

"I'm fine," she said from behind her poinsettia. "Just on my way out." She picked up the basket of fruit and struggled out to the Volkswagen.

Katie hated the thought of driving to her new apartment. It was neat and it was clean, but it was . . . blah. Inevitably she thought of her last few days in the stone house. Cindy had stayed there for two or three of them, resting quietly and organizing her thoughts and emotions. During that time the girl never spoke as freely as she had that night in the Shape-Up Room, but she and Katie had laid down the tentative framework for a real friendship. Fletch, who seemed to have to work harder to get out of the London deal than he had to get into it, still found time to share a long walk with them in the mild late December sun. That evening the three of them had sipped brandy in front of the fire while Katie told them all she knew of the history of the stone house.

And then Cindy got on a bus to Boston; Fletch hopped a plane to London; and Katie drove . . . here. For the last week the stone house had stood dark and empty.

While Katie rummaged in her bag for the key to the outside door, her landlady swung it open for her.

"I saw you coming from my kitchen window," the elderly widow bubbled. "And I said to myself, this girl is a very popular young lady. All day long, the delivery men are coming. Flowers! Packages! I let the men into your apartment with the flowers—don't worry, I watched them every second—but when the package came, by *courier* yet," she said importantly, "well, that I left on my table. I didn't feel right going into your apartment by myself," she added primly. "I'll bring it up."

By the time Katie wrestled her poinsettia up the stairs, her landlady was right behind her with the courier package. She handed it to Katie and hovered expectantly, on the chance that Katie might be one of those eager types who tears into packages on receipt. Katie wasn't.

The landlady accepted Katie's thanks, turned and went partway down the stairs. "Oh, and the telephone company called. The problem isn't with the wiring in *this* house," she said rather proudly. "It's somewhere *else* in the neighborhood. Your phone should be working in a couple of days."

Katie smiled, closed the door and groaned; already she

was suffering from too much landlady and not enough Fletch. She went into the bathroom to wash up.

That was where the flowers were. In the bathtub. The arrangement was in the shape of a five-foot-long rainbow. The colors of the spectrum varied from purple hyacinths and irises to orange day lilies and tiny yellow roses. At least a thousand blossoms were worked into the rainbow; it belonged in the Rose Bowl Parade. Katie tore open the card: "Hope your coming-out went well. Love, Fletch."

She gazed at the rainbow for a long time with an absurd, foolish grin on her face, and then noticed that where the pot of gold would be, a tiny photograph had been attached—a picture of Judy Garland in her role as Dorothy in the *Wizard of Oz,* holding her dog Toto. It would have been so easy to miss.

But what was it supposed to mean? As she moved the rainbow from the bathroom to the living room to the kitchen to the bedroom and back to the bathroom, she puzzled over it. The poignant lyrics from Dorothy's song "Over the Rainbow" meandered through her head. In the movie, Dorothy didn't know what it was she really wanted. Was Fletch comparing her to Dorothy? Saying she was being childish?

Katie took the rainbow back to her bedroom and propped it on the headboard; instantly the bedroom was a riot of color and fragrance. The cat stuck his front paws on the headboard and sniffed madly, remembering old times; he'd been housebound for a week now. Still smiling, still feeling slightly foolish, Katie turned her attention to the courier package that she'd left unopened on her dresser.

She peered at the return address on the blurred carbon mailing label—more from Fletch! She flopped down on the bed, opened the courier envelope and shook its contents onto the patchwork quilt: There were two small packages, each the size of a ring-box, wrapped in drugstore-quality Christmas wrap. Each was tied in curly ribbon, which hadn't quite been made to curl. The wrapping job was hopelessly amateurish; she loved Fletch desperately for it.

The box with tiny Santas on it had "Me First" written on its tag. Katie unwrapped it almost reluctantly; it was like tearing up a letter from Fletch. She flipped open the velvet box: A stunning round sapphire, set in a filigree of gold and hung on a delicate chain, winked back rays of light at her. A sheet of paper had been folded half a dozen times and jammed into the lid. It read, "This is for the color of your eyes, sugarplum. Merry Belated Christmas. I love you. Fletch."

All reluctance was tossed to the winds as Katie opened the second package, wrapped equally clumsily, but in dark blue paper with silver snowflakes. Inside was an identical pendant, set in the same graceful filigree—but it was an emerald. The second note, folded and tucked in the lid, read, "I never can decide if your eyes are blue or green. Happy Belated New Year. I love you very much. Fletch."

"They're hazel, you dope," she said aloud, and her eyes—blue, green, a mixture of both—filmed over with tears.

Much later Katie lay in bed, gulping down great swallows of the rainbow fragrance above her head, fingering two almost identical pendants hanging around her neck, trying unsuccessfully to sleep. No matter which way or how fiercely she drove her thoughts, they came back to one of the final scenes in *The Wizard of Oz:* the one in which Dorothy, with her eyes closed tightly, taps her red sequined shoes together and whispers, over and over, "There's no place like home; there's no place like home; there's no place . . ."

Katie had just completed the first day of the second week of shooting. She was in her dressing room, she was very tired, and she was disgusted with herself for allowing Max to talk her into wearing version number three of the black sequined leotard. Version number three was somewhat more modest than its prototype. But still. It just wouldn't do.

Max appeared in the hall outside her dressing room dragging a wheeled rack of glittering leotards behind him. "From wardrobe at last. Get a load of these, kid. What do y'think? I think they'll give the show what it needs—more sass. Dee-Dee's nuts about 'em."

Katie eyed the rack with distaste. On it hung a dozen leotards in every color of the rainbow, each with a wide matching sequined waistband. Visually they were stunning, just the thing for a trapeze artist or a rock star. But were they really for Katie, who favored soft woolens and hand-made lace?

"I can't wear them, Max," she said quietly. "And I can't do the show. None of it is really . . . me. I know you'll tell me I haven't given it a chance—"

"Wrong. I'll tell you you haven't read your contract," he interrupted.

"—but I know you won't force me to do something I'm no good at."

"Wrong again. You're good."

"I'm *competent;* I'm not great at it, Max. Being on camera is simply not my cup of tea. I need to work with real people. I need to know when I'm pushing too hard, or not enough. I need the sound of human voices, Max. Let me go." Her voice had dropped to a whisper; it was as near to begging on her knees as she'd ever got in her life.

Max took the unlit cigar from between his clamped teeth, pointed the end toward his face and stared at it, then chomped back down on it. "That would leave me with Dee-Dee."

"Right; Dee-Dee! She's become so much better in the last week, Max. Everyone in the studio says so. She has more confidence; the enthusiasm shows. She's a natural; you know she is." If Katie could have seen the bright eagerness in her face, she'd have realized that she was defeating her own cause.

"Dee-Dee couldn't choreograph her way out of a wet paper bag," Max said flatly, and turned to leave. "The answer is no."

"*I'll* do the choreography!" Katie cried instantly. That was the solution, the rainbow's end: She could design the choreography in the stone house, whenever she wasn't teaching at the Shape-Up Room. "Sure; why not? I enjoy designing a program. I'm good at *that*, I know. Max—let's talk about this. Yes?"

He tossed his cigar butt into a hallway ashtray. "You want me to send out for sandwiches, maybe?"

The next morning, the New Haven viewing audience got to see, for the first and only time, Trina Bright doing a show—which had been taped the day before—in a black sequin-waisted leotard. One of that audience, a sandy-haired businessman with angry gray eyes, was sitting in a New Haven motel room in t-shirt and jockey shorts, half of his face shaved, the other half still lathered. In his hand he held an old-fashioned, undisposable safety razor. His red-rimmed eyes were proof that, like any other transatlantic jet-setter, he needed more than one night to catch up on his sleep. During the entire twenty minutes that he sat trans-fixed before the television set, only three words escaped his lips.

"I'll be damned."

He stood up, flicked off the set and walked into the bathroom where he finished shaving in three or four impatient passes over his cheek and chin. He nicked his jaw, swore and tore off a bit of toilet paper to plaster to the cut. It kept coming off on his finger instead of sticking to his jaw. He swore again.

How could she do it? Just stand there, in front of a *television* camera, for God's sake, practically naked and

. . . cavort. And her hair; what had she done to it? He was no prude, but *this* . . . He pulled on his pants, hurried into a shirt, stood on his foot as he yanked a sock over his other bare foot, then switched feet, hopping once or twice before regaining his balance. Whatever clothing he'd had the energy to unpack the night before got rolled into a haphazard bundle and was slammed into his nicely crafted leather suitcase.

All right, so maybe he *was* a prude—where she was concerned. Dimly he seemed to remember that the bouncy blonde—Fifi, Gigi, whatever her name was—had been wearing a lot less over a lot more. But that wasn't the point. The tight knot that had been gathering in the middle of his chest twisted a little tighter. He fumbled in his carry-on bag until he came up with a bottle of antacids, dumped two into the palm of his hand and left his motel room chewing them through his fury.

Outside he winced at the sight of the red Ferrari that waited anything but demurely in the parking lot. Red, yet; it had to be red. He tossed his bags in the back and took off for station WTAT. His brilliant scheme to overwhelm Katie with riches was looking a little stupid in the morning light of downtown New Haven. He realized that it was all on short notice, but couldn't Jack have got hold of an unobtrusive *white* Ferrari for him?

She wouldn't be dazzled, anyway. She'd say, "I much *prefer* the bus; you meet so many interesting people there." Ditto the emerald and the sapphire. They were probably hanging from some window latches right now so that she could watch the sun filter through them. He downshifted and shook his head in frustration. She couldn't be cajoled; she couldn't be bought. He remembered with wry fondness the way she'd edged away from him, like a skittish colt, when first he approached her—shy, suspicious creature. If she'd only known how her aloof reserve intrigued him.

The traffic light changed to green; he wasn't paying

attention. A cabbie behind him leaned on his horn and gave the Ferrari a friendly nudge. *Red Ferraris get no respect,* he thought with disgust, and took off in a dramatic squeal of rubber which he hadn't intended; he was still getting used to the car.

How could someone so shy wear that leotard? It made no sense. Either she was a consummate actress—in which case he didn't know her at all—or she really needed the money. It was true that the stone house seemed to have sprouted a few new elegances, and Katie had moaned about some reckless shopping binge; but she couldn't be that desperate. Then why? Why?

He pulled the Ferrari into the small parking lot of WTAT, instantly picking out Katie's battered Volkswagen bug. Maybe she *did* need the money, he thought, glancing at the sad little wreck. On the other hand, she probably felt sorry for it and wanted it to spend its last weeks feeling needed. *Ah, Kate, I love you.*

He walked up to the reception desk where an efficient-looking secretary was going over some paperwork with a short, balding man. Fletch knew instantly that it must be Max; the unlit cigar butt branded him plainly.

The secretary looked up and said, "Good morning."

"I'm here to see Katrina Bright," he said abruptly; there was nothing good about the morning.

"She's in her dressing room, first door to the left," she answered, much more crisply. "Did you have an appointment?"

"I don't need one," Fletch said, swinging on his heel toward the dressing rooms. "She quits, by the way."

"Who're *you?*" Max demanded.

"The guy who got her pregnant, that's who," Fletch returned coolly.

She'll kill me for that one, he told himself as he walked away. And he was willing to bet that that was a breach of contract. Tough. Let the lawyers worry about it.

He knocked—pounded—on Katie's door. It swung open and he saw her standing there, wearing a flame red sequin-waisted leotard slit down the waist in front, revealing breasts that . . .

"Take it off," he ordered. "You're going home."

Katie stared at Fletch in openmouthed amazement. He wasn't due back until tomorrow. She'd planned to surprise him at the stone house—she still had the key. Max had been very decent about renegotiating her contract. She'd come to the station to clear out her dressing room, and she hadn't been able to resist trying on one of the new leotards. She considered them a sleazy joke, of course; but the look on Fletch's face was anything but amused.

"I'm going where?" she asked, instantly wary.

"*Home*."

"Which is?"

"New Paltz, New York."

"Sez who?"

"Sez me. C'mon; pack up." He glanced around the dressing room; obviously there was nothing left to pack. "Is this your suitcase?" he demanded, picking it up. "Let's go."

"You're crazy; I have a contract," she lied. What infuriating nerve!

"Not anymore, you don't," he said angrily.

How did he know that? Max had asked her to keep it quiet until he talked with his lawyers. "You're crazy," she repeated. What was the matter with him?

"I want you out of this job and out of that leotard, Kate. I mean it."

"What if I won't get out of either?" she taunted unnecessarily; she was embarrassed, defensive, angry.

His look was scathing. "Well, if you feel fulfilled in your role as sex queen at Station WTIT—oh, excuse me—that's WTAT, isn't it?"

She slapped him.

"I guess that's fair," he said, bringing his hand up to his face with a wry, pained look. "Tit for tat."

She tried to slap him again, but he caught her flying wrist. "We can stand here pummeling one another all morning, or we can go somewhere to discuss it, Kate. Which?"

"I'll . . . meet you in the parking lot," she choked out, horrified at the level of violence they'd reached.

He left and she ripped off the red leotard and threw it on the dressing table. It was all a sickening misunderstanding; they had hurt one another for no reason at all. Denims, a sweater and her long wool coat did nothing to dispel her chill. Her teeth chattered as she walked up to him in the parking lot. He should have been cold, too, in his light suede jacket; but if he was, he showed no sign of it.

"Kate, oh, darling Kate. I'm sorry," he said huskily, cradling her pale, shocked face in his hands, dropping light, skimming kisses on her eyelids and cheeks and mouth.

"Wait," she breathed. The whole studio obviously knew about their argument; it bruised every nerve-ending she possessed to think that now they were enjoying the reconciliation. Katie had had enough of making a public property of herself.

Hypersensitive to her need, Fletch said, "Shall I follow you to your apartment?"

She nodded dumbly, then got behind the wheel of her little car and drove out of the parking lot. Automatically she slowed down, looking for Charlotte in her rear-view mirror, before it dawned on her that Fletch had got into some sort of red car, the one behind her. With a feeling of rising, giddy relief she drove away from the station whose very call letters would forever remind her of her profound misjudgment.

She parked her Volkswagen on a tree-lined street; Fletch pulled up behind her. Her landlady—needless to say—

peeked out from her kitchen curtains and waved. "She's much better than your burglar alarm," Katie murmured to Fletch, in a shaky attempt to seem playful. *"Nothing* would get past her."

When finally Katie closed her apartment door on her landlady, station WTAT, the city of London, and the rest of the world, the first words she whispered as she slipped her arms around his neck were, "I want to go home, Fletch. Take me home."

Now it was his turn to hesitate. "Home . . . which is?"

"New Paltz, New York," she answered with the first smile to light up her face since his return. "Where else?"

"Done!" he cried, scooping her up in his arms and swinging her around. "Get the cat, pack your nightgown. Forget the nightgown; we'll send in movers. Ah, Kate," he whispered, and lowered his mouth to hers in a kiss of rapturous apology. When he released her from his kiss he said, "I made such an ass of myself at the station."

"No you didn't; you had no idea—"

"—how to get you to walk out on the show and come away with me? You're right. And frankly, in my wildest fantasies I didn't think you'd buy that macho, club-over-the-head business," he chuckled into her hair, naively pleased with himself.

His hands wandered possessively over her; Katie could feel the cheerful triumph in their touch. She smiled into the yellow linen of his shirt. "I didn't."

"Didn't what, darling?"

"Didn't buy that macho stuff." She turned her face up to his, her eyes shimmering with love and—she couldn't help it—mischief. "I quit yesterday."

"You what?"

"Quit. Yesterday. Isn't that what you wanted?" she asked, watching him with wide-eyed, unblinking innocence.

The everyday rosiness beneath his cheekbones deepened, then deepened more, into a dull ruddy flush. "Is that why you quit? Because I wanted you to?" he asked carefully.

"What do *you* think?" she parried.

"I think—" He held her away from him, trying to assess her, as if she were an exquisite art object from an epoch he didn't know well. "*I* think there isn't a snowball's chance in hell that you'd do anything just because I wanted you to." Cheerful exasperation replaced the cheerful triumph in his voice. "You win. That's fine. It doesn't matter." He wrapped his arms around her tightly, nuzzling her, rocking her, happy anyway.

But to Katie it mattered. "It'll always be this way, you know," she whispered. "You'll always push me, test me, probe me. It's in your genes. And I'll always resist; I can't help it, any more than you can. There's probably no hope for us," she said with a rush of her old fatalism.

"Gracious," he rumbled laughingly in her ear. "Are you saying that you became a TV star just out of spite? To 'resist me'?"

"No, no," she answered, treating the question perfectly seriously. "I've told you why. For the money, and the recognition. . . ."

He sensed the hesitation in her voice and coaxed her. "And maybe for something else?"

"And maybe," she repeated with a grimace, "to show my . . . ex-husband that I could be chic and svelte and—oh, I don't know—sophisticated. Blasé. You can't imagine what it was like to be so . . . full-bodied, when *she* was so thin. To be shy when *she* was so admirably at ease in a crowd. As it dawned on me what was happening between Peter and her, I got shyer, and heavier, and more fatalistic about my marriage. I remember—" Her voice dropped to a hushed, tiny whisper as she dragged out, from a hiding place in her soul, her most painful memory.

"One evening," she continued, "Peter and I were at a

party, and so was *she*. I went into the bedroom at the end of the evening to get my coat. Peter was there with . . . with her. Kissing her.'' Katie swallowed and went on. ''Like a fool I just stood there, shocked and yet weirdly triumphant —because then I knew I was right about them, you know? Peter didn't say anything. He just looked at me, and so I turned to leave. As for *her* . . .'' Katie's smile was weak, and her lip trembled as she quipped, ''Gosh. Talk about your Other Woman! As I was walking out I heard her laugh and say, 'Silly cow. She'd be pretty if she lost a few pounds.' ''

Katie exhaled, almost explosively. It was as though a captured bird, fluttering for years beneath her rib cage, had escaped at last on the rush of her sigh. ''It was quite a walloping one-two punch at the time,'' she said softly. ''For five years, up until yesterday, that sixty seconds governed my life.''

She was about to tell Fletch how the phrase ''silly cow'' had haunted her nighttime dreams and her daytime reveries, and to apologize for being so childish and emotional. But instead Fletch pressed a forefinger against her lips and said, ''Shhh.''

He left her side then, and she watched him cross the living area, scoop up the cat from an easy chair, and come back to her. She watched him glance around the rented room with a look of vague distaste—they had no memories here—and then turn to her with a look of infinite tenderness.

''Let's go home,'' he said softly.

The fire danced to a manic beat, throwing sparks high into the wide, brick chimney. Each time a gust of wind howled outside, the fire answered with a crackling laugh inside. Wind and fire: The two were old friends.

Fletch and Kate had rushed with shivering glee through the dark and cold house, lighting everything: candles, kerosene lamps, heaters, the oak fire. The house blazed with light and flickered with shadows—jumping sprites and dancing, friendly ghosts. Perfectly at home with their shadowy friends, the two had made rapturous love in front of the fire. Now they lay curled in the high-backed loveseat, complacent and tipsy with love.

"*Seriously,* Kate," Fletch insisted. "You didn't mind leaving it? The fame—well, the notoriety, anyway? . . ."

"Not if you don't mind fronting me a small loan to get the Shape-Up Room started again."

"Anything. Anything! I'll charge you the highest interest rates in the world if that'll put your proud mind at ease. Just so long as you find the time to help me raise some chickens and kids and—"

"Kids? Kids of goats, or kids of people?" She acted surprised, even a little shocked, though she was neither.

"Let's put it this way," he said slyly, nibbling at the lobe of her ear, trailing his warm lips down to the curve of her throat. "I know at least one cigar-smoking fella who wouldn't be surprised if one of these days you took a maternity leave."

Impatient, loving, he lifted her face to his, cradling the line of her jaw between his thumb and forefinger. His look was soft with adoration as he murmured, "Woman with the blue green eyes . . . I've figured out the mystery. They shine bluish when you're angry and aloof; greenish when you're loving and open."

She was radiant with happiness, light-headed with desire for him. "Oh? And what color are they now?" she teased, putting on her coolest, haughtiest look.

"The color of emeralds, my love," he said, his voice blurred and diffuse with longing. "Glittering emeralds."

Silhouette Special Edition

MORE ROMANCE FOR
A SPECIAL WAY TO RELAX
$1.95 each

2 ☐ Hastings	21 ☐ Hastings	41 ☐ Halston	60 ☐ Thorne
3 ☐ Dixon	22 ☐ Howard	42 ☐ Drummond	61 ☐ Beckman
4 ☐ Vitek	23 ☐ Charles	43 ☐ Shaw	62 ☐ Bright
5 ☐ Converse	24 ☐ Dixon	44 ☐ Eden	63 ☐ Wallace
6 ☐ Douglass	25 ☐ Hardy	45 ☐ Charles	64 ☐ Converse
7 ☐ Stanford	26 ☐ Scott	46 ☐ Howard	65 ☐ Cates
8 ☐ Halston	27 ☐ Wisdom	47 ☐ Stephens	66 ☐ Mikels
9 ☐ Baxter	28 ☐ Ripy	48 ☐ Ferrell	67 ☐ Shaw
10 ☐ Thiels	29 ☐ Bergen	49 ☐ Hastings	68 ☐ Sinclair
11 ☐ Thornton	30 ☐ Stephens	50 ☐ Browning	69 ☐ Dalton
12 ☐ Sinclair	31 ☐ Baxter	51 ☐ Trent	70 ☐ Clare
13 ☐ Beckman	32 ☐ Douglass	52 ☐ Sinclair	71 ☐ Skillern
14 ☐ Keene	33 ☐ Palmer	53 ☐ Thomas	72 ☐ Belmont
15 ☐ James	35 ☐ James	54 ☐ Hohl	73 ☐ Taylor
16 ☐ Carr	36 ☐ Dailey	55 ☐ Stanford	74 ☐ Wisdom
17 ☐ John	37 ☐ Stanford	56 ☐ Wallace	75 ☐ John
18 ☐ Hamilton	38 ☐ John	57 ☐ Thornton	76 ☐ Ripy
19 ☐ Shaw	39 ☐ Milan	58 ☐ Douglass	77 ☐ Bergen
20 ☐ Musgrave	40 ☐ Converse	59 ☐ Roberts	78 ☐ Gladstone

$2.25 each

79 ☐ Hastings	87 ☐ Dixon	95 ☐ Doyle	103 ☐ Taylor
80 ☐ Douglass	88 ☐ Saxon	96 ☐ Baxter	104 ☐ Wallace
81 ☐ Thornton	89 ☐ Meriwether	97 ☐ Shaw	105 ☐ Sinclair
82 ☐ McKenna	90 ☐ Justin	98 ☐ Hurley	106 ☐ John
83 ☐ Major	91 ☐ Stanford	99 ☐ Dixon	107 ☐ Ross
84 ☐ Stephens	92 ☐ Hamilton	100 ☐ Roberts	108 ☐ Stephens
85 ☐ Beckman	93 ☐ Lacey	101 ☐ Bergen	109 ☐ Beckman
86 ☐ Halston	94 ☐ Barrie	102 ☐ Wallace	110 ☐ Browning

Silhouette Special Edition

$2.25 each

111 ☐ Thorne	133 ☐ Douglass	155 ☐ Lacey	177 ☐ Howard
112 ☐ Belmont	134 ☐ Ripy	156 ☐ Hastings	178 ☐ Bishop
113 ☐ Camp	135 ☐ Seger	157 ☐ Taylor	179 ☐ Meriwether
114 ☐ Ripy	136 ☐ Scott	158 ☐ Charles	180 ☐ Jackson
115 ☐ Halston	137 ☐ Parker	159 ☐ Camp	181 ☐ Browning
116 ☐ Roberts	138 ☐ Thornton	160 ☐ Wisdom	182 ☐ Thornton
117 ☐ Converse	139 ☐ Halston	161 ☐ Stanford	183 ☐ Sinclair
118 ☐ Jackson	140 ☐ Sinclair	162 ☐ Roberts	184 ☐ Daniels
119 ☐ Langan	141 ☐ Saxon	163 ☐ Halston	185 ☐ Gordon
120 ☐ Dixon	142 ☐ Bergen	164 ☐ Ripy	186 ☐ Scott
121 ☐ Shaw	143 ☐ Bright	165 ☐ Lee	187 ☐ Stanford
122 ☐ Walker	144 ☐ Meriwether	166 ☐ John	188 ☐ Lacey
123 ☐ Douglass	145 ☐ Wallace	167 ☐ Hurley	189 ☐ Ripy
124 ☐ Mikels	146 ☐ Thornton	168 ☐ Thornton	190 ☐ Wisdom
125 ☐ Cates	147 ☐ Dalton	169 ☐ Beckman	191 ☐ Hardy
126 ☐ Wildman	148 ☐ Gordon	170 ☐ Paige	192 ☐ Taylor
127 ☐ Taylor	149 ☐ Claire	171 ☐ Gray	
128 ☐ Macomber	150 ☐ Dailey	172 ☐ Hamilton	
129 ☐ Rowe	151 ☐ Shaw	173 ☐ Belmont	
130 ☐ Carr	152 ☐ Adams	174 ☐ Dixon	
131 ☐ Lee	153 ☐ Sinclair	175 ☐ Roberts	
132 ☐ Dailey	154 ☐ Malek	176 ☐ Walker	

SILHOUETTE SPECIAL EDITION, Department SE/2
1230 Avenue of the Americas
New York, NY 10020

Please send me the books I have checked above. I am enclosing $_____
(please add 75¢ to cover postage and handling. NYS and NYC residents please
add appropriate sales tax). Send check or money order—no cash or C.O.D.'s
please. Allow six weeks for delivery.

NAME _____

ADDRESS _____

CITY _____ STATE/ZIP _____